EDGARD
VARÈSE

Also by Alan Clayson available from Sanctuary Publishing:

George Harrison, 1943–2001
Ringo Starr
Serge Gainsbourg: View From The Exterior
Jacques Brel: The Biography
Only The Lonely: The Roy Orbison Story
Hamburg: The Cradle Of British Rock
Death Discs: An Account Of Fatality In The Popular Song

Printed in the United Kingdom by Biddles Ltd

Published by Sanctuary Publishing Limited, Sanctuary House, 45–53 Sinclair Road, London W14 0NS, United Kingdom

www.sanctuarypublishing.com

ISBN: 1-86074-398-6

EDGARD VARÈSE

Alan Clayson

Sanctuary

About The Author

Born in Dover, England, in 1951, Alan Clayson lives near Henley-on-Thames with his wife, Inese, and sons Jack and Harry. He has written many books on music – including the best-selling *Backbeat*, subject of a major film – as well as for journals as disparate as *The Independent*, *Record Collector*, *Medieval World*, *The Guardian*, *Record Buyer*, *Folk Roots*, *The Daily Mail*, *Guitar*, *Hello!* and *The Times*. He has also been commissioned to broadcast on national TV and radio and lecture on both sides of the Atlantic. Before becoming better known as a music historian, he led the legendary band Clayson And The Argonauts in the late 1970s and was thrust to 'a premier position on rock's Lunatic Fringe' (*Melody Maker*). The 1985 album *What A Difference A Decade Made* is the most representative example of the group's recorded work.

As shown by the formation of a US fan club in 1992, Alan Clayson's following has continued to grow, as has demand for his production talents in the studio, with versions of his compositions having been recorded by such diverse acts as Dave Berry – in whose Cruisers he played keyboards in the mid 1980s – and New Age outfit Stairway. He has also worked with the Portsmouth Sinfonia, Wreckless Eric, Twinkle, Screaming Lord Sutch and members of The Yardbirds and The Pretty Things, among others. He is presently spearheading a trend towards an English form of *chanson*, and feedback from both Britain and North America suggests that he is becoming more than a cult celebrity. Moreover, his latest album, *Soirée*, may stand as his artistic apotheosis, were it not for the promise of surprises yet to come.

Further information is obtainable via www.alanclayson.com.

Contents

'Facts about Varèse's life and work are difficult to obtain. He considers interest in them to be a form of necrophilia; he prefers to leave no traces.'

– John Cage

To Antonija Pommers

Jo tālāk aizejam, jō tuvāk atgriežamies

Prologue
The One-All-Alone

'Well, you see, it is like this: when you hear the difficult music, first you say, "Oh." Then you hear it again and you say, "Ah." And then you hear it again and you say, "Ooo."'

– Pierre Boulez[1]

I still possess a 7s 6d ticket stub for The Mothers Of Invention's British stage debut on 23 September 1967 at London's Royal Albert Hall. As an excitable schoolboy from a country town in Hampshire, this show was a pivotal event that informed not so much my artistic direction but an attitude about its presentation. Through received advice from Frank Zappa, the group's leader, via the music press, I also became an even more difficult teenager during a running battle about haircuts, church and other issues with a mother who swore she'd die of shame if ever I appeared onstage with a pop group.

She survived that particular ordeal and the sound of Frank's 1960s LPs – that I was buying without first listening to them – from my bedroom, although the same didn't apply to composers that Frank said he enjoyed, notably Edgard Varèse. I'd already heard a recording of Varèse's most renowned work, *Ionisation*, without paying much attention to it when it was played by the music teacher during my ignominious career at grammar school. My general impression of *Ionisation* was that it was less turgid that Brahms's *German Requiem*, one of the set works in that summer term's academic tournaments.

However, for all my unconcern then, I bought a Varèse album in 1971 that contained six of his works (including *Ionisation*). Because

Zappa was a fan of Varèse, as I was of Zappa, I was determined to 'get into' my new purchase, but in a dark and lonely corner of my mind, a still, small voice was asking, 'How could anyone like this stuff?' Nevertheless, I persisted with it and, after about the ninth dutiful spin, it became suddenly intriguing – if still baffling – with certain sections of individual pieces assuming sharper focus.

'I don't think about the composer of pieces I enjoy listening to,' reflected Frank Zappa as cancer killed him in 1993. 'I'm only listening to the results.'[2] That's as may be, but the person who dreamed up *Offrandes*, *Octandre*, *Intégrales* and the other tracks on my Edgard Varèse LP began to preoccupy me, as he would those who were to construct the 3,440 internet sites that mentioned him at the beginning of 2002.

Back in the early 1970s, all I had was *Edgard Varèse: A Musical Biography* by Fernand Ouellette,[3] a French–Canadian poet/musician who'd organised a Varèse tribute concert in Montreal in October 1961. He was to be chosen as collaborator when, despite certain philosophical objections, the aged Edgard was toying with the idea of writing his life story. When death claimed the composer, in 1965, it became Ouellette's first biography.

Perhaps it lost a lot in translation, but when I first attempted *Edgard Varèse: A Musical Biography* as a callow youth, it failed the litmus test of whether a music book is worth buying (as opposed to just ordering from the library) in that it didn't incite in me a compulsion to listen to interrelated records. If devoid of any overriding 'angle', it wasn't even a 'good read' and, as a serious study of Varèse's life, it was short on in-depth estimation of motive and measuring of experience. Also, despite the lengthy quotes from the man himself and from all manner of other authorities, I discovered later that it contained yawning omissions, on which I was to alight with nit-picking vigilance when researching this present account.

Yet Ouellette's barely adequate, if well meant, quasi-eulogy was helpful for the periodicals mentioned in its reference notes. These I sought to investigate at source – and, in the cases of French, German and Spanish items, get re-translated.

For further reading, I am far more inclined to recommend *Varèse: A Looking-Glass Diary – Volume 1: 1883–1928* by Louise Varèse, his widow,[4] which turned morning to evening without me noticing the lengthening shadows until it got too dark to read on. While Louise didn't get around to publishing a second volume, the strength of the first lies in a sense of being there and the minutiae of the subject's daily existence, both before and after meeting the writer. Just as absorbing is Olivia Mattis's essay 'Varèse And Dada' in the more recent *Music And Modern Art*, edited by James Leggio (Routledge, 2002).

Nevertheless, while these and further relevant literature are pertinent to this saga, we must not forget that Edgard Varèse was a revisionist who tended to adjust his past to suit an evolving self-picture. As Mattis implies, he might have been, for example, more of a Dadaist than he led the media to believe with statements such as, 'I had several Dadaist friends [but] I was not interested in tearing down but finding new means by which I could compose with sounds outside the tempered system that existing instruments could not play. Unlike the Dadaists, I was not an iconoclast.'[5]

Another characteristic that emerged as I waded through oceans of archives was that Varèse often repeated himself – sometimes word for word – in successive interviews. While this was slightly irritating, the consistency of his remarks on the same matters was useful for confirmation of information and opinion.

Unlike people, verbatim accounts are uninfluenced by the fact of being observed – *litera scripta manet.** Furthermore, in the context of this present discussion, they were also more important than primary sources. Because Varèse and nearly all of his contemporaries are dead, the majority of my interviewees were either living relations for whom the *dramatis personnae* were in most instances a cradle memory at most or genre experts who, like me, knew of Edgard Varèse second-hand. I decided, therefore, to treat him as an historical figure on a par with others born during a time when Queen Victoria ruled an Empire on which the sun never set, and who grew to adulthood in the prehistoric era of recorded sound.

* The written word remains

In his creative prime between the World Wars, Varèse was responsible for 'a music that epitomises the spirit of the early 20th century', according to a *Sunday Times* review[6] of one of two major Varèse retrospectives released on compact disc in 2001. 'The great emancipator of noise,' it continued, 'transformed the clamour of big-city life into clear musical images.'[6] Yet, while aspects of *Amériques* certainly celebrate the metropolis, images provoked by the mere titles of, say, *Hyperprism*, *Density 21.5* and *La Poème Électronique* have more to do with reinforcing Varèse's basic axioms that music – or 'organised sound', as he called it – was an 'art-science', composition the weighing of 'blocks of sound' and that machines rather than traditional instruments ought to dominate the sonic vocabulary available to modern composers.

Thus Varèse anticipated the electronic ventures of less innocent cultural generations and aggravated the argument of arch-minimalists such as Steve Reich and Philip Glass that the very idea of machine-music was unnatural and 'creepy' – and so was Varèse's non-tonal output, as it ran counter to what they regarded as the true task of 20th-century classical composition, which was to narrow the gap between highbrow and lowbrow and infiltrate popular taste. Yet to a greater – if more perverse – degree than the likes of Glass and Reich, Varèse was a catalyst in the dissolving of outlines between pop, classical and jazz.

The most original and adventurous of 20th-century composers, he remains both figurehead and grey eminence of modern music, despite the so-called 'wilderness years' that followed a fruitless attempt to gain funding and spur the progress of 'organised sound' beyond devices that he found 'too timid'.[5] Among these were the two sirens found on *Ionisation* and the theremin used in horror movies and, more famously, on Varèse's own *Ecuatorial* (and, in 1966, The Beach Boys' 'Good Vibrations'). Varèse was depressed, too, by indifference to offerings like *The One-All-Alone*, a science-fiction opera, and *Espace* (alias *Symphony For The Masses*), intended as a simultaneous performance in various parts of the world connected by radio communication.

Nevertheless, with the appearance of his works on vinyl in 1950, Varèse's return to contemporary prominence was no longer out of the question. Thanks to technological advances, he was now able to create some of the 'atmospheric disturbance' that he had been hearing in his head for decades. In 1958, this was exemplified by *La Poème Électronique*, for tape alone, fed through hundreds of revolving loudspeakers in an enclosed space at the World's Fair in Brussels. The CD containing the original recording has been deleted, but a second-generation transfer from the original master is still available on *Varèse: The Complete Works* (Decca 460 208-2), a double CD that was supplied to me by Spencer Streeter of G&S Music (www.gandsmusic.com).

Spencer is one of the 'genre experts' mentioned earlier. Special thanks also need to go to Melvin Bird, Jimmy Carl Black, Jo Carpenter, Jack Clayson, Virginia Cobbs, Roddie Gilliard, Thierry Gauduchon, Alan Heal, Kevin Howlett, Mark Lapidos, Mary Parisi, Hugo Rolland and Christopher Sipkin.

I am also beholden to the BBC Music Library, the music department at the University of Reading, the National Sound Archives, Westminster Music Library, Caversham Book Shop, Caversham Public Library, the British Library, Colindale Newspaper Library, L'Institut Français, New York Public Library and other avenues of new and rediscovered evidence.

Further debts of gratitude are owed to Penny Braybrooke, Jeff Hudson, Michelle Knight, Laura Brudenell, Lisa Wright, Chris Bradford and Iain MacGregor at Sanctuary Publishing for all their encouragement and patience, which went beyond the call of duty.

Whether they were aware of providing assistance in varying degrees or not, let's have a round of applause too for Hans Alehag, Jack Belton, Stuart Booth, Bruce Brand, Billy Childish, Harry Clayson, Don Craine, Kevin Delaney, Peter Doggett, Ian Drummond, Pete Frame, Mike Gott, Eric Goulden, Brian Hinton, Robb Johnson, Garry Jones, Graham Larkbey, Jon Lewin, Jim McCarty, Steve Maggs, Peter Mound, Andy Pegg, Chris Phipps, Mike Robinson, Mike and Anja Stax, Dick Taylor, Vic Thomas, John Tobler, Clifford White – and Inese Clayson, for whom *Un Grand Sommeil Noir* assumed an unlooked-for significance.

Finally, it may be obvious to the reader that I have received help from people and institutions that prefer not to be mentioned. Nevertheless, I wish to thank them for what they did.

Alan Clayson, March 2002

1 The Burgundian

'Not everyone is lucky enough to be an orphan.'
– Jules Renard

If not common in mainland France, Edgard Varèse's surname was imprinted deeply in Corsica – where Louis XV conferred nobility and granted land to a brood of Varèses in 1772 – and the north of Italy, where many peasants were named after their native villages. In the Alpine foothills, close to the Swiss border, one such settlement mutated into a manufacturing town called Varèse, while within the hinterland of Geneva stand both Varese and Varezza.

Most families tend to claim affinity with someone vaguely famous, too. While Henri, Edgard's father, treated this with derision, Edgard would allude with quiet pride to a late 16th-century composer named Fabio Varese (or Varesus) and Giovanni Baptista Varese, born slightly later, who 'flourished' in the employ of some Milanese aristocrat and had several masses and motets published. Edgard noted, too, Felice Varesi, an operatic baritone from the same city, who, at the age of 34, sang the title role at the 1847 première of Verdi's *Macbeth*. Moreover, within Edgard's own lifetime, a cousin, Alfred Cortot, emerged as quite a well known concert pianist in France.

Whatever the real or imagined links with these musicians, the names of Edgard Varèse's paternal grandparents had appeared since the 17th century on census rolls of Pinerolo, a district of thriving tillage in the Piedmont equidistant between the Alpine Varese and the one near Genoa. This region is now Italian but was still suffering an identity crisis when Achille Varèse wed Pauline Monet, whose great-uncle had been a doctor in Napoléon's army.

The crux of avaricious squabbles between France and Italy over the centuries (as Alsace-Lorraine was between Germany and France), the Piedmont had therefore evolved into a divided land that embraced two distinct languages. The Varèses, however, spoke and thought in French and their son, Henri Pie Jules Annibal, was to settle in Paris and gain a degree in the comparatively new subject of civil engineering at the Polytechnicum Federal de Zurich.

The proverbial 'self-made man', Henri worked his way up to high office as a partner in a prosperous mining firm whose origins were traceable to the Industrial Revolution. By the middle of the century it had expanded its interests – notably into hardware and agricultural accessories – and stuck tentacles into most French-speaking territories.

On his far-ranging expeditions to inspect mines, workshops and factories, his subordinates regarded Monsieur Varèse as fastidious and given to instigating costly litigation. It was also whispered that, at home, Papa Varèse demanded and received total subservience, and was feared abjectly by his tired wife, Blanche-Marie.

Although Parisian by birth, Blanche-Marie was of Corsican stock. Her father was Claude Cartot, once a soldier in a Burgundian regiment stationed in the Middle East. On demobilisation, Claude returned to his village, Le Villars, which was located within the tributary pull of the Saône and some 150 miles southwest of the capital. Half-hidden by woodland and set amid rolling pastures and rustic calm, it lay down-river from olde-worlde Tournus, renowned for its Romanesque church, Saint-Philobert, where the highest chancel-angels wore halos of a fine mist at dusk and dawn.

It was during a visit to the big town that Claude met his future wife, Celenie Yasse, who was originally from Alsace-Lorraine. The couple settled in Le Villars for a while before investing their savings into a bistro in central Paris, on the Rue de Lancry, a stone's throw from the east bank of the Canal St Martin. Business was brisk enough to cover the rent for an apartment where the 10th arrondissement borders on the 11th. From there, it was a five-minute dawdle to 88 Rue du

Faubourg du Temple, the long main thoroughfare from the Place de la République, where Edgard Victor Achille Charles Varèse was prised into the world at 4pm on an unseasonably warm Saturday 22 December 1883.[1] Such weather was in keeping with a national mood of buoyant optimism as, making a good recovery from the country's humiliating defeat in the Franco–Prussian War, the Third Republic was about to benefit materially from the establishment of a French protectorate in Indo-China.[2] More immediately tangible was the groundwork for the construction of the most enduring mark on the city skyline: the Eiffel Tower. This was to be the *pièce de résistance* of an international exhibition of new industries in 1889. Too expensive to demolish, it was to loom over the expanding village of pavilions along the banks of the Seine during the long preparations for the Exposition Universelle, a more insidious display of national prestige, at the turn of the century.

From the cradle, Edgard was to catch and hold a Parisian accent, but the curly headed boy was frequently delivered to the care of relations in Pinerolo and, more often, to his Burgundian great-aunt Marie and great-uncle Joseph Cartot, a blacksmith, who – with their daughter Marthe, a girl of his own age – still lived in Le Villars, a sanctuary from the oppressive climate of home. There, Edgard savoured affection rather than antagonism when, for instance, he spent hours messing about with his great-uncle's mandolin, investigating sounds rather than notes.

Overall, his visits to Burgundy purchased respite from criticism, chastisement and shouting to the extent that he came to regard himself as a Burgundian who 'hated to return to my family to go to school in Paris'.[3] Small wonder, therefore, that the adult Edgard would treasure delightful and inspiring memories of the lost mellow sunshine of weeks on end in Burgundy, especially during the late summer and into the gold of autumn.

During each dispiriting train journey back to Paris, an uncomprehending loneliness would sting Edgard's grey-blue eyes, as it would anyone who had been a popular hero to his playmates one day and an object of contempt the next in a place where life had long ceased to make sense. Yet he stepped down onto the platform and, drifting like a coltish ghost through the steam hissing from the undercarriage, steeled himself to keep in check behaviour that was the norm in the affable household he'd left behind.

Papa was especially minatory about what he considered to be poor table manners – which included, for example, the Burgundian habit of devouring squelching handfuls of grapes at the close of dinner. Through Henri Varèse's purported regime of emotional fascism, the only safe noises heard during meals were the unavoidable clatterings of cutlery on plate. He had crushed Blanche-Marie's self-respect and turned her into a progressively more conscientious rather than doting mother, anxious to survive from breakfast to bedtime without invoking her husband's ire. No objective perspective made her realise that Henri's behaviour was wrong. So it was that, listless to iniquities, a gaze once tender became as hard as marble, as hard as her hardened heart. She pushed off a weeping embrace of a child who turned for comfort to the very person who was persecuting him – like Winston Smith did to O'Brien, his tormentor, in George Orwell's *1984*.

While her eldest son blamed his father for what she had become, he reserved scorn for Blanche-Marie because she allowed it to happen. Thus she earned Edgard's eventual pity rather than any filial devotion. In later life, Edgard seized upon a quote from novelist Jules Renard – 'Not everyone has the luck of an orphan' – whenever the matter of his upbringing came up in conversation.

We would like the impossible – to view videos of scenes from the Varèse dining room, or sample with his own sensory organs, say, to understand how a particular glance, word or gesture from Henri would cow his children. In every family there is always territory forbidden and inexplicable to outsiders, but, while there may have been lengthy periods of peace, it seems certain that Edgard and the others – his two brothers, Maurice and Renato, and two sisters, Corinne and Yvonne – were beaten as children and were also subjected to methods of upbringing intended to force them not to feel bitterness or anger towards their parents, even when those feelings might be entirely justified.

They were probably encouraged to inform on each other, causing them to be guardedly 'good' in order to stockpile ammunition for the defence when their cases came up shortly after the *paterfamilias* arrived home at the end of his working-day tether. Accusations would then fly back and forth and up to five faces, alight with malicious glee, would conjure up different colours along the spectrum of hostility for the defendant whenever retribution awaited, deserved or otherwise.

Despite his assertions that he was a respected and supportive eldest brother, there were doubtless reprisals by Edgard against his siblings – especially Maurice, apparently – as he researched the limits and scope of their pain and terror whenever he reckoned he could get away with it. Too much of his father lived in him – because, like Henri, he wiped from his memory the nasty, spiteful things he did – and he carried out all the usual small atrocities that boys commit, especially eldest ones.

Aggressively scruffier than Corinne, Maurice and Renato in an unsmiling photograph taken when he was about 11, Edgard had become secretive, sullen and bored at home as well as impetuous, argumentative and given to bouts of sulking when allowed to play unsupervised outside. Twice, apparently, he attempted to run away from home, but hunger grove him back to certain punishment – which wasn't just physical. For 'answering back' once, he was threatened with reform school – a sanctioned that perhaps he may have welcomed.

You could understand his attitude. Papa hit him. Mother, care-worn and peevish, snapped at him. 'You have broken mine and your father's hearts' was a recurring sentence. The others knew just how to goad their big brother to breaking point. Then they could be victorious 'victims' when he lashed out.

It was Blanche-Marie's turn during the tension of Sunday lunch. Full of accusatory delusional righteousness, she took divertive offence every time he opened his mouth. Sunday meals climaxed on occasions with her running out in apparent hysterics and the master of the house clipping Edgard's ear and sending him upstairs. What followed was commensurate with an age when 'spare the rod and spoil the child' – a phrase attributed to contemporary essayist Samuel Butler – was an approved and much-quoted maxim.

These days, it would be called 'tough love' or 'child abuse'. Whatever the most accurate term, it wasn't very effective as either a teaching aid or a display of affection – at least as far as Edgard Varèse was concerned. His father's rage and, while able, exultant application of corporal punishment drove out both a capacity for uninhibited joy and any pleasant recollections of life in a dysfunctional home. Another legacy was lifelong nervous disorders and lengthening bouts of clinical depression.

Whatever busied the loveless rooms of No.88 and, later, when the family moved to an apartment along the nearby Boulevard de Strasbourg, it was decided that it would be in everyone's interest if 'awkward' Edgard moved in with his Cortot grandparents for a while. Claude and Celenie's flat opened up like an anemone and swallowed him whole. Edgard slept and ate there and Henri and Blanche-Marie would have washed their hands of him, had they not cared enough about the good opinions of their peers to trot out formally attired children at the 'at homes', soirées and receptions that pocked the calendar of polite society. Of all his nearest and dearest, Edgard came to be closest to Grand-père Claude, especially after Celenie died suddenly in 1892, in her mid-50s. Indeed, it was Claude who had accompanied him to school on his first day there.

There is no reason to assume that Edgard's education deviated from the late 19th-century norm: an unimaginative and terrifying regime epitomised by multiplication tables chanted *en masse* to the rap of a bamboo cane on the Eton-collared master's ink-welled desk.

When he moved up to the École Polytechnique, Edgard had buckled down almost eagerly to his lessons but was soon transformed into an uninvolved student, unblinking in the monotony of, say, Euclid's knottier theorems or the gloomy Old Testament prognostications of Ezekiel. Latin had been taught from kindergarten, and although Varèse found it dull, he was later to discover a gift for languages, mastering a hidden curriculum of Italian, Spanish and English, as well as picking up enough German to get by.

Like Latin, music was seen by the likes of Henri Varèse as having doubtful practical value, except that it looked good on a school prospectus. It was taught as a kind of mathematics then, supporting the theory that a tone deaf person could write a symphony.

Edgard's interest in the subject was treated with humorous scepticism, at first, by his father, who nevertheless scraped a violin occasionally to his wife's piano accompaniment ('Playing sentimental trash,' sneered Edgard[4]). Unless a person was a scion of what Henri derided as one of these 'artistic' families, it was unwise to see music as anything more than a vocational blind alley. Varèse would insist later that he received no musical instruction until he was 17 but, while his parents frowned on any exploratory pounding with plump infant fists on the upright piano in the living room, they – in common with most other so-called gentlefolk – had paid for their children to endure piano lessons of tear-inducing discipline. As Shakespeare reminds us in *Hamlet*, 'Rich gifts wax poor when givers prove unkind.'

It was beyond them to show it, but his parents were delighted that they were getting their money's worth in that, even when not under the tutorial lash, their first-born was willing to try, try again as he sweated over Bach, Chopin and further prescribed exercises that, crucially, revealed to him that music was a science as much as an art. Edgard was also self-contained enough to disassociate it from the carping tutorials and the drudgery of daily practice.

Furthermore, he seemed ostensibly a fascinated listener to the tinklings of Handel, Mozart and so forth during those recitals that were a frequent occurrence in the 'at homes'. Indeed, if no young Mozart playing blindfold, Edgard could just about get away with performing a couple of keyboard pieces himself with digits on auto-pilot, thus exempting himself from being led forth, glistening with embarrassment and under tacit threat of future chastisement, to set a drawing-room a-tremble with a Schubert Lied or some stirring national hymn in the uncertain treble of a voice about to break.

Had he been familiar with Wordsworth, the teenage Varèse might have muttered a dry 'to be young was very heaven' as he took stock of what was becoming a miserable existence. He'd grown into a heavily built, beetle-browed nuisance, insolently dumb with passive contempt for the sarcasm of teachers who were relieved when he was absent, and in his mind he was sometimes far away in Burgundy. Hands supporting expressionless head, thick-legged Edgard – uncomfortable on the hard chair at his tiny desk – yearned for the storybook countryside, with its friendly relations devoid of complicity and disapprobation. He longed to see once again that boundless, shimmering horizon of sloping forest, rutted trackways and breeze-blown seas of grass. The harvest moon in its starry canopy would shine bright as day while, inside the house in Le Villars, the log fire would subside to glowing embers.

Then a barked command from some withered pedagogue to pay attention interrupted the reverie of a troublesome and troubled youth and Le Villars was gone. The final weeks before the end of term became very long, simmering, as Edgard was to get back to the place where his load was always lightest.

2 The Turinian

'I cannot resist that burning desire to go beyond the limits.'
– Edgard Varèse, July 1928

During what remained of his childhood, Edgard Varèse was to see less of Le Villars than Bergeggi, a resort along the same stretch of Mediterranean coastline as the towns Varese and Varezza. The family had acquired what amounted to a time-share in Bergeggi after the firm moved Henri to an office job at the Italian branch, in Turin, in 1893. Among his qualifications for the post were local familiarity, as Turin – Torino in Italian – was the Piedmont's key trading centre, located as it was at the point at which numerous tributaries flow into the River Po at the beginning of its laceration of the country from the Alps to the Adriatic.

For centuries, dray horses had dragged cargoes of goods from everywhere in the Piedmont to be loaded onto domestic barges for delivery to Turin and subsequent distribution across Italy and beyond. The investment of old money into the Industrial Revolution had expanded the city's boundaries, swallowing surrounding communities in its path. Instead of the flickering monochromatic images of hansom cabs and penny farthings that fuel common imaginings of life at the end of the 19th century, giant chimneys of blast furnaces and factories were already belching chemical waste into the skies of Europe and caking employees' poky dwellings with soot. In this respect, the Piedmont had become the most progressive state in Italy.

In Turin – as in Brussels, Birmingham, Hamburg and similarly landlocked pivots of grimy enterprise – the barges now slip-slapped along a waterfront of wharves, refineries, metal works and clerking offices. It became a confluence and terminus of road and rail connections, too, and myriad manufactured goods – from fountain-pens and typewriters to the equally new-fangled motor cars and 'boneshaker' bicycles with their pneumatic tyres – were shunted daily from Turin's quickly over-populated conurbations.

For all his later fascination with the imagery and hidden musical vocabulary of modern technology and mass production, Edgard Varèse was thoroughly depressed by the culture-shock of moving to the clamorous ennui of Turin from the ebbing urban calm of Paris, the place to be during the so-called 'gay '90s' – even though Edgard had been sheltered from direct contact with any associated bohemianism or the *l'art pour l'art* aestheticism propagated by Gautier, Flaubert, Oscar Wilde and their sort.

Yet, unprepossessing as much of it was, Turin had forged palpable opportunities for artistic development via the patronage of both its aristocracy and its *nouveau riche*. Immediately after respective 1893 premières in Milan, 100 miles to the northeast, Puccini's *Manon Lescaut* and Verdi's *Falstaff* were performed in Turin's gaslit Opera House, a venue on the itinerary of most touring companies. Among these were the Concerts Colonne, which, in 1895, enthralled Edgard as he stood in the promenade during his first experience of an orchestral concert. The programme that night included established works by Richards Wagner and Strauss and a new composition of Wagnerian persuasion by Vincent d'Indy, but it was 33-year-old Claude Debussy's evocative *Prelude À l'Après-Midi d'Un Faun* – inspired by his middle-aged *confrère* the French symbolist poet Stéphane Mallarmé – that caused the restlessness in young Varèse's eyes to vanish and wafted him into the twilight afterwards, lost in wonder and half-formed ambition. The adventure provoked a sea-change in him, and the worst era thus far of incomprehension, lamentation, deprivation, uproar, assault and domestic 'atmospheres' would follow – but not for a while yet.

In the first instance, however, *Prelude À l'Après-Midi d'Un Faun* may have inched forward an idea for what was as much a song-cycle as an opera. A one-man composer, librettist, choreographer and stage designer, Edgard was going to call it *Martin Pas* after a ripping yarn by Jules Verne he had been forced to read at the École Polytechnique.

While it seems unlikely that anything he may have heard subsequently at the Turin Opera House could have matched the intensity and as-yet-unspoken repercussions of that initial attendance, there would be other visits that enabled Edgard to shut off, however fleetingly, the harsh reality of his detested new school, the Institut Technique, where, at the dictate of his father, he was to focus principally on mathematics, science and geography. In middle age, Edgard would recall distinctly a passage in an Italian geography book about the differing speeds of the many currents that made up the overall flow of the Zambesi River. This led a 14-year-old to wonder if the same principle could apply to the sphere of sound.

While Varèse's insistence that this was a patently prophetic discovery is entirely credible, perhaps to bolster a self-image as one streetwise beyond his years, he also made himself out to be a frightful desperado, given to fighting and playing truant. A more general image – during his first term in Turin, at least – was Edgard blundering about aimlessly in the playground bustle. With or without his only companion – Jean-Yves Gauduchon, another new pupil from France – he would also be noticed leaning pensively against walls and staring moodily as snatches of foreign babble became gradually less novel and unintelligible to him and the speakers more approachable.

More sad than angry about the turn of events, Edgard's mother – now pregnant with Yvonne – viewed Paris through a rosier haze until months in Turin became years and the phantom of France as some kind of Promised Land was exorcised. Before that, Blanche-Marie's and Edgard's painful homesickness was soothed by the widowed Claude Cortot – the fist that had stopped the dyke bursting at No.88 and the Boulevard de Strasbourg – leaving the bistro to take care of itself and arriving to live with his exiled daughter and her family.

It was through his grandfather that Edgard was to enjoy the biggest treat of his adolescence – more so than the Debussy recital – when, in April 1900, he and Claude were among the 40 million visitors to the Exposition Universelle back in Paris. The Champs Elysées was as green as it had been before the migration to Turin – actually as green as when Napoléon had commissioned the erection of its Arc de Triomphe. There were still more horses than motor cars, but the old life was soon to disappear. Harbingers of what was to come were shop-windowed at the Exposition, not only in the form of the latest petrol-fuelled vehicles but also in the graceful (if expensive) curves of Art Nouveau furniture and contraptions like Danish inventor Valdemar Poulsen's magnetic tape recording machine.

If wild with excitement, Edgard's nature and upbringing reined his recounting of the event at the top of his voice when he and his voluptuously weary grandfather arrived back in stifling Turin. Besides, any euphoria aroused by the Exposition Universelle was to fade swiftly. Blanche-Marie's appearance gave both of them a bit of a shock. At 31, she was too young to have hair so grey, but as well as this, and her usual harassed forbearance, she had the detached air of a dying woman – which she was. Her eyes had a burned-out look, emphasised by purple-black blotches under them that looked like mascara that had trickled and dried on a ghastly countenance. Even when lost in melancholy thoughts, her lips would be pressed together as if holding back pain. She couldn't say specifically where it hurt most, only that the hurt hovered all over her.

Maman rarely betrayed any overt emotions in front of the ideally seen-but-not-heard Edgard. Nevertheless, on her deathbed a few weeks later, she appealed to what she called his 'better self' by burdening him with guilt. She told him that she had stayed in the marriage 'for the sake of the children' and that, as the eldest, it was now his responsibility to protect Corinne, Maurice, Renato and baby Yvonne from their father, who, she gasped, was 'a murderer'.

Let's try to be fair to Henri Varèse. To assess his character, we only have the perspective of Edgard, for whom Papa was a handy peg on which to hang all manner of frustrations. Moreover, while Henri's conduct may have been tyrannical, it wasn't atypical of many other 'masters in their own homes' in a time when the workhouse – only fractionally less severe and shaming than prison – still beckoned the handicapped, the retarded and anyone made destitute through no fault of their own. Although at this time poor children were required to attend school to the age of 12, it was easy for them to slip through the net and be put to work as soon as they could walk. All youngsters were routinely thrashed black and blue, except in the case of this or that German princeling who had a *Prugelknaben* – a boy who was spanked every time his royal highness misbehaved.

Considered quite middle-aged at 30, mothers of whatever station were immune from punishment, too, if they kept their offspring in order with a cane. In turn, a husband could, within legally prescribed limits, drive his wife to near suicide with a repertoire of mind games and physical attacks. He could slap her face and she would smile through the tears and continue to treat him with the greatest respect. Furthermore, she had to be tolerant of – or indifferent to – stray mutterings about other attachments while gripping hard on her dignity as the official spouse. It wasn't as if mistresses were uncommon or a purely Gallic phenomenon –although it was a French homily that ran, 'The chains of marriage are so heavy that it takes two to carry them, and sometimes three.'

Not long after Blanche-Marie's funeral, Henri wed Marie-Christine, a mistress known to his eldest son, if not the others. Edgard wasn't as resentful of the situation as he might have been, mainly because, for all his father's directives, she didn't put herself forward as a duplicate of his mother. Nonetheless, she was unable to change Henri, who still believed that he somehow owned the lives of both his new wife and her step-children.

As Edgard seemed to have an artistic turn, it was almost a matter of course for Henri to suppress it, having decided long ago that the boy would follow in his footsteps, even graduate like he did from the polytechnic at Zurich. Indeed, Edgard was already learning the trade – and the value of money – in the office as a part-timer in readiness for a smooth passage from school into the world of work. It was as humdrum there as it was in class and, with the relaxed disinterest of the completely jaded, he would raise his head and glower into the tedium, wondering if this was all there was. It had never been suggested that there were more glamorous options beyond the nausea of bourgeois convention epitomised by the drab security of civil engineering and its associated paperwork.

Grandfather Claude may have been a sympathetic audience when Edgard thought aloud about his life, his dreams and his aspirations, but the old man's grief for Blanche-Marie and frank exchanges with his former son-in-law had led to his retirement to Le Villars. Exasperated attempts by Edgard to discuss his future with Henri were pointless. Variations on the same theme of prevarication came up over and over again and nearly always cadenced with a blazing row. No such altercation, however, was as bitter as the one about the piano.

As it had been in Paris, there was such an instrument in the house, but Henri didn't like any of his three sons wasting too much time hunched over its keys. On hearing that *Martin Pas* had been performed at school by Edgard, Jean-Yves and some of their classmates – albeit with a mandolin as solo accompaniment – Henri lent a sour ear to his first-born's efforts one evening. With the usual splendid certainty about everything he said and did, Henri then locked the lid, covered the piano in a linen shroud and kept the key about his person.

That was more or less the end. Before it reached the stage of burly Edgard yelling, struggling and kicking as Henri whacked away, the animosity had become mostly verbal. Otherwise, hardly a word passed between father and son that wasn't a domestic imperative, and in those days Edgard, his heart full of fear and guilt and his head full of hatred, was almost permanently out of the house. '*J'aurais du tuer ce salaud!*' ('I should have killed the bastard!') was an expression that tumbled from his lips as regularly as the chorus of a chanson, both then and in later life,[2] when, without warning, as one intimate noted, 'he would be seized by cold fury, a blind, brutal hate. "Sometimes, I could kill," he once told me. "I am afraid of myself."'[2]

To Henri, the source of this characteristic, a boy choosing any of the liberal arts as a profession was almost as deplorable as a girl becoming a stripper. It was also a sure sign of effeminacy, with the words *artistic* or *musical* being as much of a euphemism for *homosexual* then as *gay* is now. With the disgrace of Oscar Wilde resonating even in Turin, Henri wondered about Edgard. He'd never shown much interest in girls, had he? More than once, Henri had observed him preening himself in the mirror, spending too long combing and stroking what was to be described as 'black, bushy, electrified hair seeming to wriggle like coils of wire'.[1] What's more, since being deprived of the piano, the shock-headed youth had taken to slouching despondently about the house. Well, he'd better snap out of it soon or there'd be dire consequences decided Henri.

After a while, it became clear to Henri that he had behaved with the utmost correctness in removing the frivolity of music from his son's reach. It was pleasing to him to note how industriously an apparently subdued Edgard applied himself to the office, if not his schoolwork, even mortgaging his spare time to earn extra money there. He would be on a decent salary sooner rather than later, now that all of that nonsense had been flushed out of his system.

The subtext of this was that Edgard was squirrelling away as much cash as he could. Part of his purpose in doing so was then non-specific but, realising that he would never get anywhere without proper instruction, much of the money went on lessons in harmony and counterpoint after he had got as far as fingering the door-knocker of Giovanni Bolzoni, director of the local conservatory. On gathering the nerve to bang it, he'd explained his needs to the maestro who, looking Master Varèse up and down, elected to take him on.

Had Edgard ever enjoyed more interesting conversations than those that evolved during the sessions with Bolzoni? The feeling turned out to be reciprocal, and Edgard proved to be such a promising (if wayward) student that Bolzoni began to waive his fee. The maestro was also well placed to recommend Edgard when a vacancy arose in the percussion section of the Opera House's resident semi-professional orchestra. When Papa got wind of this, he stormed off to Bolzoni's, where his son had already fled to seek, even supplicating him to assist an escape across the border into France. As Edgard was still a minor, this was illegal and likely to land any adult collaborators in gaol. However, Bolzoni thought that there might be another remedy.

When Henri was shown into the hallway, his wrathful glare up the balustraded stairway was met by those of Bolzoni and the wretched

Edgard – and the placid gaze of Monsignor Spandre, Archbishop of Turin. The wind taken out of his sails, Henri Varèse fell silent and seemed to deflate in front of them. There was nothing for it but for him to nod in unnerved agreement – 'dreadful misunderstanding, Your Reverence...never forgive myself' – when the Archbishop, benign personification of authority – and personal friend of Giovanni Bolzoni – suggested conversationally that, whatever misdemeanour the headstrong but talented youth had committed to merit correction, it was surely time to let him have access to the piano again. Then followed an amused telling-off for Edgard for sly and manipulative behaviour that showed disrespect towards a honest, hardworking parent.

Matters appeared to be mended, superficially, and Edgard was no longer obliged to be so furtive about slipping off to his lessons with Bolzoni and rehearsals at the Opera House. Indeed, when the conductor was indisposed one afternoon, because no one else volunteered, 18-year-old Edgard replaced him for a run-through of *Rigoletto*, perhaps the most popular of Verdi's operas.

The participants had fun, and the general verdict was that young Varèse had coped well, even with a piece so rich in melody and dramatic construction that even the most ham-fisted wielder of the baton could have managed it. Nevertheless, this was the thin edge of the wedge. Edgard had savoured the power and found that he had liked the taste. Crucially, it had made him immune to twinges of conscience at the enormity of what his heart was telling him to do.

Who could not respect the extraordinary spirit with which Varèse anchored himself to the notion that, one way or another, he was going to keep the wolf from the door as a musician, even as a composer? The answer, of course, was Henri. But it was not his scowling disapproval that jolted Edgard Varèse into raising the standard of a brief but conclusive rebellion.

The impetus came in the form of Marie-Christine, whom Henri was treating in the same boorish way that he had treated her predecessor. During one such incident, Edgard's flinching glance darted from parent to step-parent as if watching a tennis match, stopping when he perceived the old omen of assault in his father's face. The massive but brittle dyke burst and the boy's pent-up frustration against Henri, his brothers and sisters, Turin, school, civil engineering, you name it, overflowed in an interjection loud enough to be heard in Milan. Freely translated, it was along the lines of, 'Marie-Christine thinks you're a bloody bastard and so do I!'

Surely he was dreaming. The syllables hung in the air for a thousand years. Henri stared at an Edgard with an unprecedented glint in his eye, an Edgard without his thumb in his mouth. Then the silence metamorphosed from decaying shock to mad fury that exploded like shrapnel.

Panic fired Edgard into the first and last instance of violence against his father. When everything turns red as hell, you don't plan precisely what you're going to do. He saw himself round on Papa and the flat of his hand shoot out in an arc to make glancing contact with the other's spectacles. These clacked onto the wooden floor and, while Henri was grubbing around for them, Edgard scrambled out of the room and slammed into the night, looking as if he'd seen a ghost. How long he roamed the streets, taking stock, nobody knows, but come the next day Edgard Varèse had quit his parental home and wanted no welcome back.

3 The Parisian

'The dead govern us. Their lives, their laws, their traditions, their works weigh us down, poison and enervate us. Fear, the ruler of the mob, bows to their decrees, strengthens their power and sterilises any individual revolt against them.'

– Edgard Varèse, April 1932[1]

As the third millennium began not on New Year's Day 2000 but 11 September 2001, so the previous century started on 22 January 1901, when, after 63 years on the British throne, Queen Victoria, the personification of an age, died in the arms of her grandson, the Kaiser.

Others of her direct descendants dominate the dwindling royal houses of Europe today. Yet, just as the fossil monarchies linger, so the most culturally fertile decade since the Renaissance resonates still. While what tidy-minded historians define as 'modern music' began before Victoria shuffled off this mortal coil, it was between 1901 and the Great War that Stravinsky, Schoenberg, Holst and Ravel were on point of impact on the public mind. In their respective fields, so too were Freud, Einstein, Lloyd-Wright and those serving as midwives to the birth of Hollywood.

Half a world away, in Paris, Picasso, Duchamp, Léger and Picabia were just anonymous wanderers further afield in the city, but with drink inside them they were willing cult celebrities in the bistros fanning out from the Jardin du Luxembourg to the Seine's left bank and Montparnasse. In many of these, they were able to make a single *vin ordinaire* last for hours.

When Duchamp strolled in, there would be an instant scraping of chairs, a pushing away of tables, in an eagerness to come across and join him. Outside, in the narrow and steep back alleys, acolytes would fall into step at Picasso's side, devoutly questioning him on aspects of art and accepting with reverence the easy-flowing words that fell from his lips. Some would invite themselves into his Bateau Lavoire studio – which was where he was to impart one vital pearl of home-spun philosophy to Edgard Varèse: 'It doesn't matter what people say about you as long as they're talking about you.'

Although the fêted Picasso's early Parisian output was reminiscent of the post-Impressionist posters of Toulouse-Lautrec, he would soon understand that the modern artist didn't have to produce a nice picture on a specific subject any more; photography took care of that. A painting or sculpture no longer needed to be of anything recognisable. Representing nothing but itself, its sole purpose was to touch you in some way, perhaps for reasons you couldn't articulate.

This was all very well but, if parochially renowned, Picasso, Léger, *et al* – as well as later arrivals like Modigliani, Joan Miró, Diego Rivera and the Catalan sculptor Julio Gonzalez[2] – induced bewilderment, even contempt, to the 'man in the street' who recalled occasional paragraphs about them in city newspapers. They could talk all they liked about the different and still-developing 'isms', 'periods' and 'movements', but he would scratch his head over even Modigliani's portraits of fragile females with elongated necks and the clean geometry of Georges Braque's *Le Violon* before the inevitable enquiry, 'What's it meant to *be*?'

That the Left Bank – an 'artists' quarter' since the days of Rabelais – could accommodate both the figurative Modigliani and the Cubist still-lives of Picasso infers correctly that there was not yet an all-pervading 'École de Paris' with common aims and lodged rules of procedure. Indeed, very much the opposite. Mention of the artistic community in the City of Light still prompts peculiar accounts of what alleged 'insiders' claim that they either heard about or saw of the decadent fun to had there, thanks to France's relatively open-minded attitude towards sex, stimulants and escapades that improved with age. For example, there's the one about Picasso, abetted by surrealist bard Pierre Reverdy and art critic Guilliame

Apollinaire, heisting ancient Iberian sculptures from the Louvre. Then there's the tale about playwright Alfred Jarry – whose surreal and burlesque *Ubu-Roi* opened at the Theatre Antoine in 1908 – firing a vertical warning shot from a pistol to aid his queue-jumping at bus stops.

While he made himself conspicuous, Jarry was but one of what the world at large saw as a ragbag of slackers, misfits and malcontents, making clowns of themselves via daily stupors of absinthe – 'the green fairy' – and cheap wine, Jarry even going as far as dying his hair green in honour of his preferred tipple. Within the clang of the bells of St Sulpice, they led a hand-to-mouth existence in studio garrets inside crumbling townhouses that held each other up like drunkards rolling homewards after chucking-out time. It was a subworld of stinking communal toilets, a puddle of congealing vomit on the stairwell, a fresh avalanche of plaster that an irate rent-collector's pounding had dislodged onto the hallway floor and the burning of furniture against the chill of winter.

Although bordered by bustling consumers' paradises, such environs had been as a Forbidden City to Edgard Varèse when the family was resident in Paris, embracing all that his upbringing had taught him to both despise and dread. Yet romantic squalor – well, squalor, anyway – held vague, even exotic enchantment for a lad from Turin who had appeared in Montparnasse as if from nowhere in spring 1903.

Conversations about Varèse's first weeks back in Paris brought out stories of him sleeping under the arcades of the Louvre, being arrested for vagrancy, subsisting on soup made of leftovers from street markets and dressing like a tramp, at the mercy of the parish. Some of these weren't total fiction, but not that long after his arrival, he billeted himself with Jean-Yves Gauduchon, then an architecture student ekeing out an allowance from his parents in upstairs rooms in a boarding house along Rue Saint-Andre-des-Arts.

At the window, beyond the rooftops along the left bank of the Seine, Varèse could make out the morning sun climbing behind the spires of Saint Chapelle and, towering above the Île de la Cité – where Paris had been born, in the Dark Ages – Notre Dame, whose bells had once been stolen to garland the neck of a mare ridden by Gargantua, Rabelais's King Kong-like buffoon-hero.

As familiar as he was with the medieval legend on which this was based, Edgard Varèse may have permitted himself wry amusement at Gargantua's extreme strategy to outfit a horse with superfluous adornment when his own efforts simply to survive were so pathetic. To counter the dwindling of his savings from the job in his father's office, Varèse sought work as a transcriber of music – for which he was paid by the hour rather than by the page – weighing up how long he could stretch it out without arousing suspicion and thus jeopardising chances of further commissions.

As for his own music, there were so many ideas chasing through his head that it was all he could do to write them down. A red-eyed, unshaven impartiality and a quality control peculiar to himself would often occupy him until the grey of morning when Gauduchon, half-feeling his way downstairs, would notice the crack of gaslight under his friend's door. A symphonic poem entitled *Apothéose De l'Ocean* had already been completed and there were other works in progress, included something called *Chanson Des Jeunes Hommes*.

Heard only in the minds of their creator and the few he permitted to read the dots, all that remains of these pieces are titles – 'that always derives from some association of ideas in relation to the score and has, needless to say, an imaginative appeal to me personally'.[3] Nevertheless, the manuscripts must have been sufficiently impressive – and orthodox – to lurch the weather-vane of approval in Varèse's direction when he applied for admission to the Schola Cantorum, an academy founded in 1896 originally for the study of Church music and still employing – as Varèse was to reveal later to Stravinsky – 'teachers ruled like manuscript paper'.

First among equals on the interview panel, Vincent d'Indy was of a noble family for whom 'culture' was second nature. Nonetheless, his was a childhood as bleak, after its fashion, as Varèse's own. Yet he had emerged as the college's flagship lecturer, one of its directors and an acquaintance of one of Edgard's relations, the pianist Alfred Cordot (who, incidentally, Varèse disliked heartily). An ardent Wagnerian and adherent to the eternal verities of melody and harmony, d'Indy, then in his mid-50s, was one of the most acclaimed composers in Europe, just as Carl Philipp Emanuel Bach had been in the late 18th century – and, just as it did to the celebrated Johann Sebastian's son, posterity would reduce Vincent d'Indy to an also-ran.

In the context of this discussion, however, he is important for the pragmatic encouragement he lent Varèse at first, both he and Alfred Cortot pulling unbothered strings to find the young man a part-time post as a librarian and, thereby, a means of paying his way through the course. Edgard also moonlighted as secretary-companion to the elderly Auguste Rodin, but this employment terminated when a discussion about music took a nasty turn and Varèse called the most famous sculptor of the day '*un con*'.

This insult was an eternal favourite of Varèse's, and was to be applied later to d'Indy, who taught composition at the Schola and every Tuesday assembled a full orchestra for his masterclasses in conducting techniques. The college's founder, Charles Bordes, took charge of Medieval and Renaissance music, while the responsibility for counterpoint and fugue was given to a former Schola student headhunted by d'Indy, Albert Roussel, for whom Varèse 'was the phenomenon of the class because of the ease with which [he] juggled with contrapuntal artifices'.[4] Edgard was, however, no teacher's pet for d'Indy.

If never a toadying disciple, Varèse had felt inherent pride in his familiarity with the Great Composer, but mutual dislike grew rapidly between them and d'Indy became the unconscious victim of innumerable derogatory *bons mots* from the younger musician. 'His vanity would not permit the least sign of originality or even independent thinking,' sneered Varèse, 'and I did not want to become a little d'Indy. One was enough.'[4]

Comparing notes in the staff room, d'Indy and the other lecturers agreed that the new student was a being apart from his fellows, as he homed in on details that others in a given class might be too lackadaisical to consider or even notice. He was also more *au fait* than most with the historical traditions and conventions of music and his cultivation of a personal style of composition more advanced – although, as he drew from every musical and literary idiom he'd ever encountered, Varèse endeavoured to disguise his sources of inspiration in the hopes that nothing would remain aggravatingly familiar.

Yet, very much knowing his own mind, Varèse preferred discernible structure and palpable substance, as exemplified by the 'colossal majesty' of Beethoven's *Ninth Symphony*, although he regarded its creator's deafness as 'really a blessing. It isolated him from the everyday. He heard with his inner ear.'[4] Of contemporary figures, 'no one has ever equalled Puccini in writing for the voice' – although, if agreeing with d'Indy that Wagner, too, 'was a very great man, a Michelangelo of music', Varèse took exception to the scoring of the tubas designed to Wagner's specifications for the *Ring* cycle: 'Beautiful on paper but, in use, always out of tune with the orchestra.'[5]

Composers of greater antiquity esteemed by Varèse included Palestrina, Mozart ('the iconoclast who first put the clarinet into the orchestra'[5]) and JS Bach, but he identified more strongly with the more austere Heinrich Schütz – perhaps the most eminent German composer before Bach – and, of the same post-medieval vintage, Claudio Monteverdi, although he understood that, to feed their families, all were obliged to cater for the recreational whims of duke, bishop and like paymaster (olde-tyme equivalents of today's radio-station programmers). 'Many of the old masters are my intimate friends and respected colleagues,' Varèse was to declare. Paraphrasing what was to be his most famous quote, he continued, 'None of them are dead saints. In fact, none of them are actually dead. They are all alive in the present.'[6]

At this time, Varèse was also absorbing a hidden curriculum via revelatory literature that his tutors might not have deemed relevant to his ordained studies. During a restless and omnivorous debauch of reading, it was almost as if he was engaged in formal research as he voyaged evening after evening into the small hours with favoured authors hauled off the shelf at the library and carried home. Gradually, his understanding of which books were worthwhile and which were not became more acute but, although he would pass on some of this accumulated wisdom via music, he would never adopt that infuriating habit some have of airing their learning in conversation.

His taste in verse tended towards the symbolist and metaphysical – Rimbaud, de Nerval, Verlaine, Mallarmé, *et al* – but he also became familiar with the medieval minstrel's vernacular lyric poetry, especially that of François Villon, a vagabond bard of the 15th century whose adventures almost overshadowed the bitter humour of his ballades. Varèse was fond, too, of robust satire, whether from the ancient Greece of Aristophanes or the daring Renaissance vulgarity of Rabelais.

While he also got to grips with obscure German philosophers, as well as the expected Schopenhauer and Nietzsche, more pragmatic food for thought was contained in *The Musical Problems Of Aristotle* and, on the recommendation of Latin scholar Maurice Pelletier, *Hermetic Astronomy* by the 16th-century Swiss alchemist Bombastus Paracelsus, whose experiments, Varèse felt, might somehow be applied to music. He became engrossed, too, in the similar theories of Hoene Wronski, a 19th-century physicist. He also got to serious grips with Leonardo da Vinci's *Notebooks*, especially with his notion that 'waves of sounds and those of light are governed by the same laws as those of water', which was essentially what Edgard's younger self had gleaned from the pages about the Zambesi in his geography primer.

'At 20, I began to feel sound as a living material, to be formed without wilful limitations,' reminisced Varèse, who had already taken to referring to music as 'organised sound' or, more weightily, 'the movement of masses, varying in radiance and of different densities and volumes'. Thinking aloud to anyone who would listen, he 'came across a definition that seemed suddenly to throw light on my gropings towards a music I sensed could exist. Wronsky specified that music as "the corporealisation of the intelligence that is in sounds". It was a new and exciting conception and, to me, the first that started me thinking of music as spatial, as moving bodies of sound in space, a conception I gradually made my own. Very early musical ideas came to me which I realised would be difficult or impossible to express with the means available, and my thinking even then began turning around the idea of liberating music from the limitations of musical instruments and from years of bad habits erroneously called "tradition".'[6]

In 1903, such ideas verged on lunacy, certainly as far as Vincent d'Indy was concerned. In any case, d'Indy was not pleased at being upstaged by his pupils or – heaven forbid! – by direct artistic rivalry. No longer commanding terrified respect from Varèse, d'Indy was now coming across as a self-obsessive who didn't belong in a student-centred environment.

D'Indy was one of these so-called pedagogues for whom an obligation to impart knowledge to others divorces them from truer vocational purpose. In d'Indy's case, this was tending to his ambitious *Jour d'Été À La Montagne*, a symphonic opus that, premièred in 1905, embraced French folk song and Gregorian chant. In a mellow mood, d'Indy was patronising, beaming puffy smiles of condescension when, magnifying the gap between himself and the common herd, he would not believe that one such as Varèse, the son of a businessman, could glimpse infinity in *Prelude À l'Après-Midi d'Un Faune* by that upstart Claude Debussy. Usually, however, d'Indy was inclined to show involuntary disinterest in his charges, unless ideas that cropped up during tutorials could be incorporated into his own body of work.

Varèse's opinion of d'Indy was shared by others such as Paul Le Flem, from Brittany, who later became a music journalist, and by a rather eccentric mature student named Erik Satie, who was nonetheless a revered figure among younger colleagues and as out of place as Varèse in the Schola's academic routine. 'We attended d'Indy's classes,' scowled Le Flem, 'but we knew enough to absent ourselves from them when we felt we would be better occupied elsewhere.' While they may have felt that the analytical feedback from d'Indy was meagre, the appeal of being left to their own devices was enhanced, noted Le Flem, 'by plunging into the rising flood of new ideas and aesthetics then breaking out all around us'.[3]

Le Flem and, less frequently, Satie had been visitors to Varèse and Gauduchon's lodgings at Rue Saint-Andre-des-Arts, which had quickly acquired the sock-smelling frowziness still common to young male student accommodation. This was exacerbated by the free-and-easy attitude of a landlord who, as long as they didn't fall too far behind with the rent, was open-minded about tenants being carried in drunk at seven in the morning, staying in bed until the gas lamps in the street came on, leaving crockery unwashed in the sink for days and entertaining anyone with a different set of hormones in rooms so untidy that they looked as if someone had hurled a hand-grenade into them.

In this respect, Edgard Varèse, for all of the hours spent with his nose in Aristophanes or Paracelsus, was no emaciated ascetic. In Turin, he might have fled if accosted by a prostitute, but with Papa not looking he may have lost his virginity abruptly in the practised and robust caress of a painted princess twice his age who had openly exhibited her seamy charms in a bordello window.

The allure of the lofty ideals that Edgard was nurturing had not prevented him from contemplating more unlikely forums for initiating erotic encounters. Amused by the memory, Paul Le Flem could 'still see Edgard walking up to the conductor's desk when his turn came on Tuesdays, his eyes flashing defiant lightning at the girls playing the second violins, and giving the signal to begin with those thunderbolt eyes'.[3]

Such affectations flooded the libidos of the sillier females in the orchestra but, slightly older than the average student in his year, Edgard was as sure of himself with their more sophisticated sisters, who perceived a strength of character beneath his assumed hybrid of tortured artist and rough, untamed outsider. He was also good-looking. While his eyebrows were now bushier and met in the middle, they reinforced a 'mad composer' magnetism. Furthermore, the powerful build that had set him apart at school was still apparent, as were his wide mouth and dramatic, aquiline nose.

The novelist Romain Rolland, then professor of music at the Sorbonne – the University of Paris – was to portray Varèse in his early 20s as 'amazingly handsome – tall, with a fine head of hair, an intelligent and forceful face, a sort of young Beethoven'.[7] By coincidence, the hero of Rolland's Jean-Christophe magnum opus was to bear an uncanny resemblance to Varèse, for whom the writer was to evolve into something of a Dutch uncle.

Part of Varèse's charm was that he seemed genuinely unconceited about his looks. Neither was he a sexual braggart, and his carnal antics as a bachelor remain the secrets he wished them to be. However, regardless of whether this most heterosexual of men was forever tilting for the downfall of someone or other's knickers or was 'saving himself' for his wedding night, it is known that, by 1905, Varèse was courting Suzanne Bing, a diminutive and free-spirited student of modern drama then furrowing her comely brow over a second-year thesis on Ibsen at the comparatively progressive Conservatoire National de Musique et de Déclamation. Within weeks of meeting, the pair had crossed that barrier between inferred companionship and declared love.

However odd a choice Varèse may have appeared, what with his seemingly wanton poverty and estrangement from his family, Suzanne's widowed and remarried mother – a Mme Kauffmann, who dwelt on the Côte d'Azur – raised no objections when her daughter announced that she was going to marry the boy. Furthermore, according to Varèse, 'She liked me better than her own daughter and sided with me in any dispute.'[10]

Pre-marital trysts took place a couple of streets west of Rue Saint-Andre-des-Arts, in the flat that Edgard was now sharing with Léon Deubel, a poet and manic-depressive misogynist who had embraced a machismo code of morality whereby he could mess around with other girls but wouldn't stomach infidelity from Anna, his diffident German paramour (who, like Suzanne, sported unfashionably short hair). Léon was an appalling fellow, really, but Edgard liked him, even when pondering how someone so brutish and foul-mouthed could be capable of producing work of such sensitivity as *La Fin d'Un Jour* and *Souvenir*, sonnets that had already inspired in Varèse sketchy plans for orchestral pieces.

To Deubel, his pal was 'a young maestro; I get great pleasure out of hearing him play Wagner and Beethoven in the evening',[3] while Varèse was content to be a passive listener as the bard, enraged or cynically amused by everything, gave his lightning-bright imagination its ranting, arm-waving head. Nevertheless, if Edgard was as lost in Léon's shadow as Anna, the differences between the flatmates consolidated their friendship. 'When I lived with him, Deubel read me everything he wrote,' recollected Edgard. 'We spent some good evenings together, drinking white wine, which he liked very much and used to go out and fetch from the co-operative on the Rue Cardinale.'[8]

When the first flush of his wonderment at Deubel had faded, Varèse moved to the Renovation Aesthetique, which embraced the offices of a journal of the same name and served as stop-gap housing for creative folk of all nationalities, for whom it was attractive for its low rent, its communal facilities and its location, which overlooked public gardens. Among those passing through during Varèse's tenure were Modigliani, Gonzalez, Jean Cocteau, Deubel (eventually), Tristan Tzara and Sar Peladan, a novelist who struck a resounding chord with Erik Satie. Preferring the company of artists and writers to musicians, Edgard enjoyed the ambience of the Renovation Aesthetique so much that he contrived to stay for longer than the regulated time of one year during his transition from the Schola Cantorum to the Conservatoire.

Any concordat once established with d'Indy had deteriorated to the level at which the teacher was deemed by the provocative Varèse as being of the same authoritarian kidney as his father, as well as with the same short-sightedness, mental sluggishness and – if Edgard was feeling especially uncharitable – cloth-eared ignorance. Furthermore, while his artistic perspectives were yet to take concrete form, the pupil now thought of himself in a different – not lower – league to d'Indy as flare-ups between the two increased in frequency. The teacher became in turns more subtle and less courteous as Varèse's sojourn at the Schola Cantorum neared a discreditable end.

To Suzanne, he would spill out his vocational disappointments even more disobligingly, pausing in mid-tirade to speak wistfully of contemporaries of nigh-on the same age as himself. Look at Béla Bartók, whose symphonic poem *Kossuth* had received its British première in 1904, or Igor Stravinsky, composing for the Russian ballet. What about Anton von Webern, whose *Passacaglia* for orchestra had ended his affable apprenticeship under Schoenberg? Or Schoenberg himself, whose string sextet *Verklärte Nacht*, his artistic breakthrough, was causing much comment after recent performances in Berlin and his native Vienna?

How was Edgard's 'apprenticeship' at the Schola going to finish? It certainly wasn't to be with a hushed ante-room at the unveiling of any formal – and unobjectionable – Opus 1, prefaced by scripted if affectionate ad-libbing between Vincent and himself, jovial voice of experience and respectful young shaver.

The most recent butt of d'Indy's sarcasm had been Varèse's 'new messiah', a scientist named Hermann Helmholtz, who, in a publication entitled *Lehre Von Den Tonempfindungen* (*Physiology Of Sound*), outlined his investigations of sine waves, with particular reference to the 'pure' rising and falling sonic recurrence heard most commonly in the siren – which, according to a 1908 English dictionary,[9] means either 'an instrument that produces sounds by introducing a regularly recurring discontinuity into an otherwise steady blast of air' or 'an instrument for demonstrating the laws of beats and combination tones'. While it hadn't the volume then to rise above the rumble of traffic, as it would when warning of air raids in World War II, a turn-of-the-century siren would have been loud enough to tyrannise a full orchestra, had anyone had the unprecedented audacity to use it in such a context.

Edgard might have done so, had he the means and opportunity. Instead, he made himself a laughing stock to d'Indy and his followers with his envisaging of the siren's musical properties, extolling its 'beautiful parabolic and hyperbolic curves, which seemed to me equivalent to the parabolas and hyperbolas in the visual domain'. To those blinkered by rules of harmony, the joke was that you couldn't control a siren's pitch, but in the course of its oscillations it must resolve for the odd split second now and then, like the inverse of a stopped clock being right twice a day.

Nevertheless, the ricocheting facetiousness, fiery intellectual debates and dialectic gymnastics were all brushed aside when the War Office, concerned about German imperialism and correlated attacks on military detachments by disaffected colonial subjects in North Africa, sent for Edgard Varèse. The dreaded official-looking envelope that hung like a sword of Damocles over every healthy young

Frenchman fluttered onto his doormat one dark morning. The National Service call-up papers within directed Edgard to report to an induction centre and join the army for a year – a lifetime, if you're scarcely more than a teenager in love.

It was possible to hold this at arm's length by either employment in a 'reserved occupation' – on the railways, say, or in a munitions factory – or extending his period of further education. With the latter option in mind, Varèse wasted no time in acquiring immediate details and an application form for a composition course at the Conservatoire, advisedly putting down Charles Bordes and Albert Roussel as referees, rather than d'Indy.

That he was the latter's *bête noire* actually worked to his advantage during a pivotal audience on 11 January 1905 with 60-year-old Gabriel Fauré who, despite the onset of the deafness that was to blight the 20 years left to him, had just been appointed director of the Conservatoire's music faculty. His considerable reputation as a composer is of less account here than the reforms he was introducing in his unobtrusive way to the curriculum. Against some opposition, Fauré maintained that mere competence in a specific musical field was nowhere as important as graduates becoming *au fait* with all aspects of the subject, from the remote past to the very cutting edge of the day's avant garde.

On paper, Fauré was just what Varèse needed. Fauré didn't have to be told what the Schola Cantorum was like, but he listened carefully to both Edgard's tale of woe and, crucially, the radical ideas that had raised d'Indy's eyebrows. Looking the supplicant up and down, the old composer decided that it might be worth enrolling him. He could bypass the foundation year and proceed immediately to the masterclass. Varèse was also to be among the select few allowed to attend sessions at the Sorbonne with the avuncular Romain Rolland. It would be one in the eye for Vincent d'Indy, reasoned Fauré, if this Edgard Varèse proved to be a star pupil like Maurice Ravel, who had been runner up for the music category in 1901's Prix de Rome, which gave winners the opportunity to study in the Eternal City and was among the highest awards given by the French government for excellence in the arts.

Ravel had been his protégé, but Fauré's elevation to higher collegiate office meant that Varèse's day-to-day tuition was delegated to Jules Massenet – a professor of composition willing to learn from pupils whose methodology differed from his own – and the equally venerable Charles-Marie Widor, organist at St Sulpice since 1870 and a prolific if unremarkable composer. Purportedly, one presented score drew from Widor an ambiguous 'I can't say I'd advise that, Varèse, but maybe the textbooks will have to be changed.'[10] Nevertheless, an unfinished fugue by the newcomer was of sufficient promise for Widor to put him forward as a contender for both the Prix de Rome and lesser commendations.

Fauré, too, thought enough of Varèse then to invite him to musical 'at homes', and at one of these soirées there was a silence so loud you could hear it after a gatecrasher made his presence felt. It was announced that a certain Henri Varèse, Esquire – who had not troubled to remove his hat – was at the door.

Edgard had always feared that Papa might materialise again in all his glory, but not in this ghastly way. Once he had ascertained his son's precise whereabouts in Paris, Henri had mailed small cheques, noting that Edgard hadn't been too proud to cash them. Now Henri was in Paris himself, ostensibly on an assignment for the firm. With customary ruthless efficiency, he completed the prodding of indolent colleagues and sly sub-contractors about why this shipment was late, where that percentage had come from and why so-and-so had been granted that franchise. Then, with a couple of days in hand, he'd made circuitous enquiries about someone he regarded not so much as a son and heir as human property that he now had the chance to reclaim.

Henri decided that it might suit his purpose best if he exposed the situation in a public forum where no hushing-up was possible. He couldn't care less about the opinions of the effete poseurs with whom the fool had surrounded himself. It wouldn't bother Henri in the slightest if he had to make a scene, even instigate a slanging match. He was quite looking forward to thus denting Edgard's self-composure in front of musical chums too godless to know an archbishop well enough to use as a buffer-state.

Yet Henri Varèse's big moment was lost when, moistening his dry lips, a nonplussed Edgard, thinking fast, floored Fauré with a sleight of social judo by changing the subject when both his host and Romain Rolland expressed interest in receiving Varèse *père*. Relaying his felicitations via Fauré's burly manservant – not one that Henri could shove out of the way – Edgard requested his father to leave his address, after which a meeting would be arranged, sooner rather than later.

Although he'd defused what would have developed into an ugly showdown, Edgard knew that Henri realised that there would be no meeting. Biting back on his rage, Henri withdrew as if to a prepared position, intending to confront his dilettante son in the street when the party broke up. Yet tedium, cold and the memory of that unprecedented aggression over Marie-Christine (about to give birth to Edgard's half-brother) overwhelmed Henri beneath the yellow-green lamplight. In any case, bygones were unlikely to be bygones for very long. He'd be unable to prevent himself from bringing up the aberrations of Edgard's flaming youth, and the old wounds would be sure to reopen. Let the boy go to the devil with his 'artistic' rubbish. A beaten man, Henri Varèse disappeared into the night and out of his eldest son's life forever.

While his own parents had lacked warmth and intimacy towards himself and his siblings, Fauré was confused and perhaps saddened by Varèse's apparently unwarranted refusal to see a father he had kept in the dark. However, when he and Widor had pieced together those fragments of family history that they could coax from Edgard, they could surmise that the edge of violence he was investing into his music was attributable to an early life governed by trauma so profound that it might have otherwise led him to prison, lunatic asylum or morgue. Instead, his talent had been motivated and enhanced by the struggle and he had been strengthened, via adaptive powers that often surface as psychological wounds heal. If nothing else, Varèse would later prove resilient in his conquest of – or his development of a tolerance to – emotional desolation. But this wouldn't be now, nor for a while yet.

For all his 'rejecting' response to the fleeting reappearance of Henri, Edgard toed a more co-operative line at the Conservatoire than he had under d'Indy. While there was far less compounding of mediocrity there than at the Schola, he had braked his lecture-disrupting wit and attempts at scathing extremism in his coursework. As snail-paced bureaucracy delayed the granting of his certificate of exemption from National Service until September 1907, this seeming reformation may have been, in part, a strategy to stay on the right side of Authority, and an educated guess is that much of Varèse's creative output then consisted of impressionistic observations about the joys of nature, the revolution of the Earth's seasons and the transience of the individual. Suggestive of a more grandiloquent Debussy, *Prelude À La Fin Du Jour* was 'for an orchestra of 120 musicians, which is colossal', gasped Deubel,[3] to whom the handwritten score was entrusted. It was, however, not found among the 34-year-old poet's belongings after his suicide on 13 June 1913.

For other lost works, all that remain are titles – *Colloque Au Bord De La Fontaine*, *Dans Le Parc*, *Poèmes Des Brumes*, anyone? A reference to a *Apothéose De l'Ocean* was made in *La Chronique De Paris*, an events guide, and there was also a completed *Souvenir*, patchy music to a poem entitled *La Lumière Natale* and, also by Deubel, several paragraphs of prose penned specifically for Varèse's use. A text by Sar Peladan was the lyrical thrust of *Le Fils Des Étoiles*, an attempt at an opera that, purportedly, bore some similarity to a rather inconsequential 1891 work by Satie.

More successful – in the sense that it eventually found a publisher – was Varèse's *Un Grand Sommeil Noir*, a three-minute song penned in 1906 for soprano and piano. Hinged on an 1881 poem of the same title by Verlaine – one of a collection started during the latter's incarceration in a Belgian gaol – it conveyed few even half-hidden musical (if not lyrical) clues of what was to come decades later. Melodically, there was nothing to provoke frowns from the likes of d'Indy – or, possibly, Henri Varèse, had he ever heard it. While a later (and longer) arrangement for orchestra exudes a clear depth of expression, *Un Grand Sommeil Noir* ('A Deep Black Sleep') stands as tall when trimmed to just voice and single instrument.

Capturing a stark beauty, Varèse's restrained arrangement leaves a contradictory aftertaste of blissful melancholy commensurate with three quatrains concerned with the 'beautiful sadness', quietude and fading of senses that follow a gathering of final thoughts by one on the point of a death confirmed by two closing staccato chords.

There was, perhaps, a shadowy link between *Un Grand Sommeil Noir* and *Rhapsodie Romane*, a hybrid of the previous century's Romanticism and of medieval traditions (to which Varèse had been introduced by Bordes). As well as being harbingers of cultural revolution, the most radical of artists – not only composers – embody a culmination of at least aspects of all that went before. Just as Picasso had turned to Toulouse-Lautrec, Bartók's earliest output, for example, was in a Liszt–Strauss vein, while Debussy's early efforts owed much to Massenet, just as Stravinsky's work for the ballet did to Rimsky-Korsakov. Now Stravinsky, too, was listening hard to music from the Middle Ages and overhauling its primitivism – as an older contemporary, Arnold Schoenberg, had when composing *Verklärte Nacht* in the style of Wagner before stripping it of all major and minor modes and functional harmony.

Whether Varèse was as adventurous with *Rhapsodie Romane* is unlikely, but this is mere speculation, since the piece is another lost to the archives of oblivion. However, for Rolland, it evoked 'solemn convent bells, shimmering autumnal twilights, ascetic souls in prayer'[11] when performed on piano by Edgard himself in the Renovation Aesthetique's small auditorium. In the audience, Peladan visualised it as 'a profane Gregorian chant'[11] if it ever reached the desired stage of a choral production, ideally within St Philibert at Tournus, the building in which the idea had come to Varèse when lifting his eyes to the thinly clouded angels.

Inspiration of broader detail prompted the beginnings of the symphonic poem *Bourgogne*, named after the bucolic shelter from the storms of his boyhood. On occasions, Varèse would have his fill of grappling with his muse, embellishing character assassinations of Conservatoire lecturers – especially Fauré, nowadays – being drawn into pretentious and futile fireside palavers until dawn in someone's room at the Renovation and having to feed and clothe himself via perpetual mental arithmetic. That's when Edgard Varèse would activate an escape valve to a tranquillity unknown in bohemian Paris and tread the backwards path to the morning of the Earth in rural Burgundy.

In Le Villars, the rustic backwater where there was always nothing doing, Grandfather Claude – now coping with chronic rheumatism – had purchased a small house ('which was once part of a tenth-century priory',[3] Edgard told his friends) with an attached vineyard, from which he manufactured his own brand of wine.

Since moving back, Claude Cortot had become a sort of village Socrates. Sticking to the same Republican opinions, he would hold forth on a café terrace in the sun-drenched square during Sunday Mass. Drawing on his pipe and nodding with apparent understanding, he would also listen to his grandson's short-lived endeavours to lead the discussion towards dialogue for the sake of dialogue about, say, the transmigration of souls or what Yriarte wrote about the collapse of the Second Empire and what Flaubert thought he meant.

Afternoon polemics also embraced asides from Monsieur Cortot's youthful sidekick about the barrier-breaking works that he was going to compose, but this fell on stony ground as, while Le Villars wasn't peopled by brutish yokels dwelling in broken-down shacks, the village had no official musical culture – no orchestra, no opera society, not even a silver band. Yet there *was* music to Edgard's ears, not so much in a bird chirrupping somewhere but in the lonesome whistle and *diddly-dum-clicketty-clack* of the passing trains, which reminded him of the 20th century back in Paris where, as Paul Le Flem was to reminisce, 'both Varèse and myself had a pretty tough time, [experiencing] moments of extreme financial depression'.[10]

Shortly before his time at the Renovation Aesthetique was up, in the summer of 1906, Edgard had exchanged half-serious letters with his *grand-père* about sharing a Parisian flat between them but had washed up alone at the wrong end of long Rue Monge in the fifth arrondissement, where most of the city's higher educational establishments had clotted. In November, however, he and Suzanne pooled their respective musical and thespian earnings and moved sideways – in every sense – to 27 Rue Descartes, parallel to Rue Monge and just as dingy.

Their apartment was towards the river in a forlorn cluster of streets, once respectable but now sliding into seediness. As early-evening streetlamps were lit, a lone pedestrian would cross the road to avoid 'Apaches' – swaggering phalanxes of youths from the poorer vicinities directly across the Seine. Satie always carried a hammer about his person as insurance against it ever being needed against these Apaches who, bored silly and with hormones raging, might be looking for things to destroy, people to beat up.

Such amusements were potentially available in the student district, but it was less burdensome to seek such gratifications closer to home along Rue du Faubourg Saint Antoine, which accorded principal access through the disreputable suburbs just beyond the opposite waterfront. Through this Parisian equivalent of Glasgow's Gorbals or southside Chicago, Edgard Varèse was now venturing out two evenings a week – merging into the shadows when he could – on his way to conduct the Choeur de l'Université Populaire, an ensemble of working men and women that he had organised for fun and profit – and as an eye-catching addition to his *curriculum vitae*.

His ambulatory brooding was interrupted by soft come-ons from the occasional tearsheet in a doorway's dark, but even for the thick-set Varèse – a past master at verbal, if not physical, combat – the sordid thrill of being out of bounds palled when he found himself constantly outfacing the gormless menace that the local yobs reserved for interlopers. With a chuckle, Edgard would reconjure how 'some of my choristers are old enough to be my parents, but some constituted themselves my bodyguard after our late evening rehearsals, escorting me as far as the Place de la Bastille, because the young Apaches of the neighbourhood "didn't know me yet", as they put it'.[3]

With his walk to and from rehearsals thus rendered as safe for him as a frighteningly favoured musician's would be in Al Capone's Chicago, Varèse organised choral recitals at the Château du Peuple in the University of Faubourg Saint Antoine, founded in 1899 as a 'people's university'. To ensure as full a house as possible, the repertoire did not extend the limits of the avant garde past a few intriguing medieval obscurities, but Varèse's then-half-formulated musical objectives would have been beyond the Choeur de l'Université Populaire – and, for that matter, any other vocal or instrumental entity in Europe.

Lately, he had been dipping into non-European cultures at the library, notably various accounts concerning African and Maori percussion. Varèse had also been puzzled but left with a feeling that he'd like to be convinced about the daring prophecies outlined in *Entwurf Einer Neuen Astbetik Der Tonkunst* (*Sketch Of A New Aesthetic Of Music*), an essay by Ferrucio Busoni, an Austrian–Italian composer and keyboard virtuoso (specialising in Bach) some 20 years Varèse's senior. While Busoni's own music adhered mainly to established conventions, he had visited North America and been captivated by a motor-driven and cumbersome precursor of the Hammond organ and, later, the Moog synthesiser. Invented by Dr Thaddeus Cahill, a New Yorker, in 1902, this 'telharmonium' had a rage of five octaves. Cahill had boasted that it could produce any number of pitches and overtones at any dynamic level. The next phase was to link the telharmonium to electricity, of which the only convenient source was the telephone system. This meant that it could only be heard from such a receiver, although fitting a megaphone to one served as a crude attempt at amplification when the good doctor demonstrated his discovery in concert.

When holding down a teaching post in the United States, Busoni was allowed an exploratory hour with the instrument. Thrilled by the purity of sound without the attending harmonics, he had returned to Europe evangelical in his belief that 'whatever new music becomes generally acceptable, machines will be necessary, and that they will play a vital part. Perhaps even industry will have its role to play in the progress and transformation of aesthetics.' Furthermore, like Schoenberg, Busoni foresaw 'the liquidation of the harmonic system based on the diatonic scale and the opposition of major and minor keys, as well as the advent of total chromaticism'.[12]

Busoni may have started to furnish vague and distant answers to some creative dilemmas, but Varèse had a more tangible solution for the needs of his domestic life. On 5 November 1907, he and Suzanne Bing got married.

Professionally, however, Varèse had fallen out irreconcilably with Fauré and, by implication, the Conservatoire. Like Mr Micawber, he was waiting for something to turn up, which it did with some speed. Before the year was out he was presented – thanks to Massenet and Widor's independent urging – with the 'Premier Bourse Artistique' of the City of Paris. It wasn't exactly the Prix de Rome, but it involved a cheque fat enough to cover the rent for several months and even enable Edgard to send a little money to Grand-père Claude.

The prestige *per se* was sufficient for someone unknown four years earlier to be brought to Claude Debussy, who, in his mid-40s, was at the height of his fame. Heaped with all manner of honours – including the loftiest grade of la Croix d'Officier de l'Ordre des Arts et des Lettres from the Ministry of Culture – he was nonetheless far from boastful about an appointment to the advisory board of the Conservatoire, where he had amassed a reputation for being antagonistic. This was correlated with worsening health that was to necessitate an operation for cancer of the rectum, leaving him with a colostomy bag attached to his lower body for the rest of his life.

Debussy was a decade from death in 1908 when he began corresponding with this Varèse that everyone was talking about. For a while, there was a flying to and fro of correspondence – some containing examples of each other's work – between Rue Descartes and Debussy's elegant house outside the inner city limits in the oak-beamed gentility of the Bois de Boulogne. Of the same stamp as Massenet, Debussy was ready to digest new perceptions and, if not entirely in artistic accord with Varèse, to study his music with more than polite interest. 'Although the tendencies in the scores were too foreign to his nature for him to really like them,' confessed Edgard, 'he approved of them objectively.'[13] Debussy, in turn, gave a round-eyed Varèse a corrected publisher's proof of his *La Mer*, an item of memorabilia inscribed, 'To Edgard Varèse, in sympathy and with my best wishes for success, October 29, 1908.'

Warming himself at a fireplace fashioned from carved sandalwood with space for half a tree to blaze in it, an ill-at-ease Varèse had been granted his first audience *chez* Debussy one snowy afternoon the previous spring. In demand as a conductor of his own compositions as far away as Moscow, the Great Man was guaranteed employment for good money for as long as he could stand. He could, therefore, afford to be paternal. 'His response was charming,' smiled Varèse. 'He put his hand on my shoulder and said, "And have I given you cause for complaint?" Being a rebel himself, I think he liked my somewhat aggressive independence and my revolt against conformity.'[13]

Debussy, like Satie, had explored unresolved dissonance, an area that Varèse wanted to but couldn't yet absorb into his own *oeuvre*. It became clear in conversation, too, that Debussy wasn't self-deprecating, either, about a knowledge and love of ethnic sounds from Africa and Australasia.

Of personal commonality between them was Debussy's ancestral connections to the same region of Burgundy as Le Villars. Edgard was also at one with Claude in the under-handed dissection of old-maidish Vincent d'Indy – with whom Debussy shared artistic similarities, although their talents and appetites were different – and a long-standing ideological feud that provided fascinating theatre of embarrassment at this intermission or that backstage party when the veneer of brother-like harmony evaporated and the two began scoring catty points off each other.

Touching on other topics than poor old d'Indy, Edgard's sardonic humour was akin to Claude's own. Nerves had suppressed it at the beginning but, as his glass was refilled at regular intervals, Varèse's tongue loosened and he began speaking with authority of many things – Picasso, Verlaine, the Franco–German crisis, Doctor Cahill's telharmonium... 'From the many long talks I had with Debussy,' considered Varèse, 'I have kept the image of a man of great kindness, intelligence, fastidiousness and wide culture. He treated me simply as a colleague, without the least condescension. He was too intelligent to be self-important. He would say, "You have a right to compose what you want to, the way you want to, if the music comes out and is your own."'[13]

More pragmatically, Debussy tried to help with such matters as a handwritten testimonial to induce a Parisian piano firm to take seriously the proposition of permitting the young friend of none less than Claude Debussy himself unlimited use of one of its products.

Perhaps old Claude was sufficiently soft-hearted to do the same for everyone who wasn't an obvious no-hoper, for his endorsement – combined with the fading lustre of the Premier Bourse Artistique – did not improve Varèse's prospects for, although Edgard attempted to channel his vexation into composition, there were days on end when little inspiration would come and all he could do was dream and despair, gazing glumly at the cobbled courtyard below the only window in his and Suzanne's poky one-room flat, separated from the next not by bricks but by grubby sackcloth.

Bickering helped pass the time. Out of work too, Suzanne was impetuous, argumentative and given to episodes of sulking herself. Neither was she the kind of bride to be content with the love of a good man, coats for blankets and waking up shivering to the next-door tenant's open-mouthed snore. Well, the place would have revolted pigs.

If he needed another excuse to quit the house, quit the city and quit the country, if need be, wasn't Debussy encouraging him and others to 'leave the Conservatoire as soon as possible and follow the ear, rather than the rule'[14]?

Yet, no matter how much Debussy professed to disdain the self-contained, privileged caste that ruled the music profession in 'artistically constipated'[10] Paris, he remained part of the same insufferably smug and cliquey closed shop. Its members exchanged smirks across concert-hall vestibules, as if the selections on the programmes couldn't be composed in any other way or performed by any other *virtuosi* than those approved of by the self-absorbed élite, whose only contact with real life was through sycophants and payroll courtiers. No one else counted.

Sickened by this and the thought of the present tension-charged ugliness – visible and invisible – stretching ahead of him, day upon day, until the grave, Edgard Varèse stopped dithering. With Suzanne supportive of any marginally feasible means of escape, he didn't even stick around long enough to honour existing dates with the Choeur de l'Université Populaire. It was the conclusion of interminable hours of the same arguments coming up over and over again, building from a trace of vapour in the sky to a crockery-smashing Wagnerian thunderstorm.

Edgard and his concurring wife packed their cases to leave Paris. 'I was impelled by a disgust for all the petty politics there,' he fumed, 'searching for a way of escaping from myself, for a way of escaping the French cultural in-crowd and that sentiment which neutralises the efforts and the sensibilities of the most astute, the most intelligent of people.'[15]

4 The Berliner

'The function of the creative artist consists in making laws, not in following laws already made.'
– Ferrucio Busoni, 1908

All signposts pointed to Berlin. One incentive for Varèse to flee France for a while was that, following his abandonment of the Conservatoire, it postponed further the evil hour when he would be conscripted. Another was that Berlin had become, however briefly, as vital a Mecca of the arts as Paris had been. Léon Deubel had been very pro-German, although he never went as far as trying to settle there. Nevertheless, Arnold Schoenberg would. What's more, Busoni already had, and that had been a consideration during sleepless nights of repetitive, anxious talk in the Rue Descartes until one breakfast time, when not so much a decision as an assumption had propelled Edgard and Suzanne into the seething rush-hour at the Gare de l'Est, buying single tickets to Berlin.

The Great Adventure began with the rest of the day plus a night and a morning in a third-class carriage. Hot-eyed, the couple arrived at the German border, where an official gave their passports a perfunctory glance. More assured of reaching their destination, they slipped into the uneasiest of slumbers until woken by a sudden jolt during an infuriatingly slow disembarkation from some country stop. The pallor of dawn gleamed dully as the couple gazed at the very valleys where, once upon a time, the Sleeping Beauty had dreamed in her enchanted castle and sheep now nibbled the grass of ancient battlegrounds. Small, half-timbered communities flew by, intimating that more remained of the arcadian Germany of yore – or a yore of sorts in such as Wagner-worshipping 'Mad' King Ludwig's fairytale palaces in the mountain greenery of Bavaria.

Such imaginings faded as the Varèses chugged through the bustling suburbs of Berlin. The smoke-blackened backs of buildings mingled with glimpses of streets of shopping precincts and City Exchange-type architecture. Peering incuriously at the long, high train was every archetype of the Prussian metropolis: close-cropped Hermans with sausages of fat bulging over their collars, their equally stout wives window shopping ponderously alongside them; Milchcow Mädchens garbed as office secretaries; and Prince Rupert of Schleswig-Holstein reincarnated as a navvy.

Where it could, the midday sun shone shyly through the grime-encrusted glass dome of the city's Friedrichstraße rail terminus as crumpled human shapes walked stiffly with their luggage along the platform. Near a rank of hackney cabs, an elderly pipe-smoking roadsweeper pushed a broom along the gutter. A newspaper vendor in his kiosk barked the headline of the final edition of the *Berlin Tageblatt*.

The oncoming night crept closer by several hours, hours spent tramping aimless pavements and suffering alternating attacks of apprehension about the mess they might now be in, more hope than they could yet justify and a strangely flippant despair: We could still be homeless this time tomorrow and destitute next week. If we can find the fare, we'll then be back in hand-to-mouth Paris by the end of the month, probably heading for an early grave along with the likes of neurotic and improvident Modigliani and his young wife in their garret. Oh, well...

By twilight, however, Suzanne and Edgard had found a hotel that didn't look too expensive. Revived by a bath and a night between clean sheets, Varèse sought out the mercurial Ferrucio Busoni, who happened to be home, enjoying a rare day off during a never-ending concert itinerary. Owing to the rather parochial nature of the European music scene, Varèse's name rang a bell with Busoni and, like a proper showbusiness professional, he thought it might be politic to bite back on any annoyance at having his leisure disturbed and make the caller welcome. He was nevertheless flattered that the young man strove to appear so casually knowledgable about Busoni's career, including his revelations about the telharmonium and other new inventions and the intellectual challenge of his theories.

'When I came across Busoni's dictum, "Music was born free and to win freedom is its destiny",' elucidated Varèse, 'I was amazed and very much excited to find that there was somebody besides myself – and a musician, at that – who believed this. It gave me the courage to go on with my ideas and my scores. He not only corroborated, clarified and encouraged my ideas but, being as magical a talker as he was a brilliant thinker, he had the gift of stimulating my mind to feats of prophetic imagination. He was a great Renaissance lord with great depths of kindness.'[1]

Varèse learned nothing fresh from Busoni, but it was reassuring that one so eminent held views in accord with his own and was able to nutshell so articulately the scattered thoughts that had invaded Varèse's mind even before he'd left Turin.

While life with his parents seemed almost like a previous existence, he hadn't burned his boats with Paris. Besides, Suzanne began commuting almost immediately to intermittent seasons in repertory, once joining the cast of a Paris-based company touring France with Chekhov's *Uncle Vanya*.

Sometimes, Edgard, though not fond of plays, would watch his wife emoting onstage during visits to Paris to catch up with Gonzalez, Deubel, Rolland (shortly to retire to Switzerland) and other friends from the Renovation Aesthetique era, who recognised him as Our Man In Germany. In this capacity, he tried and failed to initiate dialogue between Debussy and Busoni.

Varèse also seized opportunities to network, and social encounters with both Lenin and, later, Trotsky were made out by an older Varèse to be less fleeting. Other new acquaintances seemed even more significant than they actually were. If stand-offish, Ravel nonetheless invited the Varèses to the private première of his piano suite *Gaspard De La Nuit*, along with a select gathering that included Debussy, Widor and – days away from his emigration to the USA – the internationally renowned harpist Carlos Salzedo. After the performance, Ravel unbent sufficiently to actuate a conversation with Varèse. All that they had in common was the Conservatoire, and it was heavy going until Edgard was rescued by Gonzalez.

The sculptor was among the few privileged to accompany the Varèses to Le Villars. On one of these occasions, he drew a pen portrait of Claude Cartot, which was later framed by his grandson and hung in the furnished lodgings that he and Suzanne had taken along Nassauischstraße, off Kurfurstendamm – roughly the equivalent of London's Oxford Street or New York's Fifth Avenue – in what was to become West Berlin.

Between them, Edgard and Suzanne had enough knowledge of German to make themselves understood, however haltingly, as it was, with English, the main non-classical foreign tongue taught in French schools. Gradually, phrasebooks and constant exposure enabled them to read German laboriously and gave them a local accent – slightly nasal with a quickish delivery – and the dialect that filtered from the Polish border across to the neck of Denmark.

Before he became this fluent, Varèse's stronger command of musical language gained him work as a copyist, just as it had when he'd first arrived in Paris. Indirectly, this brought him to a dinner party in the suburban home of 35-year-old Hugo Von Hofmannsthal, an Austrian playwright and lyric poet who was attempting to reach a wider audience by plundering traditional and mythical themes that were part of the common unconscious. As these relied as much on dramatic action and spectacular visual effects as mere words, they lent themselves to adaptation in the style of 'grand opera', an imprecise term that Von Hofmannsthal used to distinguish a 'serious' work from Gilbert and Sullivan-esque operetta. A writer of his calibre deserved nothing less, reckoned his new-found friend, and so it was that Hugo placed his 1906 play *Oedipus Und Die Sphinx* at the silver-tongued Edgard's disposal to turn it into a three-act grand opera, just as he had granted the more eminent Richard Strauss permission to do the same with *Elektra*, the Sophocles tragedy. Furthermore, neither of these collaborators would need a librettist. They already had one: Hugo Von Hofmannsthal.

Edgard soon shaped *Oedipus Und Die Sphinx* into a workable format. Von Hofmannsthal was so pleased with this that he tried to winkle a small advance out of his publisher and began pestering Franz Schalk of the Vienna Opera to cast his eyes over an excerpt. Looking for a more objective perspective, Varèse approximated it on piano for Busoni. When the final coda died, he glanced up from the keyboard with enquiring eyebrow. After Busoni twisted his pride into a frown with amused indifference and a few perfunctory tips for improvements, Edgard posted the score to Rolland for a second opinion and couldn't comprehend the latter's advice to ditch Hugo's 'dreary and over-erudite'[1] plot altogether in favour of some other ancient saga.

Rolland may have even suggested one for, taking his words of wisdom to heart, Varèse turned to Gargantua, a character whose eye-stretching exploits are central to Book One of Rabelais's famous five-part satire *Gargantua Et Pantagruel*. The aptly named giant of folk tradition also happened to be the subject of the fictional symphonic poem in Rolland's *Jean Christophe*. Edgard's own work, however, seemed to be progressing little further than him talking about it, citing poor health as an excuse for lack of progress.

Under no external pressure to compose, and with *Oedipus Und Die Sphinx* arousing only partisan enthusiasm, he was considering a last resort of becoming a music teacher. He had been told of a vacancy for such a post at an academy back in Paris. If they still thought kindly of him, references from, say, Albert Roussel and Charles-Marie Widor would return him to the fold. The rest of his days might then be an anti-climax, but at least he and Suzanne wouldn't be dogged by that undercurrent of financial insecurity that was already floating their marriage into a choppy sea. Their love story might have ended happily with the pipe between the teeth, the clipped beard and the brown leather elbows on the tweed jacket epitomising the principal breadwinner's adjustment to respectable middle age. During lunch hours, he might have doodled on the assembly hall's upright when not relaxing in the staff room. With the comparatively short hours of his profession, he might also have immersed himself in composition as other family men did in do-it-yourself, pottery or bowls.

What a ridiculous waste of talent, protested Romain Rolland, who put instant action over debate by penning for Varèse a letter of introduction to Richard Strauss, now musical director and chief conductor of the Berlin Philharmonic. At first, Edgard – although now by no means as timid – was as crippled with apprehension as he had been when nerving himself to knock on Giovanni Bolzoni's door.

Yet Varèse wasn't an avid consumer of Strauss's music, even though he'd noted that parts for wind machine[2] and rattling chains had been integrated into the scoring of 1898's *bravura Don Quixote*. Once thought of as revolutionary, Strauss was now regarded as a kind of Rudyard Kipling of German music, suffering a tarring with the same brush as Bruckner, Brahms and other behemoths of the outmoded Romanticism that had dominated Europe's muse since the end of the 18th century. Fuelling his detractors' often unfair derision was the received wisdom that, however polished they were, *Salome*, *Elektra* and other recent spectaculars did not match the vigour of earlier offerings that, for all their recklessly strewn mistakes, Strauss had committed to manuscript paper without any of the complacency that fame and wealth often engenders.

Critical vitriol was not reflected in market standing, however, and concerts featuring Strauss compositions – with or without the fellow himself appearing on the podium – were guaranteed sell-outs. He could command huge fees, dictating terms to fawning tour managers, and carried inordinate weight in executive decisions concerning the Berlin Philharmonic's repertoire. He was, therefore, a powerful means to an end to be carefully cultivated by any aspiring musician. Schoenberg's petitioning of Strauss, for example, had resulted in funding, constructive advice as well as a plum job at the Stern Conservatorium.

So it was that, on one spring morning in 1909 – and not really by chance – Edgard Varèse was standing on the pavement as Richard Strauss drew on elegant gloves when striding down the front steps of his town house in Kurfurstendamm. Yes, Herr remembered Romain Rolland and trusted that he was in good health. He also recalled the letter. However, although Strauss showed a faint but clear interest in Varèse – despite neither speaking the other's language very well – he could do nothing for him until he'd seen his work.

In that same year, Varèse also got in touch with Gustav Mahler, whose highly personalised style, perhaps surprisingly, he appreciated less than Strauss's popularism. While a rendezvous with Mahler was not momentous, Edgard's gradually more astute gift for self-promotion paid off when he put himself in the way of Karl Muck, quite a well known German musician who was then awaiting a destiny as conductor of the Boston Symphony Orchestra. If aware that here was a young chap openly on the make, Muck warmed to Varèse to the extent of laying on with a trowel his 'rich and original quality of invention, a lively imagination and a complete mastery of musical technique', not to mention his 'warmth, energy, unflagging determination and upright and correct conduct in the face of great difficulties confronting him in his daily life',[3] when writing on his behalf to various contacts.

Cumulatively, this and more hard-won recommendations from Busoni, von Hofmannsthal and Strauss found Edgard bits and pieces of employment by autumn, mainly assembling choirs (notably the Symphonischerchor, which was similar in outlook to the Saint Antoine ensemble), teaching counterpoint to foreign students and more transcribing.

He took on these jobs with bad grace or martyred nobility, depending on whether he was representing them to Suzanne or Strauss, who was always promising to speak to his publisher about Edgard. By degrees, however, life in Berlin grew to be nauseatingly familiar as the Varèses became more and more embroiled in cashflow problems.

It was a steady downward spiral with little peaks and troughs. Edgard's Symphonischerchor had first refusal whenever a chorale was required for the bigger productions – *Faust*, *A Midsummer Night's Dream*, *et al* – of the Berlin Deutsche Theatre with its then-novel revolving stage. Yet, by mid-1911, the only regular income he was bringing to Nassauischstraße was that from one solitary pupil, a 16-year-old Swede.

Further economic damage was inflicted via Suzanne's unplanned pregnancy and the inconvenient arrival, on 28 September 1910, of a daughter. They named her Claude, after Debussy and her Burgundian great-grandfather, who died suddenly a few weeks later. The bilious coincidence of this, on top of Deubel's suicide in June, made Edgard feel the loss of his beloved grandparent all the more sharply as no misfortune that could be philosophised away but an irredeemable emotional disaster. Deeply depressing, it was to erode Varèse's relationship with his only child, despite studied efforts to prevent Claude's infant vulnerability from showing up the Henri in him.

He was, however, inattentive as both a father and a husband, preferring to eat breakfast in the late afternoon to fuel himself for frowning over scrawls of music until the grey of morning, ignoring the squalling brat and connected disturbances as far as he was able. Occasionally, Claude would stir in him an onset of tickling, pillow-fighting high spirits, but this was more for his own recreational benefit than the baby's, according to Suzanne, who berated him, too, for behaving as though she was there only to provide refreshments as he accumulated fatigue through his obsessive composing.

By Claude's second birthday, her parents were almost permanently apart. She was now being shunted between Berlin and Montparnasse, where her mother had resumed a full-time acting career at the Vieux-Columbier, a travelling company recently formed by Jacques Coupeau, within spitting distance of St Sulpice.

As he had been over the business with Henri, Claude Debussy was bemused by Edgard's merely perfunctory communications with his wife during one of his increasingly longer stays in Paris. Indeed, if not immune from twinges of conscience, Edgard seemed less inclined to fan the dying embers of any optimism that he, Suzanne and Claude would be a family again one day than keep abreast of the cultural sensation of a given season.

In autumn 1912, the sensation was Schoenberg's *Pierrot Lunaire*. Varèse and Igor Stravinsky had been among those present at the dress rehearsal on 9 October at Berlin's Choralionsaal, although neither was aware of the other. If dismissive of the 'trashy poem'[4] that was the crux of the libretto, Varèse – and Stravinsky – had been impressed with the composer's complete suspension of tonality – albeit with keys implied fitfully – in the semi-spoken song-cycle considered an aural nightmare by many, then and now, but described as 'one of the most important foundations of 20th-Century musical experience'[5] by Peter Maxwell Davies after he had become as zealous about Schoenberg as Frank Zappa became about Varèse.

Two years earlier, Schoenberg's Strauss-ish symphonic poem *Pelléas Et Mélisande*[6] had been heard during the same week and at the same venue – Berlin's Bluthner Hall – as a programme on 10 December that included Varèse's *Bourgogne*, now finished and dedicated to his very late grandfather. To facilitate this orchestral concert debut – postponed from the previous March – the obliging Strauss had called in a favour from Josef Stransky, the auditorium's resident conductor. A-twitter with excitement, Edgard railroaded everyone he knew in the city to attend, even applying emotional blackmail to drag Rolland from Switzerland and Busoni, feverish with 'flu, from his fireside and blanketed armchair.

Just as far too many would profess to have been at the first performance of Stravinsky's ballet *Le Sacre Du Printemps* three years later, so there has been in microcosm a profound lack of retrospective honesty about *Bourgogne*. Hundreds more than can have actually been there were to recapture memories of Edgard's big night, but no ticket-holders – genuine and otherwise – have ever given any precise indication of the nature of the sounds that they had allegedly paid to hear.

Yet, to beef up an image of himself as being a man ahead of his time, Varèse's eulogists have portrayed *Bourgogne* as an ignition point for extreme reaction. However, while it didn't appeal to the more conservative musical palates, the overall opinion, as the frosty twilight struck the departing audience, was that, between them, young Varèse, Herr Stransky and the house orchestra had made nice music as part of a stimulating evening's entertainment. This was a view encapsulated in print in *Berlin Zeitung* and *Berlin Tageblatt*, each freighted with vague praise for aspects of *Bourgogne*. 'Full of fascinating radiances,'[7] wrote Alfred Kerr of the latter daily, before requesting the composer to contribute an article about his influences and approach to his work for the newspaper's *Pan* supplement. More important to Varèse was the spoken opinion of Rolland, who had noticed the influence of Strauss, Debussy and – damn him! – d'Indy, as well as the piece's 'calm, religious character'.[4]

Although the first time was the only time for *Bourgogne*, 30-year-old Edgard was so full of his marvellous achievement that 'he seemed unable to go beyond it', sighed Andre Billy, one of the Paris crowd's minor writers. 'He talked about it too much. We used to say that he'd never do anything else.'[4] Nevertheless, although nothing concrete was ever to come of it, Varèse returned to the neglected *Gargantua* and embarked on a fresh orchestral opus, *Mehr Licht*, soon renamed *Les Cycles Du Nord*. It had been prompted by a recent and intense fascination with Goethe – significantly, a scientist as well as an illustrious poet – and an unmarred view of the Aurora Borealis ('unbelievable exaltation, an indescribable sensation'[4]) sighted on a grey-green horizon when, pallid with the Dracula hours he kept in Berlin, Varèse had spent a lonely holiday in some North Sea resort when pushing his wife and daughter into the background of his life.

He and Suzanne had drifted into open separation now. When the gap became too wide for either to negotiate, so began the path to a formal dissolution of a dead marriage. It was presented in Ouellette's biography – and, to a lesser degree, in *Varèse: A Looking-Glass Diary* – as scarcely more than a mild disagreement between the parties, but, after a month in Berlin with her father, custody of Claude was entrusted by a Parisian divorce court to Mme Kauffmann in the south of France. This, on top of hurt, anger and old grievances, caused Varèse to rationalise the loss of Claude to Suzanne's family as the shedding of a burden by one who'd endured a debilitating childhood himself, bereft of a father's love. Although each always remembered the other's birthday, contact between father and daughter – and ex-husband and ex-wife – was to become more and more sporadic with every passing year.

Whilst in the early stages of thus shaking off marital fetters – and moving back to Paris – Varèse had risen from a thoughtful seat at the Théâtre des Champs-Elysées in the midst of the uproar that would drive an offended Stravinsky from the building in the wake of *Le Sacre Du Printemps*'s first airing, on 13 May 1913. It had concluded with long seconds of silence before a shell-shocked crowd reacted. For some, the piece was anathema, a crime against God infinitely worse than the obscene ascending *glissando* on a trombone.

Conversely, if beset with conflicting emotions, Varèse – like most of its champions – had seen *Le Sacre Du Printemps* coming from afar. His psyche had not boggled nor his sensibilities been upset. To him, the heavy rhythmic emphasis and percussive, grinding discords of this savage invocation of pagan ceremony made perfect and inevitable sense. He said as much when pressed, but wasn't over-effusive. What Varèse couldn't bring himself to articulate was that Stravinsky had achieved what he was still chasing. If anything, long absences in Germany had made Edgard even more of an unknown quantity in Paris than he had been before he left. Ultimately, all he had to show for his struggles since leaving Turin were the six-year-old Première Bourse triumph and the curate's-egg plaudits that had followed the one-night-only inclusion of *Bourgogne* on the bill at Bluthner Hall.

While nearly all of Varèse's other manuscripts – in differing states of completion – had been stored in a Berlin warehouse, the individual instrumental scores of *Bourgogne*, dog-eared and tattered, had accompanied him to Paris to lie forgotten in a drawer in the ground-floor flat he had rented, two minutes' dawdle from his and Gauduchon's old rooms along the Rue Saint-Andre-des-Arts.

Le Sacre Du Printemps might have been an indication that one kind of tide was turning, albeit with majestic slowness. However, the title of the popular song 'Paris, Tu N'A Pas Changé' rang true in that nothing else had altered much since Varèse had been away, except that *la vie bohème* had lost more of its 1903 allure. Social life on a low income in the middle of winter was just as complicated as ever. Yet Edgard contrived to smarten himself up for those necessary ordeals of conviviality at which he mortgaged his spare time.

The round of soirées, first nights and like occasions bred many insecurities among *illuminati* and small-fry alike, but the cardinal sin was to show them. That visible desperation was too nasty a reminder of the impermanence of fame and wealth was a pervading thought that kept Edgard on his toes at the fashionable Île Saint Louis home of Louise Fauré-Favier, *the* society hostess of bohemian Paris. There, in the midst of the hysterical chatter and rehearsed patter that accompanied such galas, the atmosphere would be laced with an essence of fine tobacco and pricey perfume, and an observer would pass up to a dozen artistic and scientific legends along a single staircase. Debussy would pass a plate of sandwiches to Apollinaire at the buffet. Fernand Léger's head would be thrown back with laughter at some vulgar joke by Jean Cocteau. Don't look now, but isn't that René Bertrand, the inventor? That chap I can't quite place, isn't he some German musician? He speaks excellent French...

Varèse was daring a walkabout, trying not to make it look like he was making an effort. He ended up at a table on the periphery of small-talk soon swamped by big-talk from Luigi Russolo, the man of the moment for *The Art Of Noises*, published in March 1913. 'Life in ancient times was silent,' he pontificated therein. 'In the last century, however, with the coming of heavy industry, noise was born.'[8] To this end, in 1911 he had built a Heath-Robinson-ish 'noise organ' that regimented on a keyboard the extraneous sounds of the everyday.[9]

The garrulous Luigi went on to predict that, as well as – or rather than – the usual strings, brass, woodwinds, *et al*, future orchestras would contain the machines – *intonarumori* – that he was presently constructing, starting with the first of his explosive *scoppiatori*, which emitted a series of pops, hisses, squeaks and thuds. On the way, too, promised Russolo, were the onomatopoeically named *crepitatori* ('cracklers'), *gorgogliatori* ('gurglers' or 'bubblers'), *rombatori* ('roarers'), *ronzatori* ('buzzers'), *sibilatori* ('hissers'), *stroppicciatori* ('rubbers' or 'scrapers') and, of course, the *scoppiatori*. Edgard hung onto every word as this Luigi person continued. He had, Russolo said, already been contracted to present an entire concert of such music in Milan next spring. The players wouldn't rely on scores so much as instructions about pressing buttons and turning handles. Among items composed already were *Dawn In The City*, *Gathering Of Aircraft And Automobiles* and *Battle At The Oasis*.

Then the conversation degenerated to luvvie platitudes and waspish remarks about other Italian 'Futurists' like Filippo Tommaso Marinetti and Balilla Pratella, who had pre-empted *The Art Of Noises* with 1911's *The Technical Manifesto Of Futurist Music.* Furthermore, Pratella had just written a rather naïve work entitled *Musica Futuristica.* Russolo thought that the standard instruments Pratella used for this were inapplicable to the 'modern' effects – motor car engines, machine guns, aircraft propellers, *et al* – that he was aiming to reproduce. Edgard chipped in by name-dropping Hermann Helmholtz, René Bertrand – whose 'dynaphone', he'd be dismayed to discover, wasn't much different in principle from Thaddeus Cahill's telharmonium – Picabia with his da Vinci-like drawings of useless machinery and a now-post-Cubist Fernand Léger, then at the fore of the French wing of the Futurist movement.

Varèse was to understand the Italian Futurists' revelling in urban *bruitisme* but disregarded noise as a means of self-aggrandising sensationalism, which was the aftertaste of what he called Marinetti's 'noise-art', as well as Russolo's cluttered and hysterical recitals in Milan and – also prefaced by a lecture from the movement's self-styled 'founder', Filippo Marinetti – as part of a fortnight-long Futurist Exhibition in London. Amplified with megaphones, the pieces, if absorbed cumulatively, were nothing more than a kind of adult update of the *Toy Symphony* that, attributed originally to Haydn, had parts for rattle, cuckoo clock, tin drum, toy trumpet and the like added to those for orthodox instruments, just as a cannon was to supplement Tchaikovsky's *1812 Overture.* Works similar to the *Toy Symphony* had been composed since by Mendelssohn, Jakob Romberg as well as others.

As it had with *Le Sacre Du Printemps*, the audience made as much row as the musicians, with some enraged customers hurling stink-bombs. But, while the concept of Russolo's noise concerts – quiet by today's megawatt standards – was applauded by Stravinsky, Satie and Varèse, among others, only the maligned Pratella was to incorporate *intonarumori* into his work, placing them alongside conventional instruments in the orchestra pit for his 1915 opera *L'Aviatore Dro.*

Two years later, Satie weaved pistol shots, a siren and the pecking of a typewriter into the scoring of his ballet *Parade*, but Varèse, in imminent retrospect, was to shrug off Russolo, Marinetti and Pratella as gimmick merchants, silly, vulgar and fake with 'no other intention in their works but a succession of titillating clusters of sound, material that is principally of terrifying intractability and no intellectual concern with anything but external sensory effect'.[10]

Anticipating synthesisers just as da Vinci had aeroplanes, Varèse was becoming more entranced with the beauty of noise as a purely musical device. Indeed, in 1926, he was to proffer one of his own works, *Amériques*, as sonic evidence of this in 'the interpretation of a mood, a piece of pure music absolutely unrelated to the noises of modern life. Actually, the use of pure sound in music does to harmonies what a crystal prism does to pure light – it scatters it into 1,000 varied and unexpected vibrations. To be modern is to be natural, an interpreter of the spirit of your own time. I can assure you that I am not straining after the unusual.'[10]

In 1913, however, Varèse was straining after gainful employment, despite the impressions he created whenever his paths crossed those with whom he was on fluctuating professional equality – usually at the soirées, which now seemed more frenzied, with the laughter shriller and the eyes as bright as the sparks from the revolver in Sarajevo that were to ignite the long-foretold Great War. While Archduke Franz Ferdinand's days were numbered, Edgard Varèse was lodging restless pleas with Parisian impresario Gabriel Astruc, whose principal client was the Russian Ballet. To get the fellow off his back, Astruc promised to lean on his agents with a view to presenting *Bourgogne* and other Varèse works – if they existed – in Vienna, Budapest and further east. Edgard himself picketed moneyed individuals like Jean Cocteau, who caved in enough to shortlist him as musical director if a project for a circus production of *A Midsummer's Night Dream* ever got off the ground.

Edgard continued to behave outwardly as if these were possibilities long after the respective trails had gone stone cold. Inwardly, weeks of inactivity bred despair of ever getting up to the next level, as had Schoenberg, Stravinsky and 22-year-old Sergei Prokofiev, whose first works had already made him one of the best known – not to say notorious – musicians in Russia.

The fish weren't biting for Edgard Varèse, and the driving and clearly futile urge to be a composer was a handicap as surely as if he had been schizophrenic or a drug addict. Perhaps Papa had been right after all. A steady job, a mortgage, even wedding bells again might be worth considering now. The alternative seemed to be a vocational road that was obscure and quiet, a dusty, wearisome road that didn't look as if it led anywhere important – although there was always a chance that it might.

What else was there, apart from just enough incentive not to throw in the towel? As 1913 mutated into 1914, Astruc's *speiling* on his new client's behalf paid off when the Mojmir Urbanek Concert Society (no, I'd never heard of it either) let it be known that they wanted a suitable conductor for a programme consisting entirely of modern French music – notably a symphony by Albert Roussel and the first concert performance of the orchestral suite from Debussy's choral *Le Martyre De Saint Sébastiene*. The Society's budget allowed for just three rehearsals with the Czech Philharmonic Orchestra before the show on the first Sunday in January at the Smetana Hall in Prague.

Who better for the job, argued Astruc, than Roussel's star pupil, who, into the bargain, had been patted metaphorically on the head by Debussy, too? Delighted, the Society secretary bragged to the press about obtaining the services of Debussy's most talented protégé. A build-up of hyperbole and goodwill made the all-important *Prager Tageblatt* – and, by implication, Prague's lesser newspapers – determined to like it, as expressed in a prosy and truism-ridden critique of how the guest conductor 'succeeded in revealing to us the very soul of the compositions. The Great Love of Art which lives in this slender young man, the nobility of his demeanour...held the orchestra under his spell and immediately captivated the audience. The recital was a musical event, and it is to be hoped that we shall soon be able to hear this enthusiastic defender of modern music again as both a conductor and composer.'[11]

During the anti-climax of the return journey, Edgard's night train hurtled through landscapes blackened but for distant pinpoints of light, like a portent of doom, both global and personal. On 28 June, the bullet severed Franz Ferdinand's jugular vein and life puddled out of him. Nine months after this set in motion the chain of events that brought about the war, *L'Intransigeant*, one of many 'anti-establishment' arts periodicals that had sprung up in France, reported that the army had caught up with 'the musician Edgard Varèse'.[12]

In March 1915, his patriotic chore started in as dispiriting a way as he could have imagined. As he hadn't been brought to the barracks on a stretcher, the induction medical was a mere formality. Next, his long, wavy hair was planed halfway up the side of the skull with clippers and he was kitted out with an ill-fitting uniform that had the texture of a horse blanket. During basic training, he was bawled at from dawn 'til dusk.

The square bashing, the boot polishing and the baiting by other soldiers, who suspected that he was 'musical', made the months drag so intolerably that he was wondering about deserting. Then came a posting to the 25th Infantry Regiment, where he functioned as a staff bicycle courier after an application to be an interpreter, with his knowledge of German, was rejected. Joining the same unit several weeks later was Fernand Léger, who, before returning to figurative painting in old age, was to become to fine art what Varèse would later be to music in his fascination with the imagery and latent artistic vocabulary of modern technology and mass production. In 1915, however, there was little opportunity for the two to compare notes because, that summer, Léger was bundled off to the trenches – and back again in a field ambulance after he was gassed.

Meanwhile, a miracle had happened for Edgard Varèse. Days away from being transferred to a machine-gun battery, he was poleaxed with a bout of double pneumonia that brought him close to death. The disease was to exact a recurring toll on his constitution, and yet it warranted Varèse's hasty discharge from active service – although not before he posed for a photograph in his battle dress, with his hair regrown to dashing-romantic length.

Weak with relief, he shacked up in yet another Montparnasse attic, this time opposite the railway station. The solitude was pleasant after the barracks, where lack of privacy had been very much the way of things.

One day, while lying full-length and head-under-hands on the bed, the door creaked open and an apparition intruded on his mental stock-taking. It seemed both unknown and familiar. Then the years rolled away and Varèse saw the face of Maurice, his second-youngest brother, richly dressed and grown in the image of his father. As far as Papa had had a favourite, it had been Maurice, the sibling with whom Edgard had felt the least empathy – although that wasn't saying much. Like the other two, if called as witness for the defence whenever a parental scolding was pending, he'd been as trustworthy as quicksand.

Now, after 15 years without contact, Maurice was a stranger bound to a speechless and staring Edgard only by the invisible chains that shackle brother to brother. Doubtless, when reporting back to the others, he would not be able to spare details when dissecting Edgard's distressed circumstances and frail physical condition with joyous vehemence. Looking around the room – which contained only the bed and a piano – with summary distaste, Maurice stood feet apart, his back to the fireplace, displaying himself to Edgard. He waited a decent conversational interval and then began to tell of his successes due to having followed in Papa's sensible and well-heeled footsteps. And then he turned the conversation to Edgard himself. You look well, Edgard. How's your career going? What happened to the big plans you had to be a famous composer? You've come a long way. By the way, how's the wife – Suzanne, isn't it? – and the baby?

Edgard loathed Maurice all over again for his present conduct, his likeness to Henri and everything else that he represented. Furious, he bade his relation a politely insulting farewell. That was the end of Maurice and, indeed, the end of anything further to do with his family. For perhaps the duration of what he – like everyone else – imagined would be a short war, it also helped finish Edgard Varèse with Paris, from where he would retreat to almost the last place on the planet that Maurice or Papa might expect to find him.

5 The Immigrant

'I have never tried to fit my conceptions into any known container.'
– Edgard Varèse, Princeton University lecture, 1959

When it entered the war in April 1917, the United States of America hadn't quite become the wellspring of everything glamorous that it would during the next global conflict. Nevertheless, its star was in the ascendant. Following President Grover Cleveland's alienation of half of Congress by his upholding of the Gold Standard, the so-called Panic Of 1893 – manifested in falling harvest prices and troops breaking up a widespread railway strike – had racked the country's economy for years. Nevertheless, the USA had crept ahead of everywhere else, technologically speaking. Whereas, for example, there were less than 1,000 private residences with telephones in Paris, there was more than ten times that number in New York. Moreover, motorised taxi-cabs and an internal railway system had covered the whole city soon after the completion in 1903 of the Williamsburg Suspension Bridge – the largest bridge of its kind in the world – connecting the island of Manhattan to Brooklyn, Queens and even the suburbs beyond.

The USA was also a safer haven for artistic radicalism, now that a vanguard on both the east and west coasts had developed independently of those in Paris and Berlin. It was certainly taking the lead in aspects of music, as was glaringly exemplified on 6 March 1913, when 'jazz' was elevated from slang via its use in the *San Francisco Bulletin* in a feature concerning singer Al Jolson, whose 78rpm recording of 'The Spaniard That Blighted My Life' had been released in that week.

Stravinsky and classical composer *manqué* George Gershwin were quite open about their knowledge and love of jazz, even though Stravinsky's *Ebony Concerto* for Woody Herman's band lay nearly three decades in the future. So, too, did Stravinsky's emigration to the States, when an acceptance of a lectureship at Harvard University in the watershed year of 1939 was but one instance of European politics making an exile of one of its finest minds.

On 18 December 1915, Europe's cutting of its own throat was among the factors – among them – that, on top of personal desolations, spurred Edgard Varèse's departure for New York on board the *Rochambeau*, a package steamer from Bordeaux. Another was the universal aunt that was the continent's cultural establishment and what he saw as its excessive thrift with regard to new music and its constricting designations about what should and shouldn't be experienced within the walls of its art galleries and auditoriums. Maybe the war would help overturn that.

This stultifying attitude was why Julio Gonzales was now a welder in a Renault car factory. It was why Karl Muck, Leopold Stokowski (from England) and even the caricature Italian conductor Arturo Toscanini – all rapturous eyes and twirled moustachios – had gladly accepted respective posts with the Boston Symphony Orchestra, the Philadelphia Orchestra and New York's Metropolitan Opera. And it was why the pianist Sergei Koussevitzky was to travel from Russia to succeed Muck in Boston as well as why the harpist Carlos Salzedo had come already from Paris to join the Metropolitan Opera, at the invitation of Toscanini, who was to surrender his baton to Arthur Bodansky, once Mahler's assistant at Vienna's Imperial Opera.

It was why Marcel Duchamp had had enough of Europe, too, and why he had turned up on May Ray's New York doorstep the previous June with a gift of a glass ball containing 'Parisian air'.

Finally, it was why Edgard Varèse found himself in real danger of starving to death in his Montparnasse hovel, and why he was berthed in the low-fare 'steerage' section to the fore of the *Rochambeau* in a bunk bed above a chap named Abel Warshawsky. With letters of introduction and enough cash to sustain him for maybe a fortnight, at best, Varèse was ready to be pushed in whatever direction fate ordained.

To fellow passengers, he became known as the bloke who pounded the ivories in shipboard concerts, but to customs officials he was just another long-haired European when, 12 uneventful days later, the *Rochambeau* negotiated the ingress of the trudging Hudson River and dropped anchor at a pier on the western shore of Manhattan, the oldest borough of New York. If jaded by travel, Edgard Varèse felt a recharge of wakefulness and then a tingle of expectancy as he and Abel Warshawsky heaved their luggage out of the dock, across Riverside Park and into the streets of the Upper West Side.

As the *Rochambeau* had pottered along the Hudson, the passengers had beheld the splendour of the 15-storey skyscrapers on the skyline, but these were nowhere to be seen in what was to be the multi-ethnic location of Leonard Bernstein's *West Side Story* nearly half a century later. In 1915, too, it was a huddled land of few illusions for hordes of ragged children as skinny and ferocious as stray cats, who catcalled and scrapped in the city's coarsest intonation while dodging both the moving traffic and the pavement-cluttering fruit-and-vegetable carts standing wheel to wheel beneath what was visible of sepia skies. High above, mothers gossiped between washtubs and clotheslines on the flat roofs of squat red-brick or wooden-frame tenements, each wrapped in an iron lacework of fire escapes. These buildings seemed to shiver as New York Transit Authority trains clattered by.

Before that winter's afternoon was out, Abel and Edgard were unpacking inside such a building, having discovered that just under $1 a day – in advance – paid for a grim apartment along West 88th Street, which they shared with a painter named Albert Gleizes and his wife. As if Varèse had jumped out of the Parisian *réfrigérateur* and into the New York icebox, there was no central heating, adequate sanitation or bathroom. Sharing the miniscule communal back yard with a finger-crushing mangle, a zinc tub could be lugged indoors whenever sufficient hot water had been accumulated on the pot-bellied stove that also provided a tenant's only protection against iced-up windows and gooseflesh. It wasn't the healthiest environment for someone lately recovered from double pneumonia. Diptheria and diarrhoea were a way of life – and death – there, too.

As the noise of his first hours on an alien continent subsided, the last sound to lacerate the air as Edgard fell asleep was an engine whistle emitting the same lone note – a high C sharp – as the one he used to hear from the carriages that passed by Le Villars.

The next morning, after some heart-searching arithmetic, he took a tram to Greenwich Village, a district towards Lower Manhattan that he'd been assured by Karl Muck was as vibrantly bohemian as Montparnasse, teeming with poets, painters, musicians and the like since the 1840s, when Walt Whitman and an ailing Edgar Allan Poe had been near-neighbours there.

His cult reputation in European centres of operation preceding him, Varèse triggered some fuss when he walked into the Photo-Secession Gallery at the Washington Square end of Fifth Avenue. Then exhibiting African and Mexican art objects, some juxtaposed with Cubist drawings from Braque and Picasso, it was one of about half a dozen fashionable locales frequented by New York's cultural lions and their hangers-on. Cutting a familiar and beautiful figure at such gatherings, Louise McCutcheon was recognised professionally, firstly as a talented writer and then as the malcontented wife of Allen Norton, a poet and journalist. Among her social conquests was Marcel Duchamp, who presented her with one of his 'ready-made' works – a chimney ventilator – and introduced her to the Photo-Secession and its proprietor, Alfred Stieglitz, whom Louise recalled as being 'a great photographer and the John the Baptist in the American desert of modern art. Stieglitz had something of the Ancient Mariner as well. He was a tireless talker, propagandist and pedagogue, and whetted my appetite by all he poured into my virgin ears.'[1]

While the effusive Stieglitz was a crucial means of *entrée* into the local arts coterie, Varèse found flattery rather than friendship or help for many months. Neither were his impressions of New York during this time reassuring. It was, so he wrote to his former mother-in-law, 'a banal city, dirty – and the inhabitants are handsome, sporty types. I see only Europeans with whom contact is possible.'[2]

Linguistically, at least, it was less like hard work for him to talk to fellow expatriates such as the wealthy painter Francis Picabia and his wife, Gabrielle Buffet. They had known Edgard in Paris and recoiled as if confronted with a ghost when answering their Greenwich door to him within a week of their arrival from Barcelona. Nevertheless, it was with the Picabias and the Mexican poet José Juan Tablada that Edgard and Abel were to first experience jazz – 'at a negro cabaret,' remembered Warshawsky, 'and Edgard found, to his chagrin, that the instruments he was dreaming of were already in use.'[3]

Abel grasped the wrong end of the stick, but the stick still existed. With the doubtful exceptions of banjo and the standard dance-band drum kit, no accoutrement of the jazz band that Varèse heard that evening (probably at Reisenweber's Restaurant) was strange to him. Yet the interweaving dare-devilry of the blaring front-line horns – trombone, trumpet, clarinet, *et al* – and piano were at as opposite an extreme to their precisely scored and comparatively mild-mannered use by Strauss and Debussy as the Earth is to the Moon.

That Varèse was as concerned with the source as the nature of sound was revealed in his first ever remarks to be published in an English-language newspaper – the *New York Telegraph* – on March 1916. 'Our musical alphabet must be enriched,' he believed. 'We need new instruments very badly. Musicians should take up this question in deep earnest with the help of machinery specialists. I refuse to limit myself to sounds that have already been heard. What I am looking for are new technical mediums which can lend themselves to every expression of thought and can keep up with thought.'[4]

This interview had come about via Karl Muck in Boston, 200 miles north on the New England seaboard. His distant recommendation also secured Varèse an agency for cash-in-hand work as a transcriber, orchestrator and tutor. There was much more demand for these services in Chicago and New York than in Paris and Berlin, where no one had ever employed him to conduct music for silent movies as they did there. Varèse even landed two or three bit parts in such films, notably as an Italian nobleman in one starring John Barrymore.

During a leaner period, he accept a disgruntled job as a piano salesman, working eight hours a day in a Broadway department store, but Varèse's chequered workload had become sufficiently lucrative by spring 1916 to allow him to move into the homely Brevoort Hotel, close to the Photo-Secession Gallery. He stayed until January 1918 in this hybrid of Liberty Hall that served meals when working musicians and repertory actors rolled in late after curtain-down and a sort of mission for Gallic migrants to the New World.

The Brevoort Hotel was actually run by two Frenchmen who employed French-speaking *femmes de chambre* and other staff and printed a translated address – '*Anciennement Brevoort House, coin de la 5me Avenue et de la 8me Rue*' – on hotel stationery. 'It was a little corner of France,' agreed Jo Davidson, a sculptor who lived in the room adjacent to Varèse's. 'The leeway I was given there for credit, as were many others, is unbelievable, and many a party I gave there, not knowing where my next penny was coming from.'[5]

Its clientèle was, noticed Louise McCutcheon, 'a mixture of arty types and French military officers and US girlfriends plus all the drinking intelligentsia of New York and their camp followers, most of them from the far corners of the United States and almost as far from their native pastures as their French colleagues'.[2]

The Brevoort was but one cell of a scene that continued to grow in impetus and became more cohesive. Maybe it was almost the point, but the most formal sense of solidarity was fixed on a movement that denied both form and solidarity. There remains bitter division about Dadaism – alias 'anti-art', 'the Avant Garde of the Avant Garde', 'art as life' – but its basic premise was that all art is muck and that anyone could create art, no matter how absurd, trivial or pretentious the end result – and there needn't necessarily be one. If the Great War made sense, why be sensible?

By most accounts, Dadaism began in wartime Zurich and spread to Berlin, Hanover – where a certain Kurt Schwitters was its sole representative – Paris, New York and elsewhere. Its principal impact was on the literary and visual arts, as demonstrated by such diverse resonances as the non-lexical 'sound poems' of Schwitters – who Varèse was to meet in 1921 – the non-committal philosophical substance of Gurdjieff and the 'nothing matters' preoccupation that is the commonly received conception about existentialism. It was also behind the taping of a groggy still-life of a vase of flowers – signed by 'the Great Masturbati' – on a wall in the Tate in the morning aftermath of some funny party I attended in London *circa* 1972. There are elements of Dada, too, in today's Stuckism (or 'remodernism'), which 'embraces all it denounces',[6] including the dead sheep and unmade bed nominated for Turner prizes in the late 1990s.

An obvious point iterated on one Stuckist document was that 'Duchamp's work was a protest against the stale, unthinking artistic establishment of his day.'[6] In unknowing acknowledgement of this, the American Society of Independent Arts refused his entry of 'Fountain' (a urinal with 'R Mutt 1917' painted on it) to its first exhibition. This overt act marked New York Dada's provocative conception.

In May 1917, Duchamp justified 'Fountain' as 'ready-made' art, 'a polemic of materialism', in the second edition of *The Blind Man*, a self-financed Dadaist periodical. His editorial also brought R(ichard) Mutt into existence via a biography that even specified his telephone number, Schuyler 9255, which happened to be that of the mother of Louise McCutcheon, author (under her married name) of 'Buddha Of The Bathroom', another *Blind Man* essay about 'Fountain'. There were also pieces by Albert Gleizes and Allen Norton, a pseudonymous poem by Erik Satie and, on the same page, an abstract sketch entitled 'Edgar [*sic*] Varèse En Composition' by Clara Tice, who by day was an illustrator for *Vanity Fair*.

Varèse's pragmatic involvement with Dadaism included two very short attacks on technique over instinct in music ('Verbe') and the Italian Futurists ('Que Le Musique Sonne') in Picabia's *391*, a monthly of the same persuasion as *The Blind Man*. He also contributed the gloomy poem 'Oblation', penned after a bar-hopping night with Picabia, Tablada and a newer pal, the Cuban writer Alejo Carpentier. Somewhere on their travels, Edgard's chat-up lines were rebuffed by a young lady on the next stool ('a woman's laugh has caused me so much pain...the sun has refused the moon a wedding ring'). Instead of romance, therefore, the evening culminated with a whisky-tinged conversation on Brooklyn Bridge ('the river is carrying past the world's unhappiness...opposite the skyscrapers bristling with amazement'[7]).

Over the next six years, further sweet nectar that dripped from Edgard's pen could be read in around 20 other Dadaist gazettes, most of them as short-lived as 'frolicky'[2] five-cent *Rogue*, founded by the Nortons in the summer of 1916 and fizzling out by December. There were also four unpublished free-form verses sent by Varèse to Tristan Tzara, one of Dadaism's founding fathers, who thought – wrongly – that he detected the influence of Pierre Reverdy.

Eager to learn, Varèse immediately laid hands on a collection of the pre-Dadaist surrealist poet's verse and also saw the connection between Reverdy's disturbingly illogical imagery and his own more slapdash efforts. Only two of those poems mailed to Tzara survive: 'Crazy Dog' and the rude 'Corona Australis'. With the unchained conviction of Dadaism's studied naïveté – modelled in Edgard's case perhaps on Parsifal, Wagner's guileless forester – these seem as devoid of ante-start agonies as an Ernie Wise play.

Edgard Varèse was also the focus of reviews, discussions and portraiture, as one whom the poet Louis Aragon – of the original Zurich group – described as 'the only musician of the Dada period',[8] while he was cited as a leader of the New York outpost[9] by self-effacing painter Alfred Kreymborg, himself a prominent city Dadaist. On 12 January 1921, Varèse was to sign the *Dada Souleve Tout* manifesto, a pamphlet later distributed at a lecture in Paris (by the derided Marinetti). Back in 1920, he had been listed by Tzara as a 'Dada president', along with the likes of Schwitters, Duchamp, Picabia, 'Miss Norton' (ie Louise McCutcheon) and Max Ernst, in the sixth edition of *Dada*, the father of all such journals.

Varèse's was a credible name to drop in Dada circles, certainly a more erudite one than that of Satie, whose music surfaced as frequently as rocks in the stream at Dadaist events. Both former Schola Cantorum students were avid intellectual conspirators, but there were no direct doctrinal despatches from either. While Varèse defended Duchamp's ready-mades as art 'which the uninitiated are not up to appreciating'[10] and claimed – in *391*, No.3 – to have composed an opus entitled *The Cold Faucet Dance* as a riposte to 'Fountain', he perceived that New York Dadaism was heading for the same elitist impasse as almost every other new art movement he'd encountered since leaving Turin. Personality masqueraded as principles, internal squabbles as crusades and the riff-raff were kept in the dark – because, tacitly, public acceptance was dreaded by the big fish in Dadaism's small pond.

Yet Dada was fun while it lasted. Varèse chuckled at the Great Masturbati-esque happenings and liked Picabia, Schwitters, Buffet, Gleizes, Tzara and Kreymborg – if not Duchamp and Allen Norton – because they shared an understated sardonic humour akin to his own – and because they liked him. 'If they were in need, I would lend assistance,' he acknowledged, 'but I am not a Dadaist. Without doubt, that's the best way to be.'[11]

As both Picabia – who left New York after not quite a year – and Duchamp were to wash their hands of the movement, so Varèse had already, and for the same reason: it didn't reconcile with a self-picture of himself as a serious artist. Nevertheless, Dadaism left its mark in Varèse's employment of seemingly meaningless syllables in later works and in a contradiction of veneration for both a machine aesthetic (as evidenced in admiration for Picabia's many illustrations of fanciful and futile mechanisms) and a pursuit of 'primitivism', qualifying this with 'in the sense that Beethoven, breaking away from the past, was primitive';[12] not for Varèse was the taking of primitivism to the conclusion of the post-Impressionist painter (and former Parisian stockbroker) Paul Gauguin, who lived out his final years on a Polynesian archipelago on the furthest edge of the French colonial empire.

In 1891, Gauguin had written to the Swedish playwright August Strindberg, stating that it was 'civilisation that brings you pain. Barbarism is rejuvenation to me.'[13] Likewise, Louise McCutcheon was to note 'Varèse's love of primitive rites and incantations, and his glorification of the percussion section'.[5] His jungle, however, was urban, as he intimated to Beatrice Wood, ceramic artist and girlfriend of Duchamp. He wanted, he told her, 'to make music of the streets, the sounds of the streetcars, the bells on horses'.[14]

That was even after he was knocked down by a vehicle that mounted the pavement while he was waiting at the bus stop outside the Brevoort in September 1916. This landed him with a broken foot and 11 weeks at St Vincent's Hospital, which – as it was in the next parallel street – sent a stretcher rather than an ambulance. The patient's depression – caused mostly by the loss of income on top of the hospital's bill – was alleviated by visits from female friends such as Beatrice Wood and the gossip columnist Elsa Maxwell. Varèse was 'well loved by women who [didn't] know him very well', scoffed Tristan Tzara.[15]

That Edgard was more popular with the ladies than most may have led green-eyed monsters to whisper to his detractors. There were also varying degrees of jealousy between the ladies themselves – particularly if they interrupted bedside canoodling that went beyond the bounds of acceptable ickiness in a medical ward.

Beatrice Wood didn't like Louise McCutcheon, probably because Marcel had been sniffing around her, but also because she seemed too resplendent in an apparent victory in her campaign to win Edgard Varèse. 'He didn't have to be famous, as far as I was concerned,' Louise asserted. 'His presence and the certainty I felt about his genius were all I needed.'[16] Their *amour* was almost like a real-life enactment of that soap-opera cliché in which the greater the antagonism between two characters, the greater the likelihood that they will eventually become lovers. Their relationship was certainly stormy enough for Louise to compare the two of them to Dylan Thomas and his volcanic wife, Caitlin,[2] although in appearance they resembled more closely the pre-war bank-robbers Bonnie and Clyde, on the evidence on a smart 1921 photograph that showed Varèse enervatingly poker-faced in tweed cloth-cap and belted greatcoat and Louise draped in furs and gripping his arm with a bright, proprietorial grin.

Seven years Varèse's junior, all-American Louise McCutcheon was born in Pittsburg, Massachusetts. At 16, she finished school at Smith College, where a gift for languages had surfaced. As if in prophecy, she became especially fluent in French. By then, the family had moved to New York. However, when her parents relocated again to Schuyler, Virginia, she remained in New York to study comparative philology whilst earning a living as a translator. Falling in with the Greenwich Village set, she met Allen Norton and bore him a son, Michael.

As it had been with Edgard and Suzanne, the Nortons' espousal was muddling on because neither partner had sufficient motivation to end it, but a trial separation was in force by mid-1917 and Louise found herself living on her own in two floors of a house in which her friends the Gleizes had also taken rooms. While on holiday in the Midwest, she sub-let her apartment to the Picabias. To the consternation of the housekeeper, the couple had no qualms about going naked in hot weather – and neither did several of their guests, among them Edgard Varèse and the dancer Isadora Duncan.

His wife's interest in Varèse didn't appear to upset Allen Norton, mainly because Louise and Edgard hadn't hit it off – indeed, far from it – when they first became aware of each other. She had been in the Brevoort bar and, scanning the room, had been brought up short by Varèse's uncomfortable stare. A few evenings later, they had been introduced casually, not long after his discharge from St Vincent's by the Gleizes, when all four chanced to be in the same Italian restaurant.

However, no matter how much Edgard and 'non-musical'[5] (her words) Louise feigned indifference then, each stayed in the picture about the other's activities, even if Louise was led to believe that his persisting limp was the result of a war wound. When they next met – at another uproarious Brevoort knees-up – Varèse, if never much of a party animal, tagged onto Jo Davidson, José Juan Tablada and Elsa Maxwell, who went back to Louise's apartment afterwards. It was a shallow though cordial occasion, occupied chiefly with banal word games, but Louise and Edgard's eyes met through the cigarette smoke. Although his lips never moved upwards, he smiled gently.

The following afternoon, he brought her flowers and asked her out. Throughout the subsequent winter, the romance ran smoothly. He proposed; she accepted – and when Varèse confronted Allen Norton with his feelings about Louise, there was less anger than amusement as he agreed to a divorce, even promising to put in an appearance with Michael at the presumed wedding reception.

Then came the evening at the Brevoort when harmless jesting between the sweethearts swung in seconds to a very public trading of insults. For nearly three months, neither spoke to the other, to the extent that Edgard wasn't immediately aware that Louise had moved away to a skylit studio flat on 14th Street – where the Hudson foghorns were audible – on the very frontier of Greenwich Village and mid-town Manhattan. Yet, as mysteriously as it had started, the tempest dropped and the two stopped fighting the situation – although she would continue to refer to him by his surname for the remainder of her long life and Varèse kept his hotel address while he shared McCutcheon's bed and commandeered a workroom in her apartment.

He was to give up his Brevoort room when he married Louise in a civil ceremony at City Hall on 3 May 1921, the week after her *decree nisi* came through. The bride's mother attended, despite disapproval that her daughter would be giving up official US residency status by wedding this Frenchman who had to keep re-applying for an extension of his visa to avoid deportation.

Yet Varèse's attachment to Louise for the previous three years had already bound him firmly to the New World. On her seventh birthday, his daughter received a miniature US flag, along with 'kisses from your Papa', who was full of praise for the United States, its people and all its works. It was also affecting his vocabulary, substituting *sidewalk* for *pavement*, *candy* for *sweets*, *ad nauseam*. No one in Britain or her Commonwealth ever talked *thataway*. Furthermore, he could now speak, read and write English past the level required for US citizenship as decreed by a law that had been passed in 1906.

'North America impresses him with a sensation of vastness and extent,' noticed Alejo Carpentier. 'For him, New York is neither jazz nor musical comedy, nor even Harlem dives. He stands apart from those ephemeral characteristics of the New World but feels himself moved by the tragic meaning which he perceives in the implacable rhythm of its labour, in the teeming activity of the docks, in the crowds at noon, in the bustle of Wall Street.'[17]

What Carpentier meant by this *kitsch* may have bewildered its subject. Yet, after a German submarine's torpedoing of a US ship on 19 March 1917, Edgard had become a spiritual North American the day before the USA joined Canada in officially taking on the might of the Kaiser. Now respected – or at least patronised – by those in the know, he was an intriguing choice to conduct Berlioz's *Requiem* in a Palm Sunday benefit show for both those Allies already wounded and the North Americans who would be.

Not stressing Varèse's negligible hand in the war so far, the press who were aware of his professional history made much of a maiden North American concert performance. Under his aegis at the 6,000-seat Hippodrome – which, situated within the shadow of New York's vast public library, usually presented circuses and vaudeville – would be an orchestra of 150 plus the Scranton Oratorio Society of Pennsylvania, a choir made up principally of miners.

We never see a man; we only see his art. Was Varèse's splendid effort – for which the volunteer maestro refused a fee from the fund raised by city celebrities – triggered by a simple wish to help or by the chance to raise his head considerably higher above the parapet? It was the same equation pursued as those pop stars that pranced before the world at Live Aid in 1984. How could we ever know?

Certainly, it lifted his new career – however temporarily – in a new country off the runway. The hero of the hour, wild-haired and animated on the podium, Edgard delivered 'a veritable blaze of power' – so reckoned Paul Rosenfeld of *The Seven Arts Chronicle*.[18] To the *Evening Mail*, too, 'Mr Edgar [*sic*] Varèse...seemed to possess the inspiration of genius.'[19] Before he'd left the building, a crowd had surrounded the handsome young conductor like friendly, if over-attentive, wolfhounds. More importantly, demands for his services reached the Brevoort before the end of the week.

One of these was for nearly a year into the future, and this was how Varèse, replacing an interned German, came to stand before the Cincinnati Symphony Orchestra in that city's music hall on St Patrick's Day 1918, presiding over items that included Satie's three *Gymnopédies*, the prelude to Wagner's *Lohengrin* – daring bad taste under the circumstances – and *Prelude À l'Après-Midi d'Un Faun* by a faraway friend soon to die after a long illness.

The local paper acknowledged that 'Mr Varèse was warmly applauded and repeatedly called to the box, the audience lingering at the conclusion of the concert to express its appreciation.'[20] His name might have been unknown still to the man in the street in Laramie or Houston, but support from such as the *Cincinnati Commercial Tribune* and *The Seven Arts Chronicle* could have bound a well placed Varèse – had he so desired – to fulfilling decades as one of North America's leading conductors of the popular classics, just like Toscanini, Stokowski and, flushed out of Russia by the 1917 Revolution, Sergei Rachmaninoff.

This, however, was not Edgard Varèse's way. Apparently unbothered about personal popularity and huge financial gain, he had already mentioned to Carlos Salzedo that he was thinking of putting together an orchestra to present nothing but contemporary works – including, hopefully, his own – and neglected pieces by older composers. Words are cheap but, by the signing of the peace treaty in Versailles in June 1919, born organiser Varèse's New Symphony Orchestra of the New York Federation of Musicians was up and running. For all participants, it was a speculative enterprise in which everyone would take a cut of net profit (if any) from performances. However, unlike ensembles of the same bent that Satie and Schoenberg respectively had just formed in Paris and Berlin, it was to be directed at the widest possible public.

With this in mind, Varèse had called a press conference in March. Predictably, there'd been a small turn-out, but he had deadpanned the customary inane and frequently impertinent questions from the more ill-informed hacks and, with unblinking self-assurance, had cut to the chase by urging support for the New Symphony Orchestra because, otherwise, 'we are, as far as music is concerned, nothing but careless bystanders, heedlessly watching the painful growth of art without doing a thing to help it along. Musical history is being made now. American composers should be allowed to speak their messages into the ears of those for whom they are intended: the people of today!'[21]

Because *The New York Times* hadn't deigned to send anyone to the conference, Varèse fired off an immediate letter that went further than merely publicising the Orchestra: 'I should like to propose a League of Nations in Art. It needs no covenants. It would exist solely in the mental attitude of the world. Only by a free exchange of art –

music, literature, painting – can one people be interpreted to another. In art, as well as in politics, we have been jarred out of our traditional isolation – and the result will be good. The contact, the emulation, the competition will spur us to greater accomplishment. What beauty and strength!'[21]

This epistle was an example of Varèse's tendency to blurt out ideas that his head hadn't yet formulated in less bombastic terms. Nevertheless, it was published as an expedient three weeks before the New Symphony's pair of concerts on 11 and 12 April 1919 at nowhere less than Carnegie Hall, New York's premier auditorium.

Commanding terrified admiration from his musicians, Varèse was a firm adherent to the leadership principle and enforcer of his own order. With single-minded zeal, he selected the repertoire himself – with items from Debussy, Busoni, Roussel, Satie and Bartók and an excerpt from one of the more obscure Bach cantatas among its highlights – and assumed self-contained accountability when, apart from a so-so review in *The Christian Science Monitor*, both of the April outings – blighted by heavy rain – were either ignored or rubbished in small paragraphs.

Under pressure to insert more conventional material, Varèse threatened to resign. His bluff was called, however, and first refusal of the resulting vacant post went to Rachmaninoff, who, while he enjoyed Varèse's company, was out of sympathy with music more modern than Chopin and Liszt. Instead, after thinking twice about Stokowski, the job went to Arthur Bodansky, as bored as Carlos Salzedo was with pandering to audience expectations at the Metropolitan Opera. Nevertheless, to keep himself in the manner to which he'd become accustomed, Bodansky moonlighted with the similarly conservative but moneyed New York Society of the Friends of Music.

For his New Symphony predecessor, a mere orchestra was too confining for what he had in mind. The war had held up progress, but Varèse saw on the horizon devices such as the ondes Martenot – 'Martenot's Soundwaves' – patented in France by Maurice Martenot after a well-received demonstration in 1920.[22] Its creator was still working on the variable pitch, but this monophonic keyboard instrument, he explained, was an aural expression of 'a flexible, seamless beam of light', capable of a variety of unprecedented tone colours – 'The impalpable sounds of dream,' Oliver Messiaen would gasp after he, like Varèse, had seized upon its ethereal combination of keyboards and strings.

For 11-year-old Oliver, then just starting at the Paris Conservatoire, such a strategy lay in an unimagined but golden future, whereas Varèse – by now well into his 30s – was vexed once again with the pressing question of whether to stay true to his strange star or seek secure anonymity. An oft-repeated quip over the next 40-odd years was that he would be just as happy growing grapes as composing. As Varèse drifted from pillar to post, from project to unsatisfactory project, in New York, just as he had in Paris and Berlin, it seemed daft to be anything but pessimistic. Yet hardship and bitter disappointment had not yet stripped him of his hard-boiled capacity to try, try again.

Since his standing down from the New Symphony Orchestra, there had been discussion – and only discussion, for many months – of him being linchpin of some kind of composers' association, born of 'an imperative need for such an organisation, the American public having been kept in practically total ignorance of the music of its own time'.[23]

Hope became attainment on 31 May 1921 with the inaugural meeting of the International Composers' Guild, chaired by Varèse and Carlos Salzedo – its 'technical advisors' – at the Liberty Club in uptown Manhattan. This was no club that convened for cosy recreation but a convergence of concern about aesthetic and economic survival. No one well known bothered with the ICG. Rather than the likes of Rachmaninoff and Toscanini, it attracted those in the same boat, or worse, as Varèse.

The most generous of the ICG's few financial patrons was a Mrs Harry Payne Whitney, a rich widow who had been on the committee of the New Symphony Orchestra, which had fizzled out not long after Varèse's departure. As Gertrude Vanderbilt, she had exhibited her own sculptures in a gallery founded by and named after her husband. Captivated as much by dear Edgard's saturnine charm as his unremitting affront to the complacency of New York's music world, Mrs Whitney granted him a monthly allowance and the use of her secretary to assist Louise with answering letters, licking stamps and distributing publicity material. Most importantly, Varèse was given *carte blanche* to choose works to be performed, while Carlos picked the musicians and rehearsed them. Both were in charge of hiring guest conductors.

The two drew up an ICG manifesto for issue two months later. Sodden with bitter ruminations, it was an attack on what Edgard perceived as the forces aligned against the 'present-day composer' and his strivings to reach an audience. Indirectly, it was also the shaking of a frustrated fist at the kind of concert-goer for whom the main purpose of the evening was to see and be seen during the intermission, the kind of person for whom the future is the past all over again, for whom 'world première' means 'final performance' and for whom praise indeed is information that a preferred composer or star conductor's latest presentation was just like the one before.

The essence of the Guild's manifesto is worth quoting at length:

> The composer is the only one of the creators today who is denied direct contact with the public. When his work is done, he is thrust aside and the interpreter enters, not to try to understand but, impertinently, to judge it. Not finding in it any trace of the conventions to which he is accustomed, he banishes it from his programmes, denouncing it as incoherent and unintelligible.
>
> In every other field, the creator comes into some form of direct contact with the public. The poet and novelist enjoy the medium of the printed page; the painter and sculptor, the open doors of the gallery; the dramatist, the free scope of the stage. The composer must depend upon an intermediary: the interpreter.
>
> It is true that, in response to public demand, our official organisations occasionally place on their programmes a new work surrounded by established names, but such a work is carefully chosen from the most timid and anaemic of contemporary production, leaving absolutely unheard the composers who represent the true spirit of our time.

> Dying is the privilege of the weary. The present-day composers refuse to die. They have realised the necessity of banding together and fighting for the right of the individual to secure a fair and free presentation of his work. It is out of such a collective will that the International Composers' Guild was born.
>
> The aim of the International Composers' Guild is to centralise the works of the day, to group them in programmes intelligently and organically constructed and, with the help of singers and instrumentalists, to present those works in such a way as to reveal their fundamental spirit. The International Composers' Guild refuses to admit any limitation, either of volition or of action. The International Composers' Guild disapproves of all 'isms', denies the existence of schools, recognises only the individual.

To Joe and Jane America, the ICG tract – if they ever read it – was as relevant to their lives as one from the Flat Earth Society, even when sloganised to 'New Ears For New Music And New Music For New Ears'. Yet, virtually by word of mouth, the first of the Guild's three Sunday concerts filled Greenwich Village Theater on 19 February 1922 with 300 'contemporary music' zealots from New York and beyond. As for its content, the ICG made haste slowly with 'mild as milk'[2] chamber pieces by minor US composers before finishing with one each from marginally better known Europeans Arthur Honegger and Eugene Goussens. The audience clapped politely and the reporter from the local *Villager* arts journal deemed it 'a historical event of the first magnitude in the world of music on this side of the Atlantic'.[24] There had even been celebratory drinks afterwards at one of Mrs Whitney's arts clubs.

The next ICG recital went well, too, despite treading on noticeably thinner ice with items from stubbornly chromatic Carl Ruggles and Henry Cowell, a pioneer of formal indeterminacy and pianos 'treated' with the buzzings and rattlings of nail files, paperclips, teaspoons and similar objects from household and office. In a knowing, nodding sort of way, Edgard appreciated Ruggles' harsh dissonances and atonal leanings and Cowell's clusters of adjacent notes – played with the forearm or flat of the hand on piano – but he remembered Karl Muck's words during their first ever conversation: 'I sometimes play music I don't like but which I know to be good – and precisely because I don't like it, it is my duty to work harder on the score.'[16]

Although Varèse had turned his back on the 'mummified European formula'[25] of European Neo-Classicism and its influence across the Atlantic, he was amenable to the Guild underwriting the first North American performance of Stravinsky's *Les Noces*, pre-empting that by the visiting Russian Ballet in 1923. Moreover, while he had reservations about Schoenberg's now fully mobilised 12-tone system,[26] he and the Guild accepted the intellectual (and financial) challenge of the US premières of *Pierrot Lunaire* as well as Berg's *Chamber Concerto For Violin, Piano And 13 Woodwinds* and Webern's *Movements For String Quartet*, all of which counterbalanced walk-outs by members of the audience with unrequited demands for repeat performances.

For Webern's gestial twin, it had been a long time since *Bourgogne*. There was, of course, an ulterior motive for Varèse assuming control of the ICG's artistic direction. Was it so unreasonable for him to hold in his heart the idea that one day his would be the composition applauded at, say, the Village Theater or, in more far-fetched daydreams, Carnegie Hall? This could only happen via the Guild; the labour of just preparing an orchestral score to submit to more orthodox outlets in New York had thus far proved pointless.

In Varèse's index of possibilities then was the notion of going for the commercial jugular by giving the people what they wanted in order to put himself in a position to give them what they ought to want. He had even been approached to write music for Broadway comedies, which would have guaranteed an income at least as regular as George Gershwin's initial $50 a week to do the same for the lavish *Scandals* revues of near-naked showgirls for the next four years.

After deep thought, however, Varèse decided, 'You can't be both a virgin and a whore. It takes a talent I don't have.'[27] Therefore, while Gershwin was figuring out 'On My Mind The Whole Night Long', a simple 12-bar blues for the *Scandals* of 1920, fellow New Yorker

Edgard Varèse had been grappling with *Amériques*, a title chosen 'as symbolic of discoveries – new worlds on Earth, in the sky, or in the minds of men'.[24]

Elaborately scored for 142 musicians, including 11 percussionists, it was estimated to last approximately 40 minutes. While one of its flute parts was reminiscent of *Prelude À l'Après-Midi d'Un Faune*, had *Amériques* been heard in its entirety then it would have been as impenetrable as a brick wall even for those battle-hardened by exposure to the polarities of Ruggles, Cowell, Schoenberg and anyone else they cared to name.

6 The New Yorker

'I became a sort of musical Parsifal on a quest not for the Holy Grail but for the bomb that would explode the musical world and allow all sounds to come rushing into it through the resulting breach, sounds which at the time – and sometimes still today – were called noises.'

– Edgard Varèse, winter 1941[1]

Shortly before he lost interest in his *intonarumori*, Luigi Russolo – with his brother Arturo – persuaded His Master's Voice to issue a brittle two-sided 78rpm disc in 1921. While this and seven bars of *Dawn In The City* are all that remain of Russolo's music, his 'line-note' system of notation is still used by electronic composers today.

If being so immortalised mattered to him, Russolo was to have an easeful death a quarter of a century later. As a commercial sound recording, the coupling of his *Chorale* and *Serenata* was considered a viable marketing exercise in the early 1920s – although sheet-music sales were what counted, in those days when the wind-up gramophone, with its vast horn, was not yet a common domestic fixture. This was partly because its volume – 'as loud as a man sings', bragged one manufacturer – and its tinny, tooth-loosening timbre caused many landlords to write into their leases a clause forbidding their tenants to use gramophones.

A record release, therefore, did not figure in Edgard Varèse's calculations as he became immersed in his most prolific period as a published composer – although this isn't saying much when comparing the handful of works that surfaced between 1921 and 1927 –

Offrandes, Hyperprism, Octandre, Intégrales, Amériques, Arcana – to, say, Haydn's 104 symphonies or, more germane to this dissertation, Louis 'Moondog' Hardin's 50 between 1984 and 1990.

Yet, while anxious not to return to transcribing or selling pianos, Varèse was no more concerned about Gershwin-sized mass acceptance or upping the pace of his productivity than a fish in a pond is about people peering at its activities from above the surface. Like an alchemist of old, he conducted the same experiments over and over again from fresh angles. 'Of course, in common with all composers who have something new to say,' he elucidated, 'I experiment and have always experimented – but when I finally present a work, it is not an experiment; it is a finished product. My experiments go into the wastepaper basket.'[2]

To all intents and purposes, he ditched 'traditional' tonality, mode and melody while assuring *The New York Times* that 'the new composers have not abandoned melody. There is a distinct melodic line running through our work, but that line is often vertical and not horizontal.'[3]

No milkman would whistle anything from the body of work Varèse produced in the 1920s or beyond. Freighted with rhythmic complexity, free atonality – an implied key, at most – and areas that defy succinct description, his compositions lived principally in raw intensity bereft of harmonic progression to the degree that Varèse forbade vibrato on the strings – because it was 'too expressive' – and, in *Hyperprism*, dispensed with strings altogether in a search for 'pure' notes.

'Stringed instruments are still the kings of the orchestra,' he grimaced, 'despite the fact that the violin reached its zenith in the early part of the 18th century. Why should we expect this instrument, typical of its period, to be able to carry the main burden of the expression of today? What we want is an instrument that will give us a continuous sound at any pitch. The composer and the electrician will have to labour to get it. At any rate, we cannot keep on working in the old school colours.'[4]

The concepts underpinning *Hyperprism* and Varèse's marginally less contentious output was more entertaining than the aural outcome for those who automatically bought tickets for a given International Composers Guild recital in order to chat about how 'interesting' it was in licensed premises afterwards. Furthermore, works by Varèse were not performed by completely willing accomplices. Some musicians pronounced his music unplayable – via what Stockhausen was to call 'the lazy dogmas of impossibility' – and Otto Klemperer, guest conductor of *Octandre*, loathed it, although he couldn't help liking Edgard as a person.

Yet, for all his fondness, Klemperer joined most other city musicians in a tendency to patronise Varèse, whose eyes were opening to the fact that, in struggling to scale the heights of his aspirations, he was providing glimpses of high comedy to many listeners. But maybe that was their loss. Already, spoofs of the ICG were triggering guffaws in revues such as youthful Grand Street Follies in the Neighbourhood Playhouse, instanced by a piece played on dustpan and brush, carpet sweeper, typewriter and glass tumblers.

Nevertheless, the ICG – and Varèse – were a *cause célèbre* and, as Picasso would have reminded him, at least everyone who was anyone was talking about him. All manner of artists passing through New York called at the Varèse household, including the Russian poet Vladimir Mayakovski; Carl Ruggles, with his rich fund of dirty jokes; and Georges Ivanovich Gurdjieff, who was regarded as either a mystic or a vainglorious confidence trickster with a fast mouth. Varèse inclined towards the latter view when witnessing a demonstration at the Neighbourhood Playhouse of physical co-ordination and control by Gurdjieff's entourage of leotard-clad initiates from his Institute for the Harmonious Development of Man in Fontainebleau.

Varèse himself was becoming known parochially as a great talker, too. It was a skill that he had inherited from Grand-père Claude and had carefully honed for intellectual self-defence in interview. If cracking back at his critics with faultless logic, clear thinking and practised sincerity, he was also a fount of 'good copy' – plain speaking laced with quirky wit and delivered in 'ow-you-say English like a collegiate Maurice Chevalier.

You're unlikely to see his oft-repeated jocularities and compact aphorisms as tabloid leaderettes or overhear them in saloon bars, but plenty were jotted down by nicotine-stained fingers. Here are some off-the-cuff examples:

'Talent does what it will; genius what it can.'

'One must know how to exhaust adversity.'

'Scientists are the poets of today.'

'There are two infinites: God and stupidity.'

'Entertainment has its place in life, just as candies and cocktails have, but health is not built on such a diet alone, nor culture exclusively on amusement.'

'The masses are, by disposition and experience, 50 years out of date.'

'An excess of reason is mortal to art.'

The members of the press who had heard of him were delighted with this alarming composer, who was to the US music scene what Screaming Lord Sutch would be to British politics – although, like Sutch, many of Varèses ruminations proved astonishingly prophetic. As da Vinci predicted aeroplanes, so Varèse did computerised notation and the synclavier – or 'a sound-producing machine, not a sound-reproducing one,' he enthused. 'It will work something like this: after a composer has set down his score on paper by means of a new graphic, he will then, with the collaboration of a sound engineer, transfer the score directly to this electric machine. After that, anyone will be able to press a button to release the music exactly as conceived, just like opening a book. Between the composer and the listener, there will be no deforming prism but the same intimate communion as that existing between writer and reader. The "interpreter" will vanish like the storyteller after the invention of printing.' He continued, 'Do you realise that, every time a printed score is brought to life, it has to be recreated through the different sound machines called "musical instruments", which make up our orchestras and which are subject to the same laws of physics as any other machine?'[5]

Information about distant breakthroughs in musical technology wended their way to Varèse by means as mysterious as those that took details of a particular brand of footwear to St Kilda, the most far-flung Hebridean island, barely a year after its appearance in Victorian London. The sphaerophon, patented in Germany by Jorg Mager, passed Edgard by, but he was among the first in New York with the word about the aetherophone and the more sophisticated theremin, both invented circa 1920 by Lev Termen (later Leon Theremin), a St Petersburg physics professor. With tone and single-note pitch – itself capable of a frequency beyond human hearing – adjustable via by the movement of one hand back and forth around a hypersensitive antenna and the twiddling of the volume control with the other, the oscillating and unearthly wails that came from both devices were to come into their own when used for incidental music in science-fiction movies, but the theremin was also to figure in Varèse's index of possibilities.

Standard orchestral instruments were nevertheless nearly all that were realistically available to him in the 1920s, as he crouched over the upright piano in his workroom. In there, *an* rather than *the* arrangement of *Amériques* had, in theory, been completed but he was drawn back to it daily, like Bluebeard's wife to the forbidden door.

Amériques was to be dedicated to 'unknown friends', namely two anonymous benefactors – probably Mrs Whitney and a Mrs Christian Holmes – who settled matters whenever the Varèses' bills mounted up. Although the equation wasn't the same as that of the Wagners and King Ludwig, or Tchaikovsky and Nadezhda von Meck, Mr and Mrs Varèse together had discovered a talent for convincing likely sponsors with money to burn that Edgard was a genius. For the time being, this meant that, with cash injections from Louise's mother, too, not only did Louise and Edgard not starve or have to rely on a 'proper' job to stay alive, but they were also able to recharge their batteries – creative and otherwise – with breaks in faraway places. For what was diagnosed as exhaustion in February 1921, no medicine could be as efficacious for Louise as cabin-class passage on the *Rochambeau* for a few spring weeks in France.

While Edgard accompanied José Juan Tablada on a cultural safari to Mexico – the poet's first visit to his native land for seven years – a legitimate colour was given to Louise's holiday in that she was able to check up on step-daughter Claude, now aged 11 and living with her grandmother high above Monte Carlo. With this duty-call done, Louise joined the Parisian social whirl by looking up Paul Le Flem, Erik Satie and other of her husband's old cronies who were still at large. Never at ease in New York, the Gleizes had gravitated back to France, and it was through them that Louise developed a fast friendship with the Chilean poet Vicente Huidobro. Among souvenirs of the trip was a tome of his (in French) containing *Chanson De La-Haut* ('Song From On High'), which was, in broad terms, to the Seine what Varèse's *Oblation* had been to the waters flowing beneath Brooklyn Bridge but as rapturous as the latter's lines were awkwardly despondent.

Varèse – back from Mexico – thought so, too, and sought Huidobro's gladly granted permission to use it as the text for the opening section of *Dedications*, swiftly retitled *Offrandes* – 'Just a very small-scale piece, a purely intimate work,'[6] he said, but one intended to be heard via the ICG on Sunday 23 April 1922 at 8:30pm at the Greenwich Village Theater in the first public performance of any Varèse opus in North America.

Aware of the chasm into which he might plunge after years of talking about the masterpieces that he was composing, Edgard steeled himself to face facts in front of an audience – if there was going to be any audience at all – that would have no qualms about letting him know just what it thought about the seven-odd minutes of *Offrandes*. Nevertheless, as showtime approached, Varèse's mood – as well as that of conductor Carlos Salzedo – was one of qualified confidence.

Finished only weeks earlier, *Offrandes* ('Offerings') was for five woodwind and three brass instruments, harp, a barely audible backwash of strings and 'fascinating rhythmic colour in a little battalion of percussion',[7] drawn, as always, from New York music academies or a pool of freelance musicians who were semi-professional, at most. To the fore, however, was Nina Koshetz, a Russian immigrant with a soprano voice more like a boy's than a woman's. She was known to convey such exquisite brushstrokes of enunciation and inflection that a fractional widening of vibrato could be as loaded as her most anguished cry. As well as 'Chanson De La-Haut', she was required to tackle the similarly oblique lines of José Juan Tablada's *La Croix De La Sud* ('The Southern Cross'), with its Dada-shaded 'advert for Oleo margarine' in the sky – a tropical counterbalance to Huidobro's 'European' poem.

Because an encore of *Chanson De La-Haut* was demanded by an admittedly partisan crowd, an educated guess is that the prodigious Nina Koshetz – like most vocalists on subsequent recordings of *Offrandes* – emerged with credit when required to pick the bones of meaning from the graphic if unhummable libretto that followed an introit dominated by flourishes of trumpet. Over murkier horns, squeaks of woodwind harmonics, *mélanges* of peculiar tone clusters and the clatters, clacks, clangs and rataplans of castanets, gongs, snare drum, *et al*, Koshetz slipped comfortably from the boiling point of '*Je sonne mon clarion vers toutes les mers*' ('I sound my bugle to all the seas') to the coquettish insinuation of the *a cappella* close of *Chanson De La-Haut*. After the bit about the margarine, *La Croix De La Sud* climaxed with a half-spoken '*Voici l'arbre de la quinine et la Vierge des Douleurs*' ('There is the quinine tree and our Lady of Sorrows') – twisting the heartstrings tightest, and all the more rewarding for its humoured restraint – before the staccato explosions that pave the way for the final purely instrumental burst in the coda.

The work of an artist in assured transition from relatively straightforward *Un Grand Sommeil Noir* to the confrontations ahead, the presentation of *Offrandes* was the last time that Varèse's music would be hailed with unconditional and unanimous enthusiasm for three years (apart from at what was, more or less, a private function at which *Octandre* was heard at the National Preparatory School in Mexico City).

Very 'off Broadway', *Offrandes* garnered only two reviews. *Music America* felt, with some justification, that it wasn't unlike Schoenberg while, present at a morning rehearsal, the less sympathetic *Christian Science Monitor* compared it to 'the racket of a street under elevated trains' until the last run through, when it had been transformed into 'a beautiful song in the modern chamber-music form'.[8]

From the participants' perspective, all that was wrong with *Offrandes* was the venue in which it had been premièred. Not only was the Greenwich Theater too small and downtown but extraneous noise from the underground trains along Sheridan Square subway beneath it undercut onstage silences and pianissimos. Therefore, the ICG started wooing mid-town auditoriums, coaxing the Klaw Theater to host the next three concerts, beginning in December.

In the interim, written badgering from the Guild had oiled the wheels of the founding of an affiliate organisation in Moscow. It was considered necessary, however, for the high command – Salzedo and the Varèses – to go in person to Berlin to establish a German branch. The subtext of this, of course, was that it gave Edgard a subsidised opportunity to retrieve possessions he'd left in storage in 1913 and for orgies of maudlin reminiscence with old pals such as Busoni, introduced to Carl and Louise as 'the man who has meant so much to me'.[9] Although visibly ailing, Busoni was willing to be caretaker chairman of the Internationale Komponisten Gilde committee, but he couldn't get to the inaugural concert at the Gesellschaft Der Freunde Halle on a foggy mid-week evening in November, regardless of *Offrandes* being on the programme. The overall attendance was disappointing because of the weather and the price of admission – if only fractionally higher than that for a Strauss recital the previous week – it came at a time when the Deutschmark had lost almost all of its pre-war value.

Simple economics caused the IKG to fold within months. Before that, Edgard suffered a more profound upset on being informed that his belongings – including early manuscripts – had been destroyed in a fire during one of the uprisings that came in the wake of the German surrender and its damaging repercussions.

Varèse was sickened by his loss but bucked up enough to have the still-lengthening score of *Amériques* copied during a weekend in hand when the party reached the first stage of the homeward voyage in Hamburg, where Karl Muck was now in charge of the city's main orchestra. Over dinner, old times were not forgotten by Karl and Edgard who also mentioned that, while travel generally circumscribed serious composition, he'd been gainfully employed in the seclusion of hotel suite and ship's cabin, developing an idea with the working title of *Hyperprism*, implying the resolving of noise into organised sound via some imagined supersonic filter.

A creative rush had *Hyperprism* ready for rehearsal two labour-intensive months after Varèse and Louise had unpacked in their apartment, which they were finding cramped. Inspection of the score alone revealed that Edgard was courting trouble. For a start, there wasn't a stringed instrument anywhere. Before a note was played of this first work by a 'liberated' Varèse on the first Sunday in March at the Klaw Theater, the absence of the customary 'kings of the orchestra' and a preponderance of percussion and blowing instruments made the assembled ensemble under the composer's own baton more a band than orchestra. Yet four-minute-long *Hyperprism* wasn't the stuff of Remembrance Day processions or Sunday-afternoon concerts in Central Park.

Relentless and often rhythmically independent tapping, crashing and banging vied with the wail of a siren, apocalyptic crescendi and a series of short, violent tonal flurries, each haloed by a singularity that separated it from the next. No matter how quasi-mathematical it appeared on paper, the overall impression was one of ramshackle grandeur. If your ears couldn't locate a linear 'distinct melodic line running through our work',[3] then all you could cling to were the vibrations in the air at any given moment.

On the night of the première, *Hyperprism* was preceded disarmingly by a Bartók string quartet, a sonata by Salzedo and ten-year-old *Wild Men's Dance* by the Russian-born pianist Leo Ornstein. Varèse's piece had a remote element of familiarity in a trumpeter's repeated high C sharp, just like the train whistle that lacerated the air every day for both the ICG concert regulars and the curiosity seekers with scarcely the vaguest notion of the music that they'd paid to hear.

Hyperprism *per se* was less intrinsically entertaining than the audience reaction to what Ouellette would call 'the first great scandal in New York's musical life'.[10] He wasn't exaggerating. Eighty years of artistic extremity later it seems milder now. Frank Zappa maintained that he was able to dance to it, but it isn't easy to appreciate how difficult and shell-shocking *Hyperprism* was in 1923. You either had to take it at face value, pretend you did or reject it altogether. There were no half measures.

While yet uncertain whether form overruled content, Varèse's deserved if still small-scale knot of devotees deduced that *Hyperprism* contained an indefinable something else as it quivered into life at the Klaw. Keeping nervous counsel, an initially gawping element didn't quite like to laugh until a titter during a sudden lull set them off.

A disaffected Average Joe's angle might have been this: this music appears to have been dismantled and each individual bar put back together at random. There's only the faintest run-on coherence as players take off in simultaneous cacophony. Making no attempt to resolve the vilest discords they can produce, they paint a sound-picture of dementia – and the tragedy is that no one, least of all its creator, seems to care how terrible it sounds.

It was a tremendous theatre of embarrassment. Within a minute, someone had to be restrained physically from climbing onstage to strike a blow for decent entertainment for decent folk. He and another lion of justice were detained by the local constabulary, who were paying what was now a routine call on ICG concerts, where so-called 'music' soundtracked intervention from the more bellicose ticket-holders. Booing, hissing, catcalls and howls of derision had Varèse glaring into the blackness, and one of the musicians and Carlos Salzedo jumped to their feet, telling hecklers to shut up. 'This is a serious work!' shouted Salzedo. 'Those who don't like it, please go!'

A good half of those present did just that when Varèse began a reprise for an audience in turmoil. What was that? Did I enjoy it? Shall I clap or jeer? What's everyone else doing?

The critic from *The New York Times* was polishing up witticisms for his column. *Hyperprism*, he would write, was 'like a catastrophe in a boiler factory'.[11] Over his typewriter on Monday morning, one of his rivals compared it to 'the big circus when clowns with broken-down trombones and kindred instruments set up a discordant din of grunts and groans.'[12]

For others, however, *Hyperprism* was a total success. While in New York to complete a commissioned fresco, the Mexican artist Diego Rivera issued an open invitation for the Varèses to visit anytime. More pragmatically, Kenneth Curwen, an executive with a London music-publishing firm, proffered a contract before Edgard left the building. If professional enough to be civil to Mr Curwen, Varèse was sceptical about his promise to get *Hyperprism* performed on British radio. What's more, the Englishman said that he'd be pleased if Edgard and his wife stayed at his house, if they wanted to be there in person when the piece filled the then-uncongested British Broadcasting Corporation airwaves.

Knowing how changeable such an ally could be, the Varèses gave themselves the best possible chance by inviting this Kenneth character over for dinner before he returned to England. Charmed by the quality of the meal and a rapport with Edgard that the backstage bustle had curtailed, Curwen would wax enthusiastically about his new discovery to his colleagues back in the firm's office in Denmark Street, London's Tin Pan Alley. 'Varèse has the crudity of genius in the making,' he would gush, 'and combines it with the subtlety that is given only to the very sincere. And he is a good cook – which I find is regarded in New York as one of the acid tests of musicianship – and if *Intégrales* is as good as his steak and peppers, it will do.'[9]

Because of similar comments like this, and the plain fact that *Hyperprism* had so divided customers and critics, it became wickedly chic for the *demi-monde* on the composer's side of the Atlantic to latch onto him, even if they had disdained to attend the Klaw Theater fiasco. Rumours of an anarchic riot there had spread, magnified and become truth. So far out that he was 'in', its perpetrator was suddenly a wanted guest at parties. If he turned up, you could hardly believe he was real.

Playing up to his new celebrity, he would fix listeners with penetrating stares, thicken his accent, and hold forth about his life, his creative torment and his blows against orthodoxy, 'sometimes in a very low and almost oppressed voice, sometimes loudly, his words hurried and tightly packed. It seemed to me that his thought and his words had assumed a musical form.'[13]

Yet, for all his tirades against established institutions, Varèse wasn't averse to the City Fire Brigade lending a siren for a performance of *Hyperprism* in Philadelphia, where it gripped harder than it would at Carnegie Hall just before Christmas when it was crowbarred between items by Berlioz and Debussy. A lot of the applause was 'ironic',[9] groaned Louise, but to some *Hyperprism* was like an antidote to pleasure on the principle that the more arduous the effort needed to appreciate something, the more artistic it is.

Nevertheless, among the alternate vilifications and Emperor's New Clothes-like effervescence, the *New York Herald* gave no subjective opinion beyond asserting that 'the name of Edgard Varèse will go down in musical history as the man who started something',[9] and Paul Rosenfeld lauded *Hyperprism* in print simply because he liked it. As well as *Seven Arts Chronicle*, Rosenfeld freelanced for *The Dial*, *The New Republic* and other magazines many commercial rungs higher than the narrowly circulated likes of *Rogue* and *Dadaglobe*, and was an important media ice-breaker who spoke directly to the consumers most likely to take an interest in Varèse.

A lifelong friendship with Rosenfeld thus began in 1923 – and so did a lifelong feud with Arturo Toscanini. Walking in on the after-hours inquest that followed the exodus of a small audience at the next ICG show at the Klaw, the great conductor instigated a spectacular public altercation with Varèse (who had a temper to match his own) after belabouring him over the Guild's propagation of a lot of what he heard as mindless rubbish. Varèse's barbed rejoinder that his antagonist 'had the mentality of a hairdresser and looked like one'[9] brought the issue close to fisticuffs before an ebbing away that left the combatants glowering at each other, muttering to respective sidekicks.

There were murmurings, too, from low in the Guild hierarchy. Even before *Hyperprism*, some had quit to form the imitative but more peaceable League of Composers, complete with an official mouthpiece in a journal with the prosaic title *Modern Music*. Yet the writing was far from on the wall for the ICG. If anything, it seemed to have weathered the recent storms and was becoming accepted as a tolerable if specialist part of the cultural furniture. Furthermore, Varèse appeared to have applied a brake to the outrage, judging by *Octandre*, which was premièred at a crowded Vanderbilt Theater on 13 January 1924 amid works by Ruggles, Webern and Berg.

Having made some sort of point with *Hyperprism*, was Varèse beginning a prodigal return to the fold? Embracing no sirens or anything unpitched, *Octandre* followed a traditional division of three movements ('Allez Lent', 'Très Vif Et Nerveux' and 'Animé Et Jubilatoire'), each with its own isolated tempo change, occurring at the same time on all instruments. There were eight of these in all – flute, oboe, clarinet, bassoon, horn, trumpet, trombone and bowed double-bass – hence the title, derived from *octandrous*, an adjective pertaining to a flower having eight stamens.

Blossoming from an oboe figure (just as a solitary woodwind had opened *Le Sacre Du Printemps*), *Octandre* unfolds as a flower does through the slow pageant of sunrise. Of all Varèse's output, *Octandre*'s controlled sequence captures the strongest visual quality. Yet, as well as the obvious portrait of nature taking its course, anyone with a glimmer of its maker's personal history could perceive daybreak piercing the blackest shadows of an idiosyncratic belligerence rising and falling in a piece less jarringly controversial than the Vanderbilt audience had been primed to expect.

If some were there to watch or join in the fun of further *Hyperprism*-esque tumult, the wind was taken out of their sails by *Octandre*'s stealthy tranquillity. Botany instead of physics, it was almost a mini-*Sacre Du Printemps*, yet bereft of human savagery. Nonetheless, having dipped his quill in anticipatory vitriol, the reviewer from the *New York Evening Post* questioned the intelligence of those customers baying for conductor Robert Schmitz to do it all again. Overall, however, *Octandre* was better received than *Hyperprism*, *The Christian Science Monitor* daring to cite it as the musical event of a year less than a fortnight old.[14]

By coincidence, an octet for wind instruments – although nothing like *Octandre* – by Stravinsky had been premièred in Paris the previous October. In the New Year, the cogs of an eagerly awaited North American tour by the Russian composer creaked into motion. He wouldn't set foot on US soil for many months after these exploratory negotiations, however, and, when he did, Stravinsky saw no reason to call on the Varèses, in the light of certain waspish remarks made by Edgard that had reached his ears.

In those days, Edgard and Louise were receiving guests in the top floor of a small house on a forlorn sideroad off Bleecker Street, Greenwich Village's most famous thoroughfare. As accommodation, the flat was only slightly less unsatisfactory than their old one, and it was clear to the landlord from day one that the new tenants were just passing through. Come spring, Louise started house hunting, but she was still looking around and reporting on likely properties in June, when Edgard left for Europe for the BBC broadcast of *Hyperprism* on 30 July – and to carry out a musical field survey.

This interlude also saw Varèse purchase in Paris a thick-ribbed, beige corduroy jacket that, despite its usual faint faecal odour, he would continue to wear for years afterwards before buying the first of many new ones exactly like it. More to the point, during his time in Paris there was a fraternal exchange of views with Ravel and Satie (whose final works, two ballets, were premièred in that year) and attendance at events that, ostensibly, weren't figurative shovels of coal in a cultural furnace to move the train of musical progress forward. Yet during a performance of Beethoven's *Seventh Symphony* one evening in the Salle Pleyel, Varèse's face was expressionless until the scherzo, when he was dazed momentarily, so he said later, with the strangest sensation of a 'projection in space – probably because the hall happened to be over-resonant. I seemed to feel the music detaching itself and projecting itself in space. I became conscious of a third dimension in the music. I call this feeling "sound projection", or the feeling given to us by certain blocks of sound. Probably I should call them "beams of sound", since the feeling is akin to that aroused by beams of light sent forth by a powerful searchlight. For the ear – just as for the eye – this gives a feeling of prolongation, a journey into space.'[15]

While this psychic episode began an indirect journey towards music that would be heard decades in the future, its most immediate outcome was *Intégrales* – marking the first time that Varèse used the term 'spatial' to describe his music – and then *Arcana*. Possibly, a piece also called *Intégrales* (and subsequently jettisoned) had been mentioned over dessert *après Hyperprism* to Kenneth Curwen, who had been confused by the première of the seemingly out-of-sequence *Octandre*. Curwen was enlightened when Varèse showed up in England to hear Eugene Goussens conduct *Hyperprism* for the conclusion of a two-hour musical documentary on the BBC's Third Programme, entitled *From Bach To Varèse*. As a distinguished composer, Edgard was made more of in London than he had ever been at home.

Also, while the BBC was as bound as any national corporation by the rigidity of union rules, some of the musicians were not coldly professional about *Hyperprism*. To drummer Ronnie Wheeler, 'The piece was of great interest to a percussion player and was written by a man who possessed an extraordinary knowledge of the resources of that department.'[9] Such an attitude during rehearsals was refreshing, after the shiftlessness of certain of those who had read the dots at the Klaw Theater and Carnegie Hall. It was, smiled Varèse, 'like coming into civilised company after being mobbed by a lot of mud-throwing guttersnipes'.[9]

While the purpose of the trip was to spectate fretfully at the on-air session at Broadcasting House, Varèse mixed business with pleasure by soaking up the sights – St Paul's, Big Ben, Westminster Bridge and our wonderful policemen. There was also that summer's wind and rain, the toyland currency and pubs that were more than just places where you got drunk. 'The barmaids are nice,' he wrote to Louise. 'They are as quick on the uptake as a Paris *voyou*.* The English might point to them as a challenge to Villon's claim that "*il n'est bon bec que de Paris*".† You know, they all called me "Dearie".'[16]

* Street urchin.

† Paraphrased, this means, 'The backchat isn't as good as it is in Paris.'

During his cheery flirtations with these pint-pulling ladies, Varèse deduced that they were irregular listeners to 'serious' music on the wireless. However, a combination of the foreign drinker's picaresque allure and what they might have read in the *Radio Times* may have coaxed one or two to tune in to *From Bach To Varèse*.

Edgard's private anxiety about any unretractable mistakes that they would hear were unfounded, however, as *Hyperprism* was played as accurately and as adequately as he might have hoped. Moreover, the day after it had first crackled across the Empire, it evoked nowhere near the same level of critical abuse as it had in the USA, the depth of vilification being the London *Evening Standard*'s description of *Hyperprism* as 'Bolshevism in music'.[17]

A performance of *Octandres* in Los Angeles a few months later passed without much comment, too, but *Intégrales* at New York's Aeolian Hall on 1 March 1925 was the vehicle of almost as much ridicule and over-ebullient praise as the first performance of *Hyperprism*. Predictably, rabid Varèse enthusiasts prevailed upon conductor Stokowski to reprise it, and Paul Rosenfeld scribbled in his notebook, 'Edgard Varèse is a genius who has the orchestra in his skin.' The daily newspapers, however, begged to differ. The *Evening Post* exclaimed that percussion-heavy *Intégrales* was like 'being in a shunting yard, a menagerie near the din of passing trains, a thunderbolt striking a tinplate factory and the hammering of a drunken woodpecker';[18] *The World* compared it to 'a battle between two groups of instrumentalists, with the percussionists winning';[18] and *The New York Times* weighed in less hysterically with 'merely noisy and extremely dull. The composer lacks the courtesy of Satie, who, with far more wit, bowed himself out of the room as soon as he realised he was becoming a bore. If you make bad noises, make them as loudly and as badly as you possibly can. Some people will be impressed.'[18]

Sitting on the fence, the *Herald Tribune*'s provided the most level-headed summary: 'Whatever you think about Mr. Varèse's *Intégrales*, you will probably admit that there is nothing like it under the canopy. It is as remote from Schoenberg and Stravinsky as it is from Debussy, Strauss and Wagner'.[18]

You can catch, say, an opaque glimpse of Ruggles here or a Stravinsky-ish ostinato there, but as a whole the ten minutes of *Intégrales* amounted, indeed, to music precedented only by aspects of its composer's previous work. Like *Octandre*, the first and third of its three sections swell from a bald motif on a single woodwind. It leans far less on thematic development than careful construction of a mood of racked, drawn-curtained menace. This is achieved through repetition of material on different instruments and slight variations – sometimes involving stomach-turning glissandi – of shape and timbre. Also surfacing are muscular brass outbursts of single notes slipping into pseudo-uncoordination and re-emergences of earlier themes, creating a half-hidden *déjà-vu* effect.

Varèse would probably hate such a comparison, but, belying its emotional resonance and non-linear arrangement, *Intégrales* was like a sonic pre-emption of 'systems painting' – all the rage in the mid-1970s – minimalist in content and meaning and so severely formulated that it made you think of striped pyjamas. An equivalent metaphor in sound couldn't be conveyed as easily as by the equal lengths of the three sections of *Intégrales* and the use of wind instruments – oboe, clarinet, horn, two piccolos, two trumpets and three trombones – incapable of vibrato. Indeed, this effect was hinted at only in the first movement, via a low-pitched percussive quiver – *wurrrr* – amid rhythms in constant flux.

Easy listening it wasn't, but a few snare drum bars – also in the opening section of *Intégrales* – had the same beat as that which, three years later, would run throughout Ravel's *Bolero*, a classic as popular as Handel's *Hallelujah Chorus*, Offenbach's *Tales Of Hoffman*, Rossini's overture to *William Tell* and more trifling items reduced to muzak.

As it had been with the overtures that he had been asked to provide for Broadway comedies, Varèse believed that it was futile for him to try to conjure up the kinda tunes folk like a-tappin' their shoe leather to when settling down to the lightest of light entertainment on North America's electric media. While capable of mannered revelling in the brashest of junk culture vomited from the wireless – dance crazes, one-shot gimmicks and further all-American piffle – it was repugnant to him as a composer. Yet the occasional manufactured noise from such a source would seize his ear in the same way as did roadworks, a dentist's drill, the boom of a gas cooker when lit, the whizzing springs and pistons of a car engine or the evening egress from the offices in the financial district towards Battery Park.

To approximate the musical properties that he could hear in them, Varèse required 'certain acoustical means which do not yet exist but which I knew could be realised and would be used sooner or later'.[19] Yet, in 1925, an attempt to orchestrate the sounds of urban life had been made by George Anthiel, a *Wunderkind* from New Jersey, whose *Ballet Mécanique*, if also in debt to Stravinsky's *Les Noces*, was almost as much a parody of Varèse and the ICG as that of the Grand Street Follies in its embrace of heavy percussion, aeroplane propellers, motor horns and bells.

Anthiel used actual bells but, more like the real thing than the real thing, a sphaerophon reproduced those required for Wagner's *Parsifal* at Bayreuth that year. It had crossed Varèse's mind to interrupt a Mediterranean holiday to attend the performance, but in the event the entire trip was cancelled, as he was embroiled with finalising *Amériques* and becoming enmeshed in *Arcana* (originally *Arcanes*), a symphonic poem in one seamless movement. The title of the piece – implying something cryptic, unfathomable, even supernatural – was proving too apt for Varèse, for whom it had rapidly 'become like a Frankenstein monster'[9] as he grappled with what he envisaged a refinement of the fully fledged artistic premises peculiar to himself. 'It is perhaps in *Arcana*,' he considered, 'that you will truly discover my thought.'[20]

Tacitly, his thought may have been guided by a reading of a new translation of Paracelsus's *Hermetic Astronomy*, just as less archaic tomes had inspired Holst when he was writing the *Planets Suite* a decade earlier. Varèse may have protested later that *Arcana* was 'a kind of tribute to the author of those words – they did not inspire it and the work is not a commentary on them',[21] but a paragraph from *Hermetic Astronomy* was to be the frontispiece of the score: 'One star exists higher than all the rest. This is the apocalyptic star. The second star is that of the ascendant. The third is that of the elements, and of these there are four, so that six stars are established. Besides these, there is still another star, imagination, which begets a new star and a new heaven.'

The emotional thrust of *Arcana* also suggests a more-than-cursory poring over the writings of Gerard de Nerval, a precursor of the French surrealist poets. Recognising the dream as a bridge between the here and the hereafter, de Nerval's investigations of his own dreams could be interrelated with his periodic committal to mental institutions until 1855, when he was found hanged from a Parisian lamp post.

Yet, moved as he may have been by de Nerval's verse and behavioural vulnerability, and stimulated again as he was by *Hermetic Astronomy*, Varèse was obliged to let *Arcana* hang fire for a while as he prepared at last for the 16 rehearsals prior to the opening nights of *Amériques* at Philadelphia's Academy of Music on 9 and 10 April 1926. Even whittled down to just short of 25 minutes it was his lengthiest work thus far, yet it does not induce restlessness in the listener and is still regarded by many as a *magnum opus*.

At Carnegie Hall the week after the première, it was preceded by items from Bach, Sibelius and Mozart, as if to infer that Varèse was their equal. That seemed to be the opinion of *The Christian Science Monitor*. 'This work, dispassionately regarded, may be said to mark a date in the history of art,' it raved. 'In all reason, it may be accounted the first absolutely original score for grand orchestra that has been made in America since the century began.'[22]

If nothing else, Varèse had become his own man at last with a staggering composition in no more than the most superficial artistic debt to anyone or anything, other than a land comparable to Gauguin's South Sea island or Byron's Italy in its potential to inspire greatness, or at least to accommodate it. 'I did not think of the title as purely geographic,' protested Varèse, 'but as symbolic of discoveries – new worlds on Earth, in the sky or in the minds of men'.[2]

Nonetheless, if *Amériques* could have stood as tall with any title that implied immensity – the Alps, say, or Ancient Egypt or Alpha Centauri – its chosen name instilled the *idée fixe* that here was an epic as identifiably North American as *Le Sacre Du Printemps* was Russian.

Beginning almost conversationally, *Amériques* advances with the grace of a fencing master on the continent's 'spacious skies for amber waves of grain' as much as on its modern but classic city architecture. A wordless and bittersweet epic that blends a sense of nostalgia within the harsh actuality of passing time, *Amériques* cannot be dismissed as an exercise in non-melodic intellectualism, a triumph of technique over instinct.

However, close study of the score – with the awareness that Curwen's first edition of this is riddled with errors – plus constant replay of *Amériques* on disc may assist comprehension of its plateaux of rip-roaring ferment as well as dovetailed subtleties, such as a solitary bar of fandango, another of a lazy saddle-tramp trot, what sounds like a motor changing gear at around the halfway mark and, to enhance its 'barbaric flavour',[23] the intermittent – and often hilarious – insertion of duck-call, whiplash, siren and steamboat whistle.

Otherwise, all that you can do is let *Amériques* envelope you with the otherworldly deliberation of a dream's slow motion in its paranormal and fragmented mindscapes of frontier forts and wide white spaces on a map of emptiness, seas of mesquite grass, trackless wastes, log cabins, oil derricks and rain-sodden nights lit by neon advertisements. An aeroplane hovers miles above the very ruts a horse-drawn covered wagon containing the pilot's father in infancy had made *en route* to Santa Rosa during the gold rush.

The inner visions evoked by *Amériques* vary from person to person and are reliant upon the mood of the hour. Listen to it in the morning and you'll hear Mexican carnivals, cattle drives along the Chisholm Trail, colonial mansions, granite-gabled haciendas, shotgun shacks and the abandoning of the Pony Express for the telegraph – the 'whispering wires' along Route 66, soon to wind from Chicago to Los Angeles. Try again in the afternoon and it'll be wide-awake optimism in Detroit, Quebec, Seattle, Atlanta and the innately decent 'sir' and 'ma'am' values of a small town in Connecticut or Idaho. Listen in the evening, and you'll descend a lonely canyon, scale its rim and take a breather overlooking the next stretch of prairie. Then you'll set forth for another purple-headed crag and journey's end.

Thus, while he alluded to the idea of things rather than the things themselves, Varèse expressed the essence of North America as piquantly as Aaron Copland was to in such works as *Billy The Kid*, *Rodeo* and others buoyed with the catchy tonality and rhythmic jollity that would brand him as American as Benjamin Britten was English. Yet, steeped in Varèse since experiencing *Hyperprism* at the Klaw, in his early 20s Copland had composed music almost as dissonant, percussive and devoid of popular appeal. Nevertheless, *Amériques* at Carnegie Hall did not make its mark in further loud and head-scratching Copland works, but the effect – rather than the precise notes of one of its unison brass ostinati – was to be replicated in his *Fanfare For The Common Man* after he decided to make a shameless fortune, *à la* Gershwin, by provisioning just plain folks with harmless entertainment.

Along the road less travelled, however, *Hyperprism*-like mayhem greeted all performances of *Amériques*. Stokowski, its very conductor, had had his arm metaphorically twisted by Varèse to persuade him to take it on. It was therefore gratifying for Stokowski to be called back to take three bows in Philadelphia. The composer, however, declined to take any, probably in the light of a minority's hissing, as reported in the local *Evening Public Ledger*, which also pondered whether 'it would be difficult to accept this work as serious music were it not for the form in which Mr Varèse has employed in its construction'.[24]

In New York, a woman raised a laugh by yelling, 'And he dared to call it "*America*"!' and readers of *The Sun* learned that 'the outbreak, moderate at first, swelled gradually to an indescribable furore. Some men wildly waved their arms, and one was seen to raise both hands high above his head with both thumbs turned down, the death sign of the Roman amphitheatre. The demonstration lasted more than five minutes.'[24]

As for the critics, there was debate about whether Varèse was digging himself an artistic rut. 'It is not so original, so daringly self-sprung, so independent as his *Hyperprism*,' averred the *Herald Tribune*, 'but in the end, the sense of power and release, the violent, irrepressible exultation of the thing makes its effect.'[24] Even loyal Paul Rosenfeld thought 'its inner coherency is weaker than that of its successors'.

Varèse had commenced the case for the defence the morning after the Academy of Music recital. 'If anything, the theme is a meditative one,' he explained patiently, 'the impression of a foreigner as he interrogates the tremendous possibilities of this new civilisation of yours. The use of strong musical effects is simply my rather vivid reaction to life as I see it, but it is the portrayal of a mood in music and not a sound picture.'[25]

Yet, before a crotchet of *Amériques* had been heard onstage, it had been all over, somehow, for one who'd lived with it for nigh on a decade. Nonetheless, this dejectingly familiar anti-climax was mitigated by re-entanglement in *Arcana* and a return to Philadelphia for its première exactly a year after that of *Amériques*, at the same venue, with Stokowski overseeing 'musicians who detested the work',[26] in the dark as they always were about its quality and shape or whether it was 'about' anything. Like insects, they could see and hear only their immediate environments.

Anthiel's *Ballet Mécanique* was among support pieces when, on 12 April 1927, *Arcana* precipitated the customary near-riot in New York with either 'genuine hissing heard above the resolute applause'[27] or 'the boos drowned by clapping',[28] depending upon which newspaper you bought. The latter comment came from *The Evening World*, for whom *Arcana* 'transmuted into tones the Age of Steel. [It is] the product of a mind adult, robust and expert and of a heart audacious and imaginative.'[28]

Varèse had had the audacity to disinter an ascending riff from *Intégrales* as one of several short recurring passages – the longest and most imperious containing just 11 notes – variously stated by a bank of strings and an augmented wind section, coalesced by a 39-piece percussion battery – including six timpani – shared between six players.

Unless you're amused by the clippety-clop of coconuts and Chinese blocks, there's little that is remotely jocular about *Arcana* – not a single saucy siren or duck's quack. Yet it is far from moribund, as it dispenses with preamble to menace the listener instantly with a pounding, urgent figure on bass instruments and timpani. This reemerges later, once as a higher-pitched, almost Tchaikovsky-like leitmotif among the interlocking themes, vignettes and segues in what is – within the parameters of Varèse's middle period – his most cyclical and harmonious opus.

The inner scenarios invoked by *Arcana* are as incorporeal as those of *Amériques* weren't, and there is a quasi-cinematic sense of crossing a dangerous limbo via jagged spasms of woodwind, xylophone and violins and a snowballing of panic offset by unsettling pressure drops to near inaudibility. A subdued coda fades to the silence of eternity – or, more likely, the void of a nihilist fond of quoting Baudelaire's 'I am a mystic at heart and I believe in nothing'. This was expressed in Varèse's endeavours, throughout the 1920s, to free his work of spiritual content by progressively reducing it to quasi-geometric simplification, like a musical Mondrian.

For his bank manager, however, reality had to be stripped down to a column of figures. According to their recent statements, the Varèses were solvent. Direct income came from royalties generated by, say, *Octandre* in Mexico City and *Hyperprism*'s Paris première in June 1927, and ICG concerts were now filling the 2,000 seats in the Aeolian Hall, closer to the heart of Manhattan.

Nevertheless, by November 1927, the days of open-handed conviviality from the likes of Mrs Harry Payne Whitney were gone. When challenged with tax bills amassed since that first concert seven years previously, investors began to take an unwelcome interest in the Guild's handling of financial affairs.

Edgard poured oil on troubled waters in an open letter that announced the accomplishment of a mission rather than cashflow problems and that, as far as the press was concerned, the dissolving of the ICG was only temporary. After emphasising both 'the vitality of our enterprise and our efforts' desired recompense', he wrote of his 'satisfaction now to see that the great orchestral organisations are following in our footsteps and are beginning to present the contemporary works of all schools and tendencies to a public now enlightened, or at least compliant. This evolution and the return to normal living [after the Great War] allow the composer today to realize his conceptions untrammelled and assure him a perfect execution by the large orchestras and their distinguished conductors.

'This happy condition frees the International Composers Guild of the responsibility which it undertook in the name of all the young composers of today. For the moment, it sees no need for continuing its concerts. It leaves to other organisations the purely managerial task of continuing to entertain the public, which now takes pleasure in hearing (thanks to its own ears) the works of its young contemporaries.

'The ICG can only live in the exhilarating atmosphere of struggle. It therefore retires at the approach of the official laurel wreath, holding itself in readiness at any time to respond to a new call to battle.'[10]

Meanwhile, a personal battle was being fought by Varèse even as his words reached a public that could be bothered to read them. Over many months, he had been feeling more and more off-colour, often waking up headachy and fevered. Complaining of insomnia and backache, too, he would greet Louise with a snarl at the breakfast table and became 'so depressed that he was in a perpetual rage'.[9] Neither a hypochondriac or malingerer by nature, he searched for feasible causes of this general malaise. As yet, no doctor had diagnosed anything specific. Until one did, all Mr Varèse could do was take more exercise.

For several weeks, he managed this with apparent ease, walking to Brooklyn Bridge and back again once a day and swimming in the YMCA pool. X-rays, blood sampling and other measures in the out-patients department at St Vincent's Hospital winkled out an inflammation of the prostate, but this wasn't grave enough to warrant either admission or an operation. Nonetheless, disgruntled by the physicians there, who spoke to him as if he was a retard while gingerly prodding his body, he elected to take the correlated notes to a recommended medical centre in Paris for a second opinion. Although it was the height of summer there, his state of health was worsened by rheumatism brought on by a stay at a hotel situated in the damp and mind-clouding humidity of L'Île Saint-Louis.

Becoming worse, doctors noticed both an abscess and that his insides were, to use his own pungent imagery, 'swimming in pus'.[9] An appointment for a cystoscopic exploration of his urinary bladder was made for a date in the near future, but in the meantime he was prescribed self-injections of silver nitrate and, as far as he was able, complete rest and avoidance of stressful situations for a couple of months. Yet, lingering in France until early December, he risked a conciliatory meal with Suzanne, with whom Claude was now living in Burgundy.

His maladies had eased considerably by spring, when he and the second Mrs Varèse took up residence at 188 Sullivan Street, a four-storey house found by Louise on a small estate in an Italian neighbourhood. While there was no front garden to speak of, just three ascending steps between the front door and a busy Village pavement, there was space for a flower bed at the back of the house, where a gate opened onto a common green tended by a gardener who doubled as the estate's janitor.

Socially, the couple had climbed a rung higher by paying a mortgage rather than rent, thanks to Louise's mother subtracting the required lump sum from her share of the inheritance – and to rooms let to students for many years to come. Moreover, Edgard's working conditions were the most agreeable he had ever known. In a room that a largish window flooded with daylight, a wild-haired search for some mislaid jotting or other would have him ready to kill someone, but overall he quickly established an order peculiar to himself when, as a medieval scribe to his parchment, he began spending a typical day seated at a desk that vied with his baby grand piano, the gongs and other large instruments that were to dominate a spacious study like a castle sinister. It bore jam jars to hold pens, pencils, paperclips and other stationery not lurking among papers sprawled across what might otherwise be visible surface. A portrait of Edgard's mother as a girl was relegated to the drawing room, but a 'No Smoking' sign, a framed magazine cutting of the eye of a hurricane and abstract paintings (including a Miró and a couple by Varèse himself) remained on the walls of the work room, while continuing to stare at the clutter from the mantelpiece were photographs of his wife, his daughter, Debussy and Karl Muck, as well as Julio Gonzalez's drawing of Grandfather Claude.

Louise wasn't certain whether her husband was joking when, on a flying visit to Le Villars during a holiday in the French Riviera that summer, he rubbed his chin over the asking price for Claude Cortot's old house. This pleasant interlude was marred only by a return journey interrupted by Edgard's cystoscopy.

This painful and humiliating procedure was not among topics breaking the ice at the table for one of the first dinner guests at No.188. Although better known now as a poet and dramatist, Paul Claudel had first entered the world of work in the French diplomatic service, rising through the ranks to become the republic's consul in Washington. One of his reasons for imposing himself on the Varèses was to ascertain how the man of the house would feel about being awarded the Légion d'Honneur for 'services to music'.

'The only use of such a decoration in one's buttonhole,' quipped Varèse unfunnily, 'is to impress the janitor.' Anyway, did he still qualify? Surely Claudel must have heard that his host had just received his certificate of US naturalisation and thus surrendered his French passport? Did Paul not gather this through the recent elevation of Edgard to the presidency of the music committee for the American Society of Cultural Relations with the USSR? No, he wasn't quite sure what it entailed – nothing at the moment – but when Varèse said 'we' and 'us' in the ensuing discussion, Claudel realised that what he meant, of course, was 'we Americans'.

7 The Spaceman

'As things are now, I shall be forced to earn a living entirely outside music.'
– Edgard Varèse to Harvey Fletcher, 1932

Now that he was a US citizen, the internationalism propagated by the ICG was forgotten as Edgard, after a token effort to revive it, threw in his lot with the Pan American Association of Composers, an organisation that endured for six years. Essentially, its aims were the same as those of the Guild, but its catchment area covered only the USA and Latin America – although it was keen to promote performances of its members' music in countries beyond those.

A necessary appointment, therefore, was that of a peripatetic chief conductor. As Stokowski had accepted a post at Philadelphia's Curtis Institute of Music, a Nicolas Slonimsky, born a Russian but resident in the States since 1923, was an obvious choice. Through him, works by Ives and Bartók had been given their first airings in North America, and he was a respected authority on music theory. Finally, although he hadn't known Varèse for long, Slonimsky's relationship with the Association's flagship composer was based as much on friendship and an intuitive understanding of each other as musicians as much as it was on a symbiotic exchange of professional services. Best man at Slonimsky's wedding, Edgard was to bestow upon the groom an affectionate nickname, '*mon méchanicien*', appropriate enough as Nicolas took charge of presentations featuring Varèse compositions on both sides of the Atlantic, trusted as he was to shape them the way in which their absent or present creator wished.

Slonimsky was to continue as Aaron to Varèse's Moses after the Association went the same way as the ICG through a combination of internal rivalry and self-interest. Nevertheless, after the wind up meeting in May 1934, Varèse, the consummate public relations man, was unbothered and philosophical as he took credit, passed blame and acted generally as one whose sane and rational views had gone unheeded. 'The Pan-American was begun because I realised that Europe was drifting back to Neo-Classicism,' he reasoned, 'or rather what is so called, because there really is no such possible thing. You can't make a classic: it has to become one with age. What is called "Neo-Classicism" is really academicism. The influence we wished to combat is a vicious thing, for it stifles spontaneous expression, and we could combat it by performing work that was alive, that spoke for itself forcefully and truly, even if awkwardly. In this connection, it is interesting to note that, for the first time in history, it is the youth that is reactionary.'[1]

Quite middle aged now, Varèse had metamorphosed into a Grand Old Man of contemporary music, revered (or not) by newcomers as certain as his younger self had been of acclaim accrued without having to compromise artistic integrity. Some would carry that Modigliani-like self-belief even as the bailiffs carted their goods and chattels away.

Times had never been – or ever would be – that hard for Edgard Varèse, but there were perceptible signs of slackening momentum. Response – good or bad – to *Arcana* had been more muted than he had been used to at musical recitals that were becoming more like tribal gatherings. To the *cognoscenti* – in New York, anyway – he was not so much a has-been as rather commonplace. Like London buses, if you missed one Varèse performance, there would be another along if you waited. Varèse at the Klaw, the Aeolian and even Carnegie Hall was still viable, financially, but there was a noticeable falling off of attendances, which were sometimes as low as half capacity.

Why not pack it in? He'd brought a respectability, however questionable, to a mocked genre. Wistfully, though, he would drink in tales of Stravinsky's and Prokofiev's tours all over North America and further afield and of Holst refusing the honorary degree offered him by Michigan University. It was small comfort that Webern had been driven to teach in order to keep alive, just as Varèse would be examining similar possibilities by the turn of the decade. Yet, if no longer supported by patrons with bottomless pockets full of money, Varèse's savings from accumulated concert earnings, plus a loan from Stokowski, was enough to keep him and Louise afloat for an estimated five years – although, towards the end, his weeks filled with more and more lessons in composition, amassed via advertisements in the *Musical Courier* trade paper.

Varèse's professional motives were becoming confused, and he was soon debating whether to proceed directly to what seemed to be increasingly inevitable. As a college tutor, even if answerable to someone like d'Indy or Fauré, he would have the safety net of a fixed salary on which he and Louise could live quite comfortably until retirement. Moreover, if he still felt that he had something to say, he would be better placed to make headway as a composer again. That was almost a cheering thought when, as 1930 loomed, he was headhunted to be director of advanced composition at the Curtis Institute, where Salzedo was already teaching harp and Stokowski was conducting. A similar offer would be made by the New England Conservatory of Music after Slonimsky took up a post there.

To a vaguer but similar end, there was also a supplicatory letter to Varèse from Ernst Schoen, one of his former students in Berlin, who had succeeded Busoni as head of the fading Internationale Komponisten Gilde. This shot in the dark was met by a foreseeable reply with its curt assertion that Varèse's future lay in the United States, rather than what he dismissed as 'perhaps the most timid of countries, with regard to academic progress. It is a shame that the same spirit of adventure that rules [Germany's] industrial and business affairs does not govern in this area, too. As for the attitude of the musicians, it is dictated by their thirst for official and academic honours: pigs racing each other to the trough.'[2]

Schoen therefore didn't know what to think when Varèse left New York to gossip as it liked and, in October 1928, commenced a sojourn of months that stretched into years in a European city that he considered as culturally obsolete as Berlin. Perhaps he imagined that Paris could be revived if he spread the word about the Pan American Association and gave his old stamping ground the value of his experiences in the USA.

Varèse began by petitioning a number of industrial corporations, both in France and North America, in an attempt to raise interest in a centre for electric-instrument research in Paris. He also inspected properties to house this proposed 'sound laboratory' and a catholic library of scores and discs intended to facilitate the realization of new music, 'because I'm thwarted by the poverty of the means of expression at my disposal. For instance, it's impossible to produce a continuous sound. The human performer, the virtuoso, ought not to exist any more. He'd be better replaced by a machine – and he will be. These ideas still astound a lot of people, but you'll see them as realities in the not-too-distant future. The composer's ideas will no longer be desecrated by adaptation or performance as all the past classics were'[3] – and are, he might have added.

This rant in *Pour Vous*, a something-for-everyone gazette, fell on stony ground for a readership affected in varying degrees by the drying up of US overseas investment and the imminent Wall Street Crash. So began the Great Depression, the global collapse of all sizes and manner of business enterprises, with attendant multitudes suddenly finding themselves unemployed.

Where did the manufacture of funny noises figure in this? When it became evident that it didn't, Varèse concentrated on the possible by opening a school of composition. Named after himself, it attracted some attention – especially after he spoke of the project at length in an interview published in *Figaro* – but it was effectively neither better nor worse than either the Conservatoire or the Schola Cantorum, except that it had a far smaller budget. As a result, it soon petered out, but not before Edgard's canvassing had worked up a small register of students. The most renowned of these was 23-year-old Andre Jolivet, enrolled after he transcribed a piano arrangement of *Octandre*.

Among those pouncing with nitpicking hope on the remotest indication of the new school's fall was Vincent d'Indy, still sniping at the reprobate Edgard after 20 years but now doing so in print, as well as over coffee in the staff room. The snigger was almost audible in the latest article he had written about modern music for the arts periodical *Comoedia*, which had just appointed Paul Le Flem as its music critic.

Everything was different, everything was the same. Cancer had claimed Fauré in 1924. Gone, too, was Satie, and Ravel hadn't much longer to go. Yet Widor, now in his late 80s, still pumped the organ in St Sulpice, and Varèse could not help but visualise others of the same vintage in some similar fixed pose doing now what they did then. Indeed, many of them still were, and towards them Edgard remained his selectively amiable self. Yet, while calls were paid on some old pals who knew how privately ordinary – even boring – he could be, others were blocked from his mind as he sought the particular company of newer and mostly younger friends who, for all their hail-fellow-well-met familiarity, would still fall silent in the manner he had once recognised in New York and London – an awestruck sense of worship mingled with a touch of scepticism, as if the famous and notorious musical maverick responsible for *Hyperprism* and *Amériques* wasn't quite real. Poet Robert Desnos, US authors Henry Miller and Anaïs Nin (whose first work of fiction, *The House Of Incest*, was nearing completion), playwright Antonin Artaud, film director Thomas Bouchard, Guatemalan novelist Miguel Angel Asturias and photographer Georges Brassai were among those contending to flop onto the stool next to Edgard Varèse in the Café Billiard, the Dome, the Petit Napolitain and the late-night Jockey-Bar, where the polemics of the afternoon would dissolve into ribald camaraderie as the artistic pot pourri boasted, spread rumours, small talked, betrayed confidences, schemed and had a laugh or a cry, depending on how their careers were going.

Of few musicians with whom Edgard rubbed shoulders then, Heitor Villa-Lobos – perhaps the only globally renowned composer from Brazil – was on the verge of leaving France when Louise Varèse joined her man in a rented house attractive to him for the name of its street, Rue de Bourgogne. Located in the heart of Les Invalides, Paris' nearest equivalent to Westminster, it was modish light years from the dump that he and Suzanne used to share in the Rue Monge. These days, Edgard and the second Mrs Varèse could also afford a weekend cottage in olde-worlde Chevreuse, where Paris bleeds into the countryside.

Visible signs of success were but one incentive for both bohemia and smart society to adulate the returned native, who had turned the USA on its head with music that raised riots. Yet the continued soaring of his reputation had as much to do with the magnetic personality of 'a man you would notice in a crowd',[2] reckoned Miller. In concurrence, Brassai was to describe Varèse later as 'a handsome man, a Maupassant with the moustache shaved off',[4] albeit with grey-flecked hair that was to become 'a shock of steel wool'[5] commensurate with 'eyes heavy with thought'[6] when he next fiddled for the front door key of 188 Sullivan Street.

By that time, too, Varèse would be up to his neck in a dramatic project with the working title *The One-All-Alone: A Miracle*. In its most ambitious state, it was a five-act opera intended to be presented like a radio-age Live Aid, with simultaneous linked transmissions co-ordinated in either Paris or New York and featuring performers in different parts of the world singing in their own languages.

The seed of this idea had taken hold just before he'd left for Paris. Since obtaining US nationality, Varèse had taken more than a layman's interest in American history, researching beyond Columbus to Red Indian civilisations uncorrupted by hand mirrors, rotgut liquor and like trade goods that began Europe's annexation of their lands. At his urging, Louise had pieced together a discernible scenario centred on a conflict between materialism and idealism, personified respectively by a villain named Arrow-Maker and – also to be played by a singing acrobat – a hero based on the *Übermensch* (superman) in Nietzsche's *Also Sprach Zarathustra*.

The character of the latter might also have been drawn from aspects of Varèse's own – or, at least, those that corresponded with Nietzsche's model. A parallel with Zarathustra's reverse-psychology attitude towards reversals[7] amused Louise: 'Varèse sometimes made assertions contrary to his deepest desire, reminding me of a cat who has tried to catch a fly and walks haughtily away, pretending that she has never had any such idea.'[8]

Likewise, when Louise challenged him about whispers she'd heard concerning the scrapping of the original *One-All-Alone* text in favour of one written by Antonin Artaud and hinged on his *Il N'Y A Pas De Firmament* (*The Firmament Is Gone*), Edgard spluttered that such a proposal was ridiculous. Actually, Artaud – who had never heard a note of Varèse's music – had been asked to do precisely what Varèse was denying but, pleading illness, had abandoned a more than half-completed job, despite increasingly rueful written enquiries about progress.

Alejo Carpentier and Robert Desnos had also pitched in ideas for what was next called *L'Astronome* and, later, *Espace*. Also, the piece had undergone a drastic rewrite. No longer a Red Indian saga, it was set now in 2000 inside an observatory in an apocalyptic world of 'fear and mystery'. Anticipating radio astronomy, it was about a space scientist who makes contact with the inhabitants – mentally superior to Earthlings – of a planet in a distant solar system. To cut a long story short, Earth is destroyed by the aliens to the sound of sirens, aeroplane propellers and a theme fingered on an ondes Martenot as spotlights – 'sonic beams' – veer fitfully before homing in on the audience, dazzling them with panic.

To realize what was evolving into a cross between grand opera and a lowbrow science-fiction film, Varèse attempted to accelerate technology by finding the finance to have special instruments constructed. However, although dusted off intermittently over the years, *L'Astronome* or *Espace* came to nothing.

While this project was haemorrhaging time and money, Varèse had been taken aback by the calm reception that the Paris première of *Intégrales* had generated, and that coverage of it reached the man in the street, if he got beyond the opening paragraph. At the Maison Gaveau in April 1929, *Intégrales* was 'a completely new one on us, but it did not provoke a riot',[9] reported Paul Le Flem in *Comoedia*, while the less predisposed *La Liberté* noted that 'what strikes you above all is the power, the pulsating vigour...a great and truly new work'.[10] To *Le Monde*, it was 'a revelation. Is it a harbinger of the music of the future? We must hear more of Varèse's music before forming a more precise opinion.'[11]

The following month, at the same venue, it was the turn of *Amériques*, albeit a version revised once again by the composer. There was also an unforeseen adjustment to be made when it was discovered that there wasn't a siren to be borrowed anywhere in Paris, and the sound had to be approximated on an ondes Martenot.

On this occasion, sections of the crowd went as crazy as their US cousins. In the pandemonium, punches were thrown and a bleeding Tristan Tzara was among several casualties requiring hospital treatment. The trouble began, reported *Le Menestrel*, when, 'with each entry of the percussion or when the moaning sirens [*sic*] spread their swelling menace, shocked voices in pit and gallery alike were provoked into shouts of rage'.[12]

As well as chronicling what he saw and heard that night, *Le Monde*'s Adolphe Piriou 'read the lengthy orchestral score very thoroughly and tried very hard to enlighten myself. Then I put myself in the position of the ordinary listener. It was impossible, essentially, for Mr Varèse to be followed and comprehended. All of these laboratory experiments destroy music rather than revitalise it. There is nothing more difficult than to compose a new musical tune [*sic*] with a beginning, middle and ending.'[13]

Not understanding what was going on any more than Piriou but having tried hard to appreciate his pal's *Amériques*, Robert Desnos resorted to snooty and purple prose in his write up for *Le Merle*, telling readers of 'an arduous, virile transcendence in successive stages in which the most delightful first fruits were resolved into human continuity – tireless, persistent strivings towards a new summit. We held our breath as we followed this masculine endeavour. Yet what new breezes blew against out faces! Human music, playing simultaneously upon our muscles and on our capabilities of dreaming.'[14]

Oh gawd. But wait! There's more: 'Half the audience was howling its indignation in the face of a manifestation strong enough to turn their pathetic little lives on their heads, those very voices meshing with the orchestra. Impenetrable music, proof against all assault, shut against all intrusion and emitting the most powerful emotions it has been our privilege to experience for many, many years.'

That was the last performance of *Amériques* for decades, and the fellow at the centre of the furore beat a calculated retreat to the smaller and more exclusive Salle Chopin, within the arty Pleyel building on the edge of the city limits. There, on 14 March 1930, Varèse himself conducted *Octandre* and *Offrandes* and everyone clapped politely. He also took part in a round-table debate with Carpentier, Desnos, Huidobro – all the usual shower – on the future mechanisation of music. His principal contribution to the otherwise inconsequential chit-chat was the futuristic notion of loudspeakers placed in specific points that would allow sound to travel through space, crossing from speaker to speaker and striking the ears from any chosen direction.

Stereophonic sound wasn't to be regarded as a worthwhile commercial proposition for almost another 30 years, but in the teeth of the Depression there were various minor breakthroughs and well meant blind alleys. In 1930, a Friedrich Trautwein built the electrophon (renamed the trautonium), a close relation of the theremin but with greater capacity for glissandi and vibrato. Although it attracted the creative attention of German *enfant terrible* Paul Hindemith (witness 1931's *Concertino For Trautonium And Strings*) and, of all people, Richard Strauss, it – like the theremin – was subsequently used mostly in films.

Nevertheless, Varèse attempted to contact Leon Theremin in Russia, hoping to find a cure for being 'handicapped by a lack of adequate electrical instruments for which I conceive my music'.[2] He was also made aware of the activities of an 'anti-Varèse' in 29-year-old Harry Partch, a Californian who, in 1950, torched 14 years' worth of piano concerti, string quartets and symphonic poems and started from scratch, writing music to the 43-notes-to-the-octave scale he'd devised for the crychord, the zymo-xyl, the quadrangularis reversum and further non-electronic instruments knocked together from scavenged materials, such as the job-lot of light-bulbs that were the main elements of his Mazda marimba.

Accepting that Partch had no sympathy for music derived from modern technology, Varèse was to be fascinated by titles like *A Soul Tormented By Contemporary Music Finds A Humanising Element* and

The Cognoscenti Are Plunged Into Descent While At Cocktails, despite their considerable lengths and repetitive polyrhythms, and had already spoken out against 'the division of the octave into 12 semitones'. It was, Varèse pointed out, 'purely arbitrary. There is no good reason why we should continue to tolerate this restriction.'[15]

In 1933, Partch visited New York, where he met an amazing young man called John Cage. While awaiting his destiny as formulator of chance operation, the 'prepared piano' and *4'33"*, his famous 'silent' piece, Cage studied under Arnold Schoenberg, who insisted that 'in order to write music, you have to have a feeling for harmony.' At this, Cage confessed, '"I have no feeling for harmony." Schoenberg then said I would always encounter an obstacle, that it would be as though I came to a wall through which I could not pass. I said, "In that case, I will devote my life to beating my head against that wall."'[16]

An admirer of Varèse, Cage was waiting likewise for technology to catch up with the sounds he heard in his mind and, conversely, sought to boil down music to its rawest state. To this resolve, Varèse recognised that primitive humankind relied on nothing but percussion for instruments. Moreover, such limited and acoustic resources still fed the imagination of those untroubled by the dos and don'ts that traditionally affect creative flow. Random examples are Malayan *ketimum* or 'water-splash' music (hydro-percussion); Buddhist monks chanting to accompaniment from *kei*, *taiko*, *hachi*, *nyo* and other beating implements and any number of drum solos in jazz.

In 1930, Amateo Roldan, conductor of the Havana Philharmonic Orchestra, composed *Ritmicas V* and *Ritmicas VI*, the first formalised works for an all-percussion ensemble. The world might have been the talented Roldan's oyster, but unfashionable Cuba was enormous enough for him. He was also a half-caste, which made fame difficult for him to reach.

At any rate, his *Ritmicas V* and *VI* were to be totally eclipsed by a new work that Edgard Varèse had been brooding on for over a year. *Ionisation* – a scientific term for chemical decomposition by electricity – was judged by the discerning Olivier Messiaen to be 'very high among the artistic creations of the 20th century'.[17] Bearing the same relationship to Roldan's folky *Ritmicas*es as dairy butter to Tablada's low-fat Oleo margarine in *La Croix Du Sud*, '*Ionisation* is a classic,' agreed Chou Wen-Chung, a bespectacled Chinaman who was to loom large in Varèse's legend, 'not for the commonly held reason – the first serious work for percussion only – but because it demonstrates that Varèse's concept is successfully applicable even when no definite pitches are present, the supreme test for his goal of liberating sound.'[2]

Strictly speaking, *Ionisation* wasn't quite 'for percussion only'; while it was written for 13 musicians playing an assortment of unpitched instruments, including anvils, there were also parts for high and low sirens and, for the final 17 bars, glockenspiel, bells and piano.

When expressed diagrammatically, the piece resembles sonic architecture. Unison changes of time signature occur during 14 unequal 'episodes' or rhythm collages created by instruments – some constructed specifically for *Ionisation* – with individual timbres detailed with cheese-paring exactitude (and usually to create maximum resonance) in directives preceding the score. For instance, Varèse prescribed soft mallets for the playing of the timpani, the bass drums to be laid flat, the sirens to be operated by hand rather than mouth and, if possible, Cuban rather than Mexican maracas.

For all to see on the title page was a dedication to Nicolas Slonimsky, who was to take charge when (or if) the Pan American Association dared risk *Ionisation* in the context of a public concert. No one else would. Indeed, Slonimsky said as much when he turned up at *chez* Varèse in June 1931 with his Pan-American Association conductor's hat on to smoothe the rough edges of the Orchestre des Concerts Straram in preparation for two presentations at the Maison Gaveau. The programme included *Intégrales*. If not back by popular demand, this piece's 'acoustical geometry'[18] by now provoked far less lukewarm a response than it had in 1929. *Excelsior* magazine provided the most glowing testimonial, considering *Intégrales* 'the apotheosis of these recitals. Despite its scientific title, the work is not unaccessible and purely cerebral. Of all those presented here, it is perhaps the most profoundly human. It frees the lyricism inherent in pure timbre. Never for a moment does *Intégrales* go beyond the charmed circle of music.'[19]

Portrait of the artist as a film actor: Varèse landed bit parts in silent movies after his arrival in New York in 1915

Vincent d'Indy, principal lecturer when Varèse studied at the Schola Cantorum in Paris, but 'I did not want to become a little d'Indy; one was enough'

Novelist Romain Rolland. The hero of his *Jean-Christophe* magnum opus was modelled on Varèse

At the St Sulpice organ, Charles-Marie Widor, to whom Varèse's day-to-day tuition at the Paris Conservatoire was delegated

Gabriel Fauré (SEATED) with Trio Cortot-Thibaud-Casals, an ensemble containing Varèse's detested cousin Alfred (FAR RIGHT)

Claude Debussy (STANDING) in 1910, at the height of his fame, at his home in the Bois de Boulogne with 28-year-old Igor Stravinsky, Varèse's artistic rival and eventual friend

German conductor Karl Muck, who lent pragmatic support to Varèse in Berlin 'in the face of great difficulties confronting him in his daily life'

Dresden, 1911. The hard-won recommendations of Richard Strauss (SEATED CENTRE) and lyricist Hugo von Hofmannsthal (CENTRE BACK) found Varèse much-needed employment during his sojourn in Germany

Varèse in his workroom at 188 Sullivan Street

The house in New York's Greenwich Village where Varèse lived and worked for 40 years

Maurice Jacquet, Lucienne Boyer, Edgard Varèse and General Count Charles de Fontnouvelle plan the programme – which was to include the première of *Density 21.5* – for a 1936 concert in aid of the Lycée Français in New York

Jazz colossus and near-neighbour Charlie 'Yardbird' Parker was so in awe of Varèse that he didn't dare speak in the presence of one who was an everyday sight in Greenwich Village

Elaine Music Shop (EMS), a Manhattan-based record firm of no great merit, were the first to issue Varèse's works on album

Yannis Xenakis and a bespectacled Le Corbusier (CE Jeanneret) during their collaboration with Varèse on *La Poème Électronique* for the 1958 World's Fair in Brussels

Varèse during rehearsals for *Déserts* with Bruno Maderna

A drawing of Varèse by John Minnion, reinforcing the public image of the stock 'mad composer'

Frank Zappa and Pierre Boulez, Varèse's most eminent champions, meet the press in Los Angeles in summer 1989

The honorific plaque on the wall of 188 Sullivan Street, in a country that adopted Varèse as one of its own

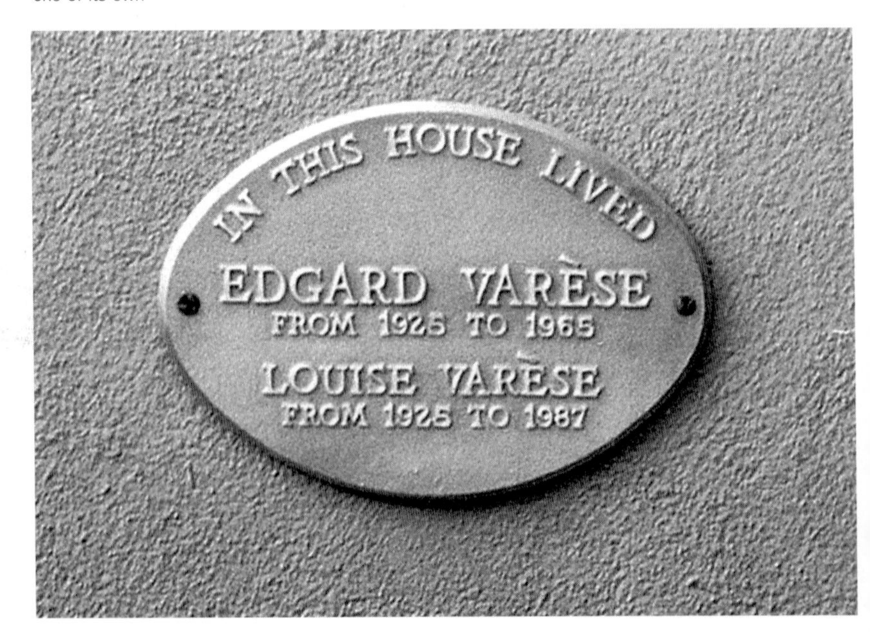

Neither did it go beyond the 'charmed circle' of that Parisian arts crowd who, united in play, were photographed at the same premières, covered the same exhibitions and sampled the same stimulants. Hardly likely to be slotted between a magician and a juggler at the Olympia, France's most capacious music hall, performances of *Intégrales* and anything else from Varèse's *oeuvre* were high-culture affairs. His devotees were of the type that browsed in bookshops and for whom 'culture' – watching Cocteau films and guffawing knowingly during a Shakespeare comedy – was second nature. Magnifying the gap between themselves and the great unwashed at the Olympia, such snobs attended the second *Intégrales* at Maison Gaveau as a cultural duty, first and foremost. Being entertained or grasping the humour in the artist – not *artiste* – rated a poor second. Edgard Varèse, as a cultural phenomenon in Paris as much as New York, had less to do with any given recital of his music *per se* than with the behaviour of most of its consumers.

Varèse knew the type well. When buttonholed by *The Musical Courier* to comment on a spate of youthful suicides and the journal's moral crusade against other dangers threatening US artists living in Paris, he allowed that 'there may be a certain wicked – if we must have that word – Paris made up of the international derelicts, rich morons and their hangers-on – pretentious individuals and neurotics. Its influence is nil and it attracts only its own kind.'[20]

The objects of his contempt treated Varèse with deadly seriousness. No culture-vultures worthy of the named found the belches of the bassoon 'funny' or the screeches of the violin 'irritating' as his music appeared to dart randomly from section to indissoluble section. In any case, they scarcely listened anyway, because each was preoccupied with thinking deeply about what to say afterwards, preferably something glibly jaw-dropping enough to match the erudition of the conversations they had overheard in the foyer at a previous such event. Often, these nuggets either didn't mean anything or were the mere parroting of received opinion, but they could convey the impression of volumes of worldly insight way above the head of anyone who hadn't picked up buzz-words or fragments of cleverness logged when skip-reading the arts sections in various papers.

Those of a more self-improving persuasion wondered if they'd been had but were convinced that this *Intégrales*, or whatever he called it, was something that only the finest minds could understand. It was an intellectual rather than aesthetic experience, even if it was like incidental music to some wild dream that makes perfect sense until the sleeper wakes. For anyone who remembered it, *Le Sacre Du Printemps* at the Théâtre des Champs-Elysées in 1913 seemed almost melodious by comparison. You'd think that this Edgard Varèse had been either drunk or enjoying some private joke when he composed it.

Back in the USA, Varèse had been as much a victim of all the drivel that had been written and spoken about him as anyone else, but now he wasn't so dazzled to imagine that he wouldn't be superseded by some fresher sensation and rendered bitterly old fashioned within the measure of a day. Before the game was up, he and Louise, defying the Great Depression, established a pattern in Paris whereby they moved rapidly onwards and upwards to homes that were always improvements on the one before. After the Rue de Bourgogne, it was a secluded mews in the most verdant part of Montparnasse, other than its cemetery. Then it was north to Passy, a village-like suburb with close proximity to open countryside.

Among their visitors there was Miguel Angel Asturias, then living on the other side of the Seine. Once, on bidding farewell, he had presented the Varèses with a signed copy of his *Legends Of Guatemala*. Edgard was struck less by Asturias's prose as his insertion of a Mayan incantation to tribal gods in the same exultant, nature-worshipping vein as the framed and calligraphed 'listen to the exhortation of the dawn' text from Sanskrit that was to be found among the crystals, joss-sticks and like wares in new-age shops towards the close of the millennium 70 years later.

As posthumous record releases demonstrate, Varèse couldn't arrive at a firm decision about whether a bass soloist or – perhaps more evocative – a male chorale should sing (and, in places, speak) the words after his imagination had been captured by Asturias's psalm-like chant as surely as Don Quixote's by the windmills of Castile. Neither was Varèse sure whether an ondes Martenot or two theremins should augment an equally prominent piano and pipe organ, as well as an eight-piece brass section and the now-customary polyrhythmic percussion. The title of the new work, *Ecuatorial*, so he would preface the score, 'is merely suggestive of the regions where pre-Columbian art flourished. I conceive the music as having something of the same elemental, rude intensity of those strange, primitive works. The execution should be dramatic and incantatory, guided by the imploring fervour of the text, and should follow the dynamic indications of the score'.

Without this background information, the only point of reference for emotive interpretation of *Ecuatorial* is in its title. Brash if obliquely exciting vocal and instrumental sounds, especially the unearthly high-pitched careen – *eeeeeeeee* – of bending pitches from the electronic instruments, worried me into a mild sensation of unfocused paranoia. If I felt like that seven decades of cultural extremity later, imagine the mass effect at *Ecuatorial*'s eventual – and almost secretive – première in New York in 1934, particularly as on that occasion Spanish was intoned through a megaphone at an English-language audience.

Between its piano introit and coda of squealing theremins, if there was so much as a tang of ancient South America in the *Ecuatorial* music, it wasn't overt, although Slonimsky, an expert on the subject, may have been consulted while he remained in Paris to conduct *Arcana* – 'a grandiloquently stylised nightmare', gloomed *Le Feuilleton Du Temps*, 'a nightmare dreamed by giants'[21] – before doing likewise at Berlin's Beethoven Halle, a performance that rendered listeners 'at times bored, at times irritated, sometimes inadvertently amused'.[22]

Of course, the early 1930s wasn't the most opportune time to present *Arcana* in Germany. Shortly to be appointed Chancellor, Adolf Hitler was already in the process of gaining supreme control of every aspect of national life, including culture. His musical tastes ran to Mozart, Beethoven and, naturally, Wagner, whose operas were 'the drug that kept him alive. He was transported into the blessed regions of German antiquity, which was for him the ideal world, the highest goal of his endeavours.'[23] So inspired was the teenage Adolf after catching *Tannhäuser* at Linz Opera House that he worked on a

Wagnerian opera of his own for three or four weeks before his butterfly concentration alighted elsewhere.

On rising to power, Hitler encouraged the elimination of what he considered to be degenerate, 'un-German' music. Civic howls of agreement led to a Reich-wide ban on performances of Hindemith's opera *Mathis Der Maler*, for example, because the (soon-to-be-exiled) Frankfurt-born composer's radical approach to harmony and counterpoint was considered 'decadent' – and so, eventually, was Webern's. What chance, therefore, did Varèse's 'Bolshevism in music'[24] stand in a country where a wireless would be switched off automatically if it was broadcasting anything remotely avant garde, because its depraved cacophony threatened to subvert all that was good and true?

Yes, the Führer might have his faults, but pouring active scorn on this rubbish while succouring the Fatherland's classical heritage wasn't among them – although he might have been more liberal had he read Varèse's interview in *La Liberté* on 13 February 1933, the 50th anniversary of Wagner's fatal heart attack. 'The reaction against Wagner gave us a composer like Debussy,' explained Varèse, 'and that in itself is something. Music definitely needs a new Wagner, a force that will wake it up and pack a few punches. We need a great Romantic, since it is my opinion that all great creators, whether in science or art, have been Romantics. Genius is Romantic. It is the work that is Classical, after it has survived the test of time.'

Yet, under the Nazis, even Richard Strauss, that most Teutonic of then-living composers, had been oppressed by government intervention in artistic matters. Unlike Hindemith – along with Schoenberg and Bartók – he was not, however, willing to let it force him from his home or prevent his music from being heard.

Not so ambivalent was Igor Stravinsky, whose family estates in his native Russia had been confiscated by the Soviet authorities. Now settled in France, he had found the Parisian première of *Arcana* poignant and had meticulously pinpointed precise bars that contained similarities to his own works. Bitching back, Varèse declared, 'Stravinsky is finished. Schoenberg is of much greater importance, but on the other hand, while Schoenberg's music will undoubtedly leave its impression on the future, his "system" is unlikely to. This "system" of atonality simply does not exist, it is a fallacy of thought, for we feel a tonality whether or not we deny its presence.'[24]

Schoenberg's own comments are not recorded. If suffering from declining health, his wanderings on fleeing Nazi Germany had brought him back to the Jewish faith of his childhood and to California, where he was obliged, like Webern, to keep body and soul together by lecturing and teaching privately.

Edgard Varèse was also confronted with the possibility of having to do what he could second best, as he talked more frequently about lack of work. How often had *Amériques* been performed, compared to *Le Sacre Du Printemps*? Once payment of musicians, hire of the venue and other overheads had been deducted, the Pan American Association's concerts – far fewer than those of the ICG, if more widespread – were so close to break-even point that Varèse didn't know whether to spend his share of the net profits on a pair of shoelaces or a box of matches.

To purchase respite, however brief, from a stagnant future of blackboards, armchaired tutorials and Brahms' *German Requiem*, Edgard felt compelled to pen entreaties to the likes of Dr Harvey Fletcher, director of acoustical research in the Western Electric laboratories of the Bell Telephone Company. One epistle from Paris late in 1932 ended thus: 'It would be a great joy to me to be able to collaborate uninterruptedly with you. Will you be so good as to consider seriously my request and let me know your opinion?'[25] The only trick he missed was signing off as 'your most humbly obedient servant'.

Although sympathetic, Dr Fletcher was ruled by Great Depression economics and so paying someone, however eminent, to undertake 'acoustical research in the interest of pure music'[25] was scarcely a priority when cutbacks in all departments at Bell meant plummeting wages and also added to the previously unimaginable unemployment crisis. Again, where did the manufacture of funny noises figure in this? Did 'pure music' feed children, no matter how potent this Varèse guy's later contention that 'the emotional impulse that moves a composer to write his scores contains the same element of poetry that incites the scientist to his discoveries'?[26]

After Fletcher's reply had wended its way across the Atlantic, Edgard gaped at the 'I regret to inform you' sentence and then the paragraph that began, 'We are here to improve the value of the investor's dollar. Electronic music struck the board of directors as a losing proposition.'[25] Realising then that the only art that concerned Western Electric was the art of making money, Varèse was still loath to accept the finality of the decision. He mailed back a nakedly desperate letter, pleading – to no avail – that, 'as things are now, I shall be forced to earn a living entirely outside music, and my preoccupation is the fear of having to go into something where I should no longer have the time nor opportunity for the work in sound, which is of such vital importance, to say nothing of my composition. That is why I am looking for a situation in a company organised for the sort of work in sound where my collaboration would have value and be worth a pecuniary return. To make money does not interest me. I only desire to have sufficient for my actual needs so that, not having to worry about money, I can give all my energy to work.'[25]

Without waiting for a response that might never come, Varèse pursued the same objective by applying for a fellowship in another US organisation, the John Simon Guggenheim Memorial Foundation, possibly because a relation of Guggenheim had been a member on the New Symphony Orchestra's committee (albeit one instrumental in the original ensemble's downfall). A request came for further details of the proposals. Varèse replied immediately, stressing that for many years he had been corresponding with René Bertrand with regard to developing the dynaphone, 'which we hope will have a sound more in keeping with our age'.[27]

Consequent silence from Guggenheim and other potential backers left Edgard with his pride smarting as he and Louise quit a city that had also disappointed them. They chose an indirect route back to New York via Spain, socialising mainly with the fine-art community. Among its leading lights were Salvador Dalí, Oscar Dominguez and Joan Miró, the subject of a proposed biopic by Thomas Bouchard, who had been wooing Varèse to write the music. Then, after spending the summer in Barcelona and Madrid, the couple split like an amoeba,

Louise going on to Grenoble on an assignment connected with her work as a translator while Edgard remained in Spain, from whence they sailed for home on 27 September 1933.

Varèse was, therefore, still in Europe when *Ionisation* was premièred at Carnegie Hall on 6 March. He must have eaten his heart out, particularly as this *l'art pour l'art* opus triggered no disruptions and was reprised to thunderous acclaim, even if some of it was for the 'wrong' reasons. Just under six minutes long, and containing no tonal dissonance, it remains the most inviting composition from Varèse's American period. Certainly, it's the one that still trips most easily off the tongue whenever he is discussed by the sort of people who, although claiming not to be especially musical, would automatically buy a ticket for a town-hall classical concert. Some applaud the cool nerve of a piece consisting of just percussion, just as they might have done against the tidal waves of derision for Russolo's gimmicky *intonarumori* at the London Coliseum in 1913. Others enter the auditorium believing that every work by Varèse is somehow a joke. Yet, although there are moments of levity in *Ionisation* – mostly via the sirens' unaccompanied overhangs and sudden cuts on point of decay – it was 'this terrible and marvellous work'[28] to Paul Rosenfeld, who also rated it on a par with 'its prodigious elder brethren', meaning the likes of *Pierrot Lunaire* and *Le Sacre Du Printemps*.

The experience lingered for Rosenfeld the next day in 'streets full of jangly noises. The taxi squeaking to a halt at the crossroads recalls a theme. Timbres and motifs are sounded by police whistles, the bark and moan of motor horns and fire sirens, mooing of great sea-cows steering through harbour and river, chatter of drills, in the garishly lit 50-foot excavations. A thousand insignificant sensations have suddenly become interesting, full of character and meaning.'[28]

At the piece's second performance – paired with the 'raucous cacophony'[29] of second-billed *Ecuatorial* – a year later at the same venue, *The New York Times* wouldn't be so sure when, after dismissing 'caterwauling' *Ecuatorial*, it pondered whether the tuneless *Ionisation* 'could hardly be called music'.[30] *The Musical Courier*, nevertheless, had perceived the same appalling beauty as Rosenfeld in

Ionisation, although it shrouded its review in condescension: 'Varèse's latest effort contains almost nothing of traditional tonal quality, being scored for various Gatling-gun species of percussion, a dolorous and quaintly modulated siren [*sic*], sleighbells and an ingenious instrument that imitated the voice of an anguished bull. Towards the end of this strange work, which moved even earnest devotees to smiles, there was a slight undercurrent of the lyrical in the muted tones of a piano and a celeste [*sic*].'[31]

Innocent of the Big Apple's *sang-froid*, coverage of performances of *Ionisation* in Havana in the following month and in San Francisco that July was much more enthusiastic. 'Atonal phantasmagoria,' raved the *San Francisco Examiner*. 'So striking. So novel, and at the same time so beautiful that it catches your breath.'[32] *The Los Angeles Times* followed suit with 'Not one serious listener would have missed the impressiveness of this work. Emotional depths are touched by *Ionisation* as by a sculptural masterpiece of geometric abstraction.'[32]

The most memorable piece in his portfolio, *Ionisation* still overshadows far worthier items and was the closest Varèse would ever come to spreading beyond the intellectual fringe. Readers of widely circulated daily newspapers – who may or, most likely, may not have heard *Ionisation* – learned about this fellow who had turned noise into music and had become the wildest act going in the classical – and every other musical – field.

No time would have been better for an international tour of *Ionisation* and a retinue of companion pieces, conducted by either the composer himself or, failing that, Nicolas Slonimsky. Yet Varèse chose to vanish almost immediately from the public eye. His return to Sullivan Street was so unapproachably low key as to be almost cloak-and-dagger. Few were made aware that he was cocooned there for the mere weeks before he and Louise boarded a train for Mexico. Belatedly taking Diego Rivera at his word, they arrived at his opulent home in Mexico City for an extended stay, beaming from the depths of brimmed hats and sunglasses.

Such a meeting of minds made theoretical sense. Rivera was as provocative in his area as Varèse was in his. The Mexican's untitled

New York mural, for example, had been erased for what was considered its blasphemous and anti-American content. When he repainted it in Mexico City, it was displayed only on specific occasions, but otherwise covered in heavy drape curtain to protect it from being defaced by Roman Catholic and right-wing militants. Later, hellfire sermons were to preach of the divine wrath that would fall on Rivera for sheltering Leon Trotsky, exiled from the USSR for his advocacy of a worldwide communist revolution. In 1940, Trotsky would be assassinated in the same house where the Varèses had imposed themselves on Rivera seven years earlier.

After a warped fashion, Trotskyism had infiltrated Spain and spread via the Soviet Union's hand in the internal unrest that served as a dry run for the Second World War. Its basic contention of democracy versus totalitarianism, liberty against fascism, drew disparate fighting forces from all over the world like iron filings to a magnet. The talk of the hour in Mexico City was of the growing unrest, and the official outbreak of the Spanish Civil War was five months away when Edgard Varèse took his seat in a packed Carnegie Hall one Sunday evening in February 1936 for a big-names-in-good-cause gala concert in aid of the Lycée Français in New York.

When cornered about Spain or, indeed, any other inflammable topic, Edgard would exchange a sidestepping smile and bark no revolutionary rhetoric, not a solitary statement that might be construed as openly doctrinal (unless you count 'War is a destructive and chronic accident and art a living, permanent force'[25]). He was, however, active in a sweepingly dispassionate way in verbally supporting pacifism and dissident popular opinion, and he also gave vent to anger at harrowing and multiplying accounts of atrocities committed by all factions congregated in Spain.

Because it exposes a point of view, every work of art is in some respect political, even *Density 21.5*, a new Varèse opus, heard by many listening to its debut at the Lycée Français extravaganza as an instrumental lament for those distracted times. Written a month earlier, *Density 21.5*, his only work for a solo player, endures as an atonal *Lark Ascending* for flute, but not just any flute. Just as Fauré composed a piece specifically for a one-handed pianist he knew, so *Density 21.5* was peculiar to Georges Barrère, principal flautist for the New York Philharmonic Orchestra, who possessed a unique instrument forged from platinum, the precious metal with an atomic density in grammes per cubic centimetre of – you guessed it – 21.5.

Since its première, every bar of *Density 21.5* has been cut, dried and dissected by academia, but there wasn't so much as a passing reference to the piece by any reviewers of the Carnegie Hall show. Expecting barbarous *Ionisation*-like magic, all they got was mere music.

For the first time, no one took any real notice of an Edgard Varèse composition, albeit one penned for the benefit of a virtuoso as much as the audience. The elegant swoops from mellow drone to harmonics on the very edge of the instrument's range went in one ear and out the other, and the piece wasn't quite long enough for either a trip to the toilet or to order a drink for the intermission.

Thus began a major episode of clinical depression that lasted for months as New York at large forgot the existence of Edgard Varèse. Recovery sat ill with wounded pride, so he leaned on every media connection he could to publicise *Espace*, exhumed after an overnight guest at Sullivan Street was shown the manuscript and, drawing on a cigarette, had nodded in apparent agreement when his hosts suggested that he write a new libretto for its new title, *Symphony For The Masses*.

Edgard, you see, had struck instant rapport with 35-year-old André Malraux, seen at the time as a paladin of the French novel. His latest effort, *L'Espoir* (*Man's Hope*), was centred on the Spanish Civil War. Indeed, his main purpose in travelling to New York in the spring of 1937 was to solicit medical aid for nearly 10,000 soldiers and civilians prostrated by homelessness, bloodshed and disease as they fled before the might of Francisco Franco, the fascist general soon to assume dictatorship of the country.

Malraux was therefore amenable to being trotted out by Varèse at a press conference organised by his publishers, Random House, in the reception area of the Mayflower Hotel. When the older man took the sensationalist lead, two neat phrases buzzed among the newsgatherers: 'the *Red Symphony*' and 'the *Symphony Of Revolution*'. These titles stuck – and so did the information that the choral passages 'would include negroes. Mr Malraux added that it would also include Russians and that he had no doubt that the symphony would be performed immediately anywhere they might wish in Russia. Mr Varèse will call upon new electrical instruments, he said, and will have sections of the orchestra and chorus wired to amplifiers in different parts of the auditorium so that the music will at times hit the hearer on the back of the neck.'[33]

The net result of all this palaver was a few days of headline hogging and Varèse's presidency of a committee that eventually raised enough cash to buy an ambulance for the Spanish cause. Meanwhile, young Malraux, having achieved as much of his objective as possible, had returned to Europe with no intention of contributing a single word to *Symphony For The Masses*. So it was that *Density 21.5* would be the last Varèse composition to be performed for 15 years.

8 The Villager

'Stravinsky needed about 13 years. Schoenberg, a more original composer, is taking a still greater time. Varèse, unsurpassed in invention, bolder than Stravinsky and subtler than Schoenberg, may require the most extended period of all.'
– WP Tryon, *The Christian Science Monitor*, 4 October 1928

Behind the red paint-blistered door down Sullivan Street, Edgard Varèse's surroundings filled him with dispiriting reflections. His stomach was permanently knotted and his head ached constantly as he endeavoured to face changing circumstances. Gloom spread from him like cigar smoke. A society based more than ever on the compounding of mediocrity and profit versus cost would not provide facilities or any further funding to prevent the snuffing out of his chosen career. This, along with the legacy of his upbringing, was the principal cause of the mental havoc that had him swinging from daytime lethargy to nocturnal contemplation of suicide as his pulse quickened during long periods of cold-sweating wakefulness in bed.

You always hurt the one you love and, sure enough, as well as taking on more translation work to make ends meet, Louise found herself acting more as a hospital orderly than as a passionate *inamorata* in these days. The wretchedness of her devotion cut ever more deeply as Edgard took it for granted that he was the only one permitted to flare up, have neuroses and be unreasonable, and that there would always be another dismal morning in which to bridge the emotional abyss of the night before. Day after day, Louise talked him through his latest paranoia; watched him destroy, Harry Partch-like, the only copies of manuscripts;

endured his alternate self-flagellations and outpourings of home truths; bore the drip-drip of hovering aggravations and let him fulminate and bluster without reproach from muttered trepidation to Hitlerian screech.

So unnerving were Edgard's histrionics one evening that, fearing he might do himself a mischief, Louise railroaded him into seeking psychiatric help, but he infuriated her by either not keeping the appointments or, when he did, by provoking pointless arguments and making silly attempts to persuade the doctor to prescribe poison for a mercy killing. In an era when clinical depression wasn't recognised as an emotional disease, he was advised bluntly to snap out of it and pull himself together. He was advised to stop playing the tortured, highly strung, misunderstood genius and do a hard day's work for a change.

Before downing tools as a working composer, Varèse was capable of conquering writer's block sufficiently to set the metronome and knuckle down to work almost eagerly. However, after he'd sat at the piano for a while or bashed about on the gongs in front of the unused fireplace, the telephone might ring. If not, dinner would be getting cold or an interesting programme just beginning on the wireless. Maybe he would try again tomorrow after he had stimulated his muse with a challenging book – Henry Miller, say, or Saint-John Perse.

Days would trudge by without a glimmer of an idea as the inner suspicion grew that he had bitten his talent down to the quick. The hunger to create might have been sharper had a carrot of commercial urgency been dangled before him, but with no one paying for him to survive while composing, all of his particles of music began to sound the same. Hyperactivity deferred into glazed languor and, bathed in tedium, Varèse's mind would wander anywhere but to the unpaid job in hand. So he turned into my definition of an intellectual: someone who reads a lot and thinks a lot but does nothing.

His very name a millstone around his neck, Edgard Varèse was lost and fading while Messiaen's *Fêtes Des Belles Eaux*, scored for six ondes Martenots, was performed in the open air in 1937 at the Paris Exposition, and up-and-coming John Cage's *Imaginary Landscape I* – a blend of sine waves, cymbals and treated piano – was shortly to be pressed onto disc.

For Varèse, there would be isolated public performances of *Offrandes* in 1938 and *Hyperprism* 11 years later, but otherwise the only way in which *Octandre*, *Hyperprism*, *Ecuatorial* and all the rest of the seemingly forgotten classics could be enjoyed by anyone interested during his 'wilderness years' was by reading published scores that got rarer by the week. Any new compositions since *Density 21.5* were either scribblings at his work desk or computed in his brain while he mooched drowsily to the nearby convenience store for a newspaper. He felt sometimes as if he had never taken a bow at Carnegie Hall, stoked up all that controversy or been the one who'd had everything it took back in the early 1920s, when first he'd touched the brittle fabric of fame – if that was the word.

Well into his 50s now, if Varèse was, indeed, finished – like he'd insisted Stravinsky had been a couple of years earlier[1] – what next? Growing grapes? Perhaps the only option was to do something else entirely, as he had expressed in the letter to Dr Fletcher. Because he hadn't toed an orthodox line, the music business certainly wouldn't look after him, in the sense of finding him employment, now that his time in front of the footlights was up. Dejecting, therefore, was the curtness of impresarios and agents too busy to reply to his letters, return his telephone calls or even invite him into the office when his unsolicited arrival was announced by the receptionist.

However, an undignified demise in New York, the heart of the US entertainment industry, was arrested when his application for a position as resident composer for the duration of the next academic year at the Arsuna School of Fine Arts in Santa Fe led to a favourable telephone interview. As Louise was overwhelmed with commissions to interpret Rimbaud, Proust, Saint-John Perse, Simenon, Beckett and too many others, Varèse arrived alone in the New Mexican city midway through the summer term. The populace learned of his coming through an article in the *Santa Fe New Mexican*, based on an interview containing the usual spiel about 'sonic beams' and 'movement of sound masses'.[2]

These phrases also cropped up at the newcomer's maiden public lecture – with 'The Music Of Our Time' its prosaic title – which took place on a Sunday afternoon that August in the local arts centre, and was immediately followed by a reception in his honour. Among several intricately chiselled homilies attributed to Varèse in the *Santa Fe New Mexican* the next day were 'On the threshold of beauty, art and science must collaborate'; 'I tell people I am not a musician. I work with rhythms, frequencies and intensities', and 'Tunes are merely the gossips in music'.[2]

If anyone was anticipating interfering eccentricity at college that autumn, Varèse's initial six-week course, 'Music As Living Matter', centred on composition and orchestration and adhered to the traditional usages of harmony, counterpoint and the common chord – with set works from Beethoven, Brahms and Ravel – on the grounds that it was necessary to know the nature of the formula if you intended to break it. 'I do not in the least regret having learned to master these jigsaw puzzles,' smiled Varèse, 'and even now sometimes amuse myself with quite similar games.'[3] Only in the final half-term in 1937 did he so much as touch on the avant garde and his own works, and only in his very last lecture did he mention electronic instruments, referring to them as 'sound producers'.

Along the way, Varèse also founded an *a cappella* choir of 40 singers. Although he hadn't intended it to be heard publicly, it was to be the main attraction at a concert during one of the college's near-perpetual fundraising drives, this time for a new piano.

The subtext of such willing participation in extramural events was his anxiety to hold onto this post, with its comparatively short hours and long holidays, and the fact that his students had grown fond of him for his musician's slang, his Maurice Chevalier accent from which a Noo Yawk twang peeped out – and, crucially, his infectious enthusiasm for his subject.

Into the bargain, Santa Fe was in a part of the country that was more agreeable than New York to a man suffering from a depressive illness and – so he'd insisted to Louise – claustrophobia. Semi-tropical, with almost zero humidity for most of the year, New Mexico was more like the lyrical scenario of 'America The Beautiful' than anywhere else that Edgard had ever been. It was also an area that, geographically, most resembled Burgundy of blessed memory, especially after rain and the irrigated rivers flowing from the Sangre de Cristo mountains transformed scrubby grassland to a land rich with pumpkins, chillies and excellent wine.

Sante Fe, moreover, was a charming metropolis, full of light and space, and one of the oldest cities in the Union. Founded by Spaniards in 1610, it will claim almost as much affinity to Mexico as the United States for as long as Spanish is taught as a second language in its schools; Mexican décor adorns its homes and fajitas and jalepeño peppers are on its restaurants' menus.

Varèse returned to New York for the Christmas break in what was – by recent standards, at least – a genial, almost happy frame of mind, and come the New Year, as the railway miles to Santa Fe sped by, he was rubbing his hands at the thought of lessons. However, all good things must come to an end, but after his contracted year at the Arsuna School was officially over, in August, there followed a postscript the following month, when further vintage Varèse was annotated in the *New Mexico Sentinel*:

> 'Beauty seems to affect some people as a personal affront.'
>
> 'It is not the artist who is ahead of his day but the general public that is always behind the times.'
>
> 'You cannot raise beauty out of a formula.'
>
> 'It is imagination that gives form to dreams.'
>
> 'Men set themselves a goal and, having attained it, are satisfied and grow paunches. In their complacency, they forget that their only future now is death.'[4]

As he himself aged, Varèse would feel progressively more secure in educational institutions. Thus, within weeks of dumping his luggage in the hallway of No.188, he was off to deliver a series of lectures and run a course at the University of Southern California in San Francisco. It turned into a working holiday, more or less, as he lodged in a penthouse apartment overlooking an acre or so of oak, redwood and wild iris. In the middle distance from the roof garden, the view embraced the Golden Gate Bridge and its riverside park's gently sloping greensward. Further away, Edgard could make out the sweeping hills of Marin County, the palm-tree-studded coastal roads and the blue curvature of the Pacific Ocean.

A home help was removing the washing from the line on the roof where Edgard was enjoying the late autumn sunshine and keeping out of the way on the morning when, rather than being lugged up narrow stairs, a piano was winched into his studio via pulleys attached to the guttering. Bawled directives from below punctuated questions put to Varèse by a young female correspondent from the French-language *Courier De Pacifique*. Perhaps he was affected by the circumstances under which it was being conducted, but he appeared to regard composition as no more or less a craft than that of 'a manual worker'.[4]

Such self-depreciating pragmatism endeared him to this slip of a girl, who, as well as noting the Fascinating Older Man's ubiquitous corduroy jacket 'worn over a thick, turtle-necked grey wool pullover', listened courteously as he spoke in the old way about *Espace* as if it was still going to happen. His voice trailed off. 'The giant had halted on the threshold of infinity,' she marvelled. 'His conception was about to infringe the boundaries of what is possible.'[5]

Varèse conducted her to the studio, where the piano was now being tuned, and started talking again, not stopping for another 20 minutes, although the gist of this fresh dialogue could be summarised by isolating a single sentence that appeared over-optimistic at the time: 'My work is in the future. I've barely begun.'[5] Then, heaving himself up from his chair, everything hushed again. 'I need to piss,' said Edgard Varèse importantly, as if it wasn't a thing he did every day. His interviewer thought that she'd never been more overwhelmed by anyone in her whole life.

For Edgard, San Francisco would always be remembered for both the standing ovation triggered by the performance of 16-year-old *Offrandes* in the Community Playhouse in February 1938 and the re-emergence of the tell-tale symptoms of the prostate complaint that had sapped him a decade earlier. The organic deterioration that had taken place since that time meant that matters could only be mended by an immediate operation.

Hours later, his sticky eyes parted and there was a whisper of a smile as his hand tightened in that of Louise, direct from another time zone with travel-tousled hair and rings under her eyes. Still green about the gills, he was discharged and instructed to convalesce for two months with bland food, afternoon naps and teetotalism.

The university postponed the remaining lectures, and muddled on with the course as best it could while the Varèses tried to derive what advantage they could from the situation. They decided to spend several weeks in Los Angeles, as soon as Edgard had marshalled his thoughts in an essay *cum* letter of introduction titled 'Organised Sound For The Sound Film' and felt fit enough for pavement-tramping and rounds of telephone calls to film studios who might be looking for a soundtrack composer who wasn't like Elmer Bernstein, Rodgers and Hammerstein, Johnny Mercer, Dmitri Tiomkin or newly arrived Miklos Rozsa. George Anthiel had been down that road already and had strayed far from the car horns and buzz-saws of *Ballet Méchanique* by capitulating to churning out assembly line background muzak for the 'talkies' to suit the conservative demands of Hollywood.

Two producers – Boris Morros and André Dumonceau, Anthiel's principal employer – agreed to meet Varèse for lunch. The outcome, however, was as he might have expected. Yes, you have interesting ideas, Mr Varèse, but the reason why no one else has invited you to discuss them is that Hollywood has enough composers already, thank you. What's more, they conform to the orthodox clichés that, if it is heavily laden, don't distract from the onscreen action. It's offensive, we know, but it's necessary to pander to the assumed desires of the lowest common denominator of movie-goer. This has nothing to do with specific sequences of notes but, instead, recurring and archetypal audio symbols that indicate, say, a love scene (slushy violins), battle (trumpets and berserk xylophones), suspense (hissing hi-hat cymbals and fingersnaps), outer space (sine waves). Get the picture? A series of chords minus the thirds equals 'medieval'. Theremins mean horror – although we hear that, in his next movie, *The Lost Weekend*, Billy Wilder will be letting young Miklos Rozsa use one to simulate an alcoholic blackout.

With a show of kindness, Dumonceau advised Varèse to investigate other territories. Look at Sergei Prokofiev, who was cornering the celluloid market in the USSR. His *Ivan The Terrible* masterpiece for Eisenstein would be deemed a 'visual opera' by *Variety*, and before that *Lieutenant Kijé* and 1938's *Alexander Nevsky* would have Prokofiev getting away with altering the natural balance of the orchestra by shoving microphones virtually inside the necks of the brass instruments in order to obtain deliberate distortion. 'Organised sound for the sound film' or what? Rather than stand on the podium, Prokofiev sat in the control room alongside the director to ascertain what was actually going to be heard by the customers. That just wasn't done in Hollywood.

Nice work if you can get it, Sergei. Shrugging off the expedition to Los Angeles as one more exercise in futility, Edgard Varèse resumed his duties at the University of Southern California. He had developed into quite a polished and engaging public speaker, very professionally staying the phantoms of inner chaos when at the lectern that supported his notes. Besides, he was too used to dealing with full orchestras to have qualms about being the cynosure of up to 800 eyes at once in the one red-brick building among the college's Spanish-colonial stucco.

The students warmed to his onstage personality and entered into voluble dialogue with him when an open forum followed the formal lecture. While the latter was becoming predictable to the diphthong to Louise, it was all new to the Californian arts students riveted by her husband's final talk, on 5 June 1939, of liberation from the tempered system, a pitch range extending in both directions, 'new harmonic splendours obtainable from the use of sub-harmonic combinations now impossible',[6] increased differentiation of timbre, an expanded dynamic spectrum, the feasibility of sound projection in space, unrelated cross-rhythms... 'Composers who are gifted with an inner ear have heard for years a new music,' he concluded, 'which the old instruments cannot produce for them.'[6]

When faculty and students milled about afterwards, Varèse let slip in the noise of conflicting conversations that his own composing well wasn't as dry as might be imagined. Perhaps it was connected with the often surreal landscapes of the arcadia of desert bloom around Los Angeles that gave way to scrub, searing sunlight and spookily flat sandscape when you turned your back on city bricks. What was to become *Déserts* was more now than a mere twinkle in his eye. It would be over a decade in gestation, but 'a work in which an important part is given to a large chorus' would be at the heart of an unanswered letter to Leon Theremin in 1941. 'I want to use several of your instruments,' Varèse continued, 'augmenting their range as I did for those I used on *Ecuatorial*. Would you be so kind as to let me know if it is possible to procure these and where? Also, if you have conceived or constructed new ones, would you let me have a detailed description of their character and use?'[7]

Yet the feeling persisted still that Edgard Varèse had shed the bulk of his artistic load – even though the cultural wounds he'd gouged in the 1920s had been acknowledged in the release of a few excerpts from his works on crackling 78rpm shellac – as exemplified by the third movement of *Octandre* leaking to Europe and thence to obscurity via Britain's newish Gramophone Company (later EMI) as Part 15 of Volume V of the *Columbia History*, compiled by Percy Scholes, editor of a journal called *Music And Youth*, and conducted by Walter Goehr, a former pupil of Schoenberg, who had fled from Germany to England in 1933.

Coupled with *Duo For Two Violins In The Sixth-Tone System* ('first movement – *allegro moderato*') by Alois Haba – once on the committee of the International Composers Guild – *Octandre* had printed beneath its title the bracketed composing credit '(Varèse)', a name that meant nothing to the general public, apart from those who reaped deep and lasting satisfaction from studying raw data on record labels.

This and precious few other scratchy discs were all Edgard believed there would ever be, but they could be bequeathed to his first grandchild, Marilyne, born to Claude in Monte Carlo. Other than poorly selling scores that not even Kenneth Curwen would reprint now, what else would she or anyone else have to remember Edgard Varèse the composer? That was a sobering thought for him especially, as he and Louise were homeward bound to New York just as France and Britain declared war on Germany. This added to Edgard's misery at leaving California as he stowed the luggage and seated himself in the railway carriage. While he grinned askance at Louise's attempts to cheer him up during the long journey, now and then he seemed far away and a shadow of unspeakable despair would cross his countenance.

Tired and foul-tempered by the time they pulled into Grand Central Station, he had no idea what to do next, although the situation wasn't entirely desperate. Very likely, all would be well, with Louise bringing in money well into the foreseeable future. His chances of gaining further lectureships were quite good, and indeed these – as well as more fruitless assaults on Hollywood – would have him flitting back and forth across the continent over the next few years. What nagged him in the autumn of 1939, however, was the weeks of job-hunting ahead, the uncertainty, the self-employed artist's constant undercurrent of insecurity.

Moreover, Varèse, like everyone else, knew that the United States would be actively supporting the Allies against the Axis powers, and sooner rather than later. The last global bust-up had been unremarkable for its encouragement of new music, and this Second World War was even less likely to be abundant with state funding and foundation grants for the likes of Edgard Varèse now that middle-aged veterans of Mons, Ypres and Passchendaele had rubbed it in that war wasn't as much fun as it had been when the mythical knights of old had gone forth to win their spurs.

Yet Varèse was hopeful that from the 'inferno now raging in Europe will come a spiritual and aesthetic renaissance so much needed today. I dare believe it will. I look forward to a complete revision of values and a restoration of the things of quality to the high, unusurped place that is rightfully theirs.'[8] Viable developments towards this end were being made, both directly and otherwise, because of the hostilities rather than despite them. Advances in the quality and scope of tape recording, for instance, came about as a by-product of the war, with a certain Paul Buff gaining sufficient knowledge of electronics in the US Marine Corps to set up a recording studio in California on demobilisation and, in 1944, Alexander M Poniatoff founding Ampex, a US-based recording-equipment company and a name that combined his initials and the first syllable of the word excellence. The latter tag came to be justified after its patenting of the subsequently widely used 400 model three years later.

As infinitesimal a cog in the machine as Paul Buff provisioning the distant bloodshed, Edgard Varèse did his bit with a chin-up Pageant of Liberation spectacular, in which he conducted Berlioz's stridently rabble-rousing arrangement of *La Marseillaise*, just as he had the same composer's *Requiem* at the Hippodrome a fortnight after the Germans had torpedoed their first US ship, in 1917.

With all manner of Gallic celebrities resident in New York lending their names in support, Varèse was also the brains behind choral concerts held under the auspices of the newspaper *Pour La Victoire* to benefit the Co-ordinating Council of French Relief Societies and, later, in aid of the American Friends Service Committee for the relief of the children of France.

Assembled by Varèse in 1943, despite a pronounced shortage of male singers, the Greater New York Chorus specialised in the Renaissance, Baroque and folk music of France – forms that, as he was to inform *Pour Le Victoire*, 'have been overlooked for too long by all but a handful of music lovers. I want to rescue these, the wonders of our country's choral music, from oblivion.'[9]

His war efforts were rewarded when he agreed, finally, to accept the Légion d'Honneur – although he didn't bother attending the investiture ceremony in Paris. His excuse was that he had been deluged suddenly with various cinematic projects, principally in collaboration with Thomas Bouchard, who now shared a house with Fernand Léger in mid-town Manhattan. While Bouchard's long-mooted film biography of Miró hadn't been abandoned, it had been set aside while he got to expedient grips with one about Léger, with mutual friend Edgard selecting excerpts from *Octandre*, *Hyperprism*, *Intégrales* and *Ionisation* for the soundtrack.

When this was premièred at the Sorbonne on 5 April 1946, Varèse, back in New York, was purportedly hard at work on incidental music for *La Naissance d'Un Tableau*, another Bouchard biopic about another painter, Hippolyte-Prosper Seligmann. Strictly non-Hollywood, too, it was seen only in French-speaking regions, where it disappeared swiftly from general circulation, considered to be too erudite for the ordinary movie consumer – although it continued to receive occasional showings in specialist film clubs and arts centres.

Varèse's contributions to *La Naissance d'Un Tableau* may have been lifted wholesale from *Espace*, which, in its entirety, was a lost cause, for all his fine words to *Courier De Pacifique*. Nevertheless, something called *Étude Pour Espace* was heard by an invited audience at New York's New School for Social Research on 23 February 1946. It was never to be performed again, although the displeased composer immortalised it on tape for transfer to three privately pressed sides of (subsequently lost) 78rpm disc. This may give an indication of its length.

For Chou Wen-Chung, a 23-year-old studying composition at the New England Conservatory of Music, this recital may have been a first experience of Varèse, who wielded the baton while two pianos and a percussion ensemble underscored a 22-voice amateur choir cantillating disjointed bits and pieces. If there was an oracular message there, it was heavily veiled, but Chou Wen-Chung was among the few who comprehended it and admired the courage and integrity of a composer who walked such a taut artistic tightrope without a safety net.

Crossing the state border again a year later, Chou Wen-Chung was drawn to another concert at the same venue, where, with the same personnel, Varèse conducted a concert entitled Modern Music Of The 16th And 17th Centuries, which embraced items by Couperin, Monteverdi and Schütz. Now an unashamed fan, Chou Wen-Chung worried when his idol flagged, cheered when he rallied and glowed when, ultimately, he went down well, earning critical acclaim for his abilities as a choirmaster and his probably unparalleled knowledge of the period.

Soon, Varèse would be serving the young man as tutor, careers advisor and father confessor – and may have revealed another area of expertise to Chou Wen-Chung. Anticipating Pop Art, but harking back to Dadaism's observed revelling in junk culture, Edgard was surprisingly *au fait* with the popular music that effused from the radio. He was especially fond of that lurid strain of musical comedy that merged burlesque, swing, mock-schmaltz and genres that defy succinct description – sometimes within the same song – when instrumental and vocal virtuosity were used to neo-Dadaist effect in the crafted mindlessness of such as Jimmy 'Schnozzle' Durante's 'Inka Dinka Doo' and Spike Jones And His City Slickers' million-selling mangling of 'Cocktails For Two'.

This interest infiltrated some of his lectures, evidenced in joking asides about the destitution of those driven to make the 'bloop-bleep' responses for Danny Kaye on his opus of the same title and in warnings that the maddeningly catchy chorus of, say, 'Chickory Chick' by Evelyn Knight And The Jesters would be with listeners to the grave.

Such quips were inserted on the spur of the moment as, in the highest traditions of jazz, Varèse took to improvising around themes, sometimes abandoning his lecture notes altogether like an AJP Taylor of music[10] – just as he did when holding forth about 'Composition And 20th-Century Music' at Columbia University on New York's Upper West Side over the summer of 1948.

If anything, he was in too much demand as a lecturer. It was a good problem to have, but it may have contributed to the combination of depression and exhaustion that confined him to bed throughout Christmas and the New Year. It was during those weeks that he received the news about the sudden death of Paul Rosenfeld, the critic who had championed him since that first Berlioz concert in 1917.

A tribute concert to Paul smouldered into form at the Museum of Modern Art on 27 January. Almost as a matter of course, the show included *Hyperprism*, the opus that Rosenfeld had risked his reputation to defend a quarter of a century earlier. Now there was no riot, no catcalling, no critical rubbishings. In an age when the novelty value of most cult figures tends to be short-lived, acknowledging roof-raising applause for a composition for which he'd once been metaphorically lynched afforded Varèse a crooked smile, as he was never to be sure whether *Hyperprism* was liked in absolute terms or for reasons connected with the almost visible wave of goodwill that washed over the entire event. Yet, whatever the audience's overall motive, for newcomers to contemporary classical music, it was as disquieting as it had been at the 1924 première. 'Varèse opened up new horizons not with his electronic works,' thought Chou Wen-Chung, 'but, in the '20s, with his works for conventional instruments.'[8]

Hyperprism was not, therefore, a curio from the recent past, nor was Varèse spoken of as if he had become an old nag put out to grass – although the fellow was never seen to do a stroke of work. While he could stroll unrecognised through a department store only two subway stops away, he was, noted Luigi Dallapiccola, 'the King of Greenwich Village. He knew all the bars; he chatted with everyone, a miracle of simplicity hiding beneath one of the most complex personalities.'[11]

If renowned already as an endlessly inventive jazz saxophonist, Charlie 'Yardbird' Parker was so in awe of the local legend that he didn't dare go near Varèse, let alone speak in the presence of one who was an everyday sight shopping for groceries, watching the open-air chess tournaments in Washington Square or sipping Turkish coffee in the window of Romany Marie's café.

As Parker was fresh from the mental hospital where his heroin addiction had taken him, his reticence was understandable, but other artists weren't so coy. Dallapiccola was but one of many young composers who introduced themselves or mailed unsolicited letters to Varèse in the late 1940s, regarding him as less like an admired elder brother than a favourite if slightly batty uncle. John Cage, Krzysztof Penderecki, Henry Cowell, Morton Subotnik, Karlheinz Stockhausen and – just – George Crumb were the most illustrious of these, but who knows if Ilhan Mimaroglu, Earle Brown, Adolf Weiss, Jacques de Menace and other names were as obscure then as they are now?

Of them all, Varèse empathised most with Chou Wen-Chung, perhaps seeing much of his younger self in this son of a well-to-do family who had elected not to return to his native China. There, he had gained both a degree in civil engineering and a scholarship to study architecture at Yale. In New York, however, free of his parents' influence, he'd joined Slonimsky's masterclass and was considered a student of sufficient promise to be brought to Edgard Varèse, who agreed to teach him privately, one to one.

As a consequence, Chou Wen-Chung as a composer was to produce worthy syntheses of western and eastern music and occupy a place below the salt – but a place all the same – in the Valhalla of modern classical music. In this discussion, however, he is important for his emergence as the Boswell to Varèse's Dr Johnson.

At the long table in the red-and-blue dining room in Sullivan Street, the host came across as 'a man of immense wit', wrote Chou Wen-Chung. 'He had a wealth of jokes, anecdotes and was ever ready with repartee.'[8] The Varèses also kept an excellent table, although regular guests knew that the invariable dessert would be white grapes, in deference to Edgard's boyhood in Burgundy.

Of his old friends, Henry Miller – who had devoted several pages to Varèse in 1945's *Air-Conditioned Nightmare* – was still around, as was Carlos Salzedo. Varèse had also befriended poverty stricken Béla Bartók, after he'd washed up in New York and had attended his funeral in 1945.

Bartók's refusal to accept direct offers of financial help had contributed to his death. More robust but just as poor and proud was Louis Thomas Hardin, alias Moondog. If Varèse was uncrowned king of Greenwich Village, Moondog was a bastard prince. As much an 'anti-Varèse' as Harry Partch, he owed far more to Aaron Copland, George Gershwin and even Miklos Rozsa than Stravinsky and Schoenberg. Like Partch, he made his own instruments. These were played when he and his wife, Suzuko – plucking the lute-like samisen – busked for spare change in mid-town Manhattan. Moondog also had 'image' enhanced by blindness and garb of army blankets, and a sort of helmet that made him look like a cross between a Druid and a Norse jarl when at his customary pitch in Times Square. Yet Moondog was not a figure of fun. Instead, he was revered too by Charlie Parker, as well as by Dizzy Gillespie, Eric Dolphy Miles Davis and other jazzmen.

Varèse was aware of Moondog and perhaps identified with his vocational dilemma, whereby nothing much was guaranteed to happen, year in, year out. Yet the tide began to turn when, partly at the instigation of the US High Commission, Varèse spent 1950's wet summer in Germany as the most venerable guest lecturer at a newly established international school and annual festival of music in Darmstadt, near Frankfurt.

There already was Pierre Boulez, a former pupil of Messiaen. Like Nicolas Slonimsky, Boulez was to be better known as a conductor than as a composer and, like Edgard Varèse, had gone against the wishes of his parents in becoming a musician. In his early 20s, he was flattered but not immediately comfortable when the Great Man spoke with him. Yet others – among them Luigi Nono and Luciano Berio – weren't as self-conscious, as here was the kind of person with whom one or other of them might find himself chatting easily about a technical problem or a musical theory, only to be told by somebody later, 'That was Edgard Varèse, you know.'

None of them realised, of course, that, if he pretended nonchalance, Varèse was as keen to learn from them as they were from him. While in Europe, too, his inner ear was cocked to discoveries further afield. In Paris, the ondes Martenot was still going strong, most conspicuously as an integral part of Messiaen's *Turangalîla-Symphonie*, premièred the previous year. Paris also cradled the explorations of *musique concrète* trailblazer Pierre Schaeffer. He and his team were ensconced in the Radiodiffusion Studio as founders of the Groupe de Recherches Musicales, recording sounds not thought of as musical, running them at different speeds, in canon and on up to half a dozen record turntables at once.

The first 'work' of this type was Schaeffer's *Étude Aux Chemins De Fer*, featuring a whistling top recorded onto a 78rpm disc with a closed groove in order to ensure continuous replay. Next up was *Études Aux Casseroles* (ditto with saucepan lids), which likewise wasn't seeking a musical objective as much as a demonstration of what the studio could do nowadays. Pitch variation was achieved *in extremis* by finger pressure and sound balance by simple twiddling of single volume and tone controls on each machine. Any given performance – referred to cautiously as a 'concert of sounds' – was a case of hoping for the best.

Schaeffer praised Varèse for approximating the same effects with ordinary orchestral instruments, while Varèse envied the creative freedom and use of equipment Schaeffer and others enjoyed now. That was just what he'd wanted all those years ago from Western Electric, the Guggenheim Foundation, *et al.*

As for the sounds emitted from the Radiodiffusion Studio, however, Varèse felt the same about them as he had about Russolo's noise machines – ie they were intriguing but of no real musical consequence. Significantly, he never employed the term *musique concrète* – or, indeed, 'electronic music' – in reference to his own output. Neither were these terms used in the sleeve notes – themselves flawed by factual errors – when Elaine Music Shop (EMS), a Manhattan-based record firm of no great merit, issued four of Varèse's works – *Octandre*, *Intégrales*, *Ionisation* and *Density 21.5* – on one of these new-fangled ten-inch 33rpm vinyl long-players – LPs – replete with picture sleeve. At the recording sessions, the New York Wind Ensemble and the Juilliard Percussion Orchestra were supervised by the composer and Frederic Waldman, who had conducted *Hyperprism* at the Museum of Modern Art.

Perhaps the story might have ended there, but the future of Edgard Varèse – with just 15 years left – was not to be the past all over again.

9 The Netherlander

'A work composed by a lunatic.'
– *Le Monde* on *Desérts*, 4 December 1954

In 1947, Varèse had his closest brush with movie stardom since his walk-on part in the John Barrymore flick. Although there was no way he wasn't going to do it, Boris Morros – perhaps as punishment for that Hollywood business lunch – had to go through the abject ritual of prevailing upon him to kindly compose a short parody of violinists tuning up, horn valves sliding prelusively and so on in imitation of an orchestra readying itself for an imminent performance. An overture to an overture, it would be ideal for the opening scene of an eponymous comedy-drama Morros was to be co-producing about Carnegie Hall for Federal Films and the RCA Victor record company.

Shortly after the cameras rolled, however, Varèse sensed that *Carnegie Hall* no longer had what he considered to be a credible screenplay (about a cleaner whose son becomes a famous pianist). It had been remodelled since with a vacuous plot that connected each section of what amounted to a straightforward concert of the lightest of light classical music – and, at RCA Victor's insistence, an 11th-hour cameo had been squeezed in for singing bandleader Vaughn Monroe, best remembered now for the cowboy ballad '(Ghost) Riders In The Sky'.

Citizen Kane it wasn't, and the most fitting epitaph for *Carnegie Hall* was to be critic James Agee's 'the thickest and sourest mess of musical mulligatawny I have yet to sit down to'.[1] The story goes that Varèse was so beset with misgivings about it that he didn't cash the cheque for his services but kept it about his person in order to at least threaten to hand it back as if on cue, should he be too affronted by necessary modifications that catered for the needs of the re-adjusted celluloid action. Sitting in at one pre-production rehearsal on a soundstage with an orchestra, something snapped within Edgard when he noticed the removal of enough bars to unbalance the structure of the opus he had titled *Tuning Up*. Within minutes, he had sprinkled the ripped-up cheque over the seated Morro's head, systematically gathered every sheet of music from each individual player's stand and stormed out of the building.

Whether or not this incident ever took place, what is hard fact is that Varèse disposed of the scores – although, rooting through his mentor's archives, Chou Wen-Chung was to come upon enough rough drafts and photocopies of *Tuning Up* to piece together a version suitable for recording in 1994. While this might not have been how Edgard intended, it would have fulfilled Morro's brief, with the droning unison surges of strings winding up or down to A in the approved fashion, tiny 'solo-ettes' and last-minute sectional rehearsals of a few isolated bars, expressed via quotes from *Intégrales*, *Amériques*, *Arcana*, *Ionisation* and what is almost but not quite 'Yankee Doodle', the ditty popularised during the American War of Independence.

To Boris Morros, Edgard's withdrawal from *Carnegie Hall* was regrettable but by no means disastrous and, with hardly a break in schedule, the film was completed ahead of deadline. Furthermore, at least it reached cinema screens, unlike a later – and untitled – film project involving Varèse and actor/director Burgess Meredith. However, as a favour to Meredith, Varèse allowed a scrap of one of its musical sequences, referred to as 'Dance For Burgess', to be used in the Broadway musical *Happy As Larry*, which closed the week it opened in June 1950.

If 'Dance For Burgess' was typical of its content, it's hardly surprising that *Happy As Larry* proved an injudicious investment for its backers. Burgess may have contrived a way to dance to it, but it's difficult to picture the music *per se* imprinting itself on the audience's memory like 'Maria', 'I Feel Pretty' *et al* in *West Side Story*, whose composer, Leonard Bernstein, was then engaged in 'long talks about opera versus whatever this should be. Maybe I should wait until I can find a continuous hunk of time to devote to the project.'[2]

Whereas 30-year-old Bernstein – who was, incidentally, friends with Varèse in a showbiz kind of way – worked on *West Side Story* on and off for the next seven years, Varèse had dashed off 'Dance For Burgess' – probably extracted from *Espace*, in any case – when he was in the throes of writing *Déserts* and was unable to find any further 'continuous hunk of time' for further contributions to Meredith's unhappy musical. Constructively, there is little to say about the minute and a half of 'Dance For Burgess', except that it is a pastiche almost as semi-comical as *Tuning Up* and contains as many flashbacks of every familiar trackway of Varèse's output. He could have written it in his sleep.

Why waste time and trouble on duds like *Happy As Larry* when all Varèse had to do was sit back and let the royalties others were earning for him roll in? Now hailed as a modern classic – ie a standard work by someone younger than Debussy and Strauss – as Messiaen had elevated it long ago, *Ionisation* was performed in several US and European cities over the next few years, climaxing with a London outing in 1957. That same year, *Octandre* reached Tokyo and *Arcana*, Cologne. Shortly after *Ionisation* was premièred in Rome, Paris heard *Octandre* and *Density 21.5* for the first time, too, and the New York radio station WQXR broadcast *Mind Over Music*, a two-hour programme devoted to Varèse, for which he deigned to be interviewed.

While it was satisfying to receive such recognition, belated though it was, Varèse didn't regard looking forward to the past as healthy, even at his advanced age. Now that the development of taped electronic music had stirred him from vocational slumber, here at last was the ghost of a chance to realize the music that he'd been nurturing in his head – what he called 'atmospheric disturbance' – almost from the beginning.

The concert stage, for all its thrilling margin of error, was less alluring now than the closed doors of the recording studio, where human mistakes could be retracted and the sounds of normal instruments doctored. At the turn of the decade, Pierre Henri, one of

Schaeffer's crew, had invented the photogene, a device that enabled users to change with greater accuracy the speeds at which sound information is recorded.

Much more significant for a wider world – and, indeed, in the history of music – was the loading into delivery vans of the first batches of domestic tape recorders. These, however, would be beyond the means of most households for years. Nevertheless, the two-track Ampex 400 was already commonly employed in professional studios and was the basis of the first faltering public performances of tape-collage music. More lucrative than these dabblings was the electric guitarist Les Paul's superimposition of his instrument several times over by bouncing back from one Ampex to another. After adding the soprano of his then-wife to the result, Paul entered the Top Ten in the music-trade journal *Billboard*'s newly established record sales chart three times in 1951 alone.

Les Paul is also credited with the discovery of the whooshing effect produced by two tape recorders relaying the same information fractionally out of synchronisation. Its technical term, *phasing*, was among *square wave*, *crossfade*, *white noise*, *EQ*, *envelope*, *tape loop*, *microtone* and further then half-understood jargon that pocked conversations between Varèse and Pierre Boulez, who was in the USA in 1952, partly to study the latest innovations in sound production.

Compared to the electronic ventures of the 1960s and beyond, these were crude. Furthermore, Boulez gauged, in his comprehensive shadowing of engineers at work in New York, that North America was no more advanced than Europe, and indeed less so when compared to complexes operational in Eindhoven (financed by the Philips record firm), Milan (where John Cage would soon be working) and, embracing West German Radio and the pressing plant for Deutsche Grammophon, Cologne. As a recommendation, Karlheinz Stockhausen was omnipresent there and coming closer than either anyone in New York or the fellows at the Radiodiffusion-Télévision Française – RTF– in Paris to the mathematical exactitudes of 'pure' electronic music.

Varèse became better equipped to do likewise on receiving an Ampex 400 from an anonymous donor – although the package bore a

New York postmark. After clearing a space for it, and knotting his brow over the attendant instruction manual, his workroom began a gradual mutation into an Aladdin's cave of linked-up tape recorders, editing blocks and jack-to-jack leads.

He was in virgin territory, at first, but after much trial and error Varèse spliced together four different lengths of tape to underscore three minutes of Thomas Bouchard's laboriously conceived film about Jean Miró, the one he'd been mithering about since 1933. Shot in colour, *Around And About Jean Miró* was a slow-moving one and a quarter hours long, but its music was a qualified triumph in that *The Procession Of Verges* – while far from being the most brilliant opus in its composer's portfolio – was like an atonal Gregorian chant, conveying an atmosphere commensurate with the final torchlit leg along narrow Spanish streets of a day-long religious parade – in which Death the skeleton and guilt-stricken penitents, yoked together by heavy chains, are persistent if minor visual symbols surrounding Mother Mary in her crown of candles and a wooden Christ thrice the size of the Roman soldiers shouldering it.

Reduced to a technical exercise, however, *The Procession Of Verges* may be viewed as a foretaste of *Déserts*, for which Varèse lugged his Ampex as far afield as Philadelphia to sample *in situ* sounds from sawmills, ironworks and various factories. After trying in vain to wriggle out of a prior commitment to write a piece for the Louisville Symphony Orchestra, he also took his tapes – months later than first mooted – for final refinements at the RTF studios, where Schaeffer, Henri and their cohorts were engaged in recording the first *bona fide musique concrète* album, to be issued on the French Ducretet-Thompson label in the New Year.

When he had decided that *Déserts* was completed, Varèse estimated that it would last for fractionally less than a marathon 30 minutes and would consist of three pre-recorded interludes between four 'episodes' played by 20 musicians using woodwind, brass, percussion and a piano, which were utilised in much the same manner as they were in *Ionisation*. There would be no pauses between sections, but at no juncture would outlines dissolve between electronic and acoustic modes. Nevertheless, the switches from one to the other were neatly done and not instantly obvious to anyone who wasn't following the score. In this respect, it helped that the layers of treated noise on tape contained percussion as well as sounds edited and collaged to emulate certain written sequences of notes played by the 'live' instruments – and vice-versa, recalling Schaeffer's comments about Varèse achieving the same result with an orthodox orchestra as the RTF did with all its console facilities.

As was his wont, Edgard's grip on both budget and physical practicality loosened when confiding to a newshound's notepad. *Déserts*, he assured the *New York Herald Tribune*, was to be an *Espace*-ish mixed-media presentation which, as well as the orchestra and the tape-operator, required a projectionist to show an accompanying film of 'not only physical deserts of sand, sea, mountains, snow, outer space and deserted city streets, but also this distant inner space where man is alone in a world of mystery and essential solitude. Visual image and organised sound will not duplicate each other. For the most part, light and sound will work in opposition in such a way as to give the maximum emotional reaction. Sometimes, they will join for dramatic effect and in order to create a feeling of unity.'[3]

Although Varèse's train of thought had chugged 40 years into the future, this anticipation of video imposition on a listener's imagination was no more than wishful thinking. There had never been much more than irresolute attempts to excite any of his contacts in the film industry into so collaborating in the première of *Déserts*, pencilled in for June 1954.

Déserts stood or fell, therefore, on its musical content alone. Considering that Varèse was often castigated for a reliance on intellect rather than instinct and for an overriding concern to delve into the essence of sound rather than emotion, it was disturbing how profound and mercurial my own response has been over the decades to an opus that, depending on my mood, can be orchestrated tinnitus, the soundtrack to a drunkard's nightmare, the most terminal opus ever written – or where both 20th-century classical music and pre-conceived primitivism begin and end, sonic testimony to Albert Camus's oft-quoted 'A man's work is nothing but this slow trek to rediscover through the detours of art those two or three great and simple images in whose presence his heart first opened'.

Varèse's heart may have first opened in the straitened circumstances of his youth, but now he had the means to express any number of 'simple images' without caring whether they provided glimpses of unconscious if toilsome comedy to the majority that tolerated more than five minutes of such as *Déserts*, or if his work proved to be beyond the wildest dreams of those to whom it reached out and held forever.

I continue to plant a foot in both camps after listening consecutively to *Déserts* and *Amériques*, which I perceive as the opposite side of the same coin, the green pasture to the barren...well, desert of *Déserts*. Because I am aware of the geographical area that sparked the composer's muse, when the mental images become describable, they begin with urban sprawl spreading from Los Angeles, a residential hinterland built by the book amid tangles of shopping precincts and industrial zones connected by droning arteries of traffic. This thins out to a scorching, dust-dry plain, bleached bones and desolate panorama, silent bar startling and solitary eldritch cries. Unless you find water, you're a dead man.

Yet, as Varèse had reminded the *New York Herald Tribune*, there are other deserts too, and the final episode evoked in me that in the background of the Pre-Raphaelite painter William Holman Hunt's 'The Scapegoat', beneath leaden skies, a swamp borders the stagnant shallows of a tideless inland sea dotted with animal skeletons and rotting driftwood. These and the effect of the coyote howls from the Californian wilderness jut from *Déserts* in the sudden swelling of horns from mid-range to shrill high from banks of sustained chords and single pitches.

For the more conservative cultural pundits, the advent of this major new work by Edgard Varèse was like the heart-sinking return of the Ancient Roman general Caius Marius, who, back from growing old in exile, was elected consul and thus given leave to vent a remorselessly bloody rage, tinged with insanity, upon the Eternal City, precipitating its spiritual decline.

Originally, the *Déserts* première was to have taken place in June 1954 in New York, but this was thwarted by the US Musicians' Union's hand-wringing about the use of recordings depriving flesh-and-blood players of work. However, there had been an out-of-town preview of sorts when, with bad grace, Edgard had given the Louisville Symphony Orchestra short weight with *Trinum* – an item in three movements ('Tension', 'Intensity' and 'Rhythm'), which was actually episodes of *Déserts* minus the electronic segments.

After much prevarication, the full-scale version of *Déserts* was delivered by the National Orchestra on 2 December 1954 at Paris' Théâtre des Champs-Elysées for both the hundreds in its over-priced seats and the unseen millions listening to what was only the second 'live' concert to be transmitted on French radio. If not on the scale of Moses re-appearing before the Israelites from the clouded summit of Mount Sinai, the audience would surely shuffle into the foyer afterwards, having participated in the proverbial 'something to tell your grandchildren about'.

Despite having no appetite for lunch that day, Varèse – who had remained in France after his sessions at the RTF Studios – vomited with nerves minutes before the evening began with a eulogy from master of ceremonies Pierre Boulez. Then he fidgeted through the endless centuries of a Mozart piano concerto and Tchaikovsky's *Symphonie Pathétique* before conductor Hermann Scherchen tapped his music stand and counted in the tubular bells that clanged the opening bars of *Déserts*.

As it entered its tenth undaunted minute, some of the more elderly critics exchanged nervous glances. Who'd have thought that the old lad still had it in him? Already, audience reaction mirrored that towards *Le Sacre Du Printemps* nearly 40 years earlier. 'Mutterings at first,' noted the man from *Le Monde* with appalled joy, 'waves of vigorous protest mingled with sporadic applause, ladylike tut-tuttings, shouts of "That's enough!", "Shame!" and so forth. The seats in the theatre were, thank heaven, bolted firmly to the ground.' Under the editorial lash the following morning, he concluded that *Déserts* was 'a work composed by a lunatic',[4] thus supporting mob opinion epitomised by a remark overheard on the pavement afterwards: 'That Mr Varèse ought to be shot without ceremony. No, what am I saying? That would make even more noise. He'd be delighted!'

However, with a whole week in which to gather his thoughts on the matter, the reviewer for *L'Express* lauded 'a healthy admixture of "for" and "against". The violence of the hostile reaction – which was opposed immediately by an enthusiastic ovation – is proof of the daring and the crucial energy that the work aroused.'[5] To *La Gazette Litteraire*, it was 'the musical event of the year!',[6] but *Carrefour*'s bald statement that 'many imagined Varèse to be a flaming youth of 22, when he is really a man of 70 summers'[7] was the most pointed indication that Edgard Varèse was back, rejuvenated and contemporary, debunking the myth of an artistic death.

As if in acknowledgment of this, a rush of energy after the concert banished sleep that night. On listening hard to a muffled recording made with a hand-held microphone, Varèse forsook celebratory after-hours roisterings to pump his adrenaline more profitably into trying to improve the sound quality at the RTF console. In the grey of morning, he grabbed what rest was feasible before taking an edgy train ride to Hamburg, where *Déserts* was to headline over Stockhausen's *Kontra-Punkte* not quite a week later.

That the latter work was a product of the Cologne studio paved the way for a reception of the Varèse epic that was less polarised than it had been after Mozart and Tchaikovsky in Paris. Information that the next *Déserts* recital in Stockholm passed without incident, too, was relayed to Varèse, now back in France to pre-record an edition of a radio series of in-depth interviews called *Entretiens*, a chore he shared with the likes of George Brassens, Jean-Paul Sartre and Marc Chagall. Presenter Georges Charbonnier drew from his eloquent and forthright guest nothing that he hadn't said 100 times already to the US media, namely reasonable and direct explanations for 'a work composed by a lunatic' and everything else put to him. 'Toeing the line has so become the rule on radio,' thought *Combat* magazine, 'that it's quite surprising to hear someone whose voice cuts straight through the expected amiable platitudes.'[8] Indeed, Varèse gave such a good account of himself that his discourse was transcribed for publication in a special edition of the arts periodical *L'Age Nouveau* in May.[9]

Entretiens also kept Varèse in articulate trim for a stint as principal attraction at a conference that was to close with a lecture at New York's Bennington College on 16 May 1955, the day prior to North America's first encounter with *Déserts* via a water-test before selected friends and media at the National Guard Armory, under the direction of Frederic Waldman.

Buoyed by the *New York Herald Tribune*'s 'a noble work by a noble musician'[10] laudation, *Déserts* went public at City Hall on Wednesday 30 November 1955. A few scattered boos were smothered by a standing ovation for 'an astonishing *tour de force*...an epoch-making piece in an experimental sense. Varèse – like Monteverdi in the 17th century – is the first big musical mind to take up the materials of a new musical experience and put them to really serious uses. He ranks far ahead of most other tape experimenters, and whatever we think of his music, we must accord him full musical "big league" status.'[11]

If ever there was one, a forewarning of what was to come next was made in *The New Yorker*'s belief that 'Mr Varèse's next logical step is the total elimination of human performers, a step that would remove his activities from the concert hall, thus freeing him from music and music from him.'[12] Other newspapers, however, weren't so sniffy about the local-boy-made-good, who was elected to the National Institute of Arts and Letters before the winter was out.

A more pragmatic honour was in the air, too. It was to be bestowed through the machinations of Charles Eduard Jeanneret (known to posterity as 'Le Corbusier'), who had been in Paris to catch *Déserts*. For better or worse, he was a Christopher Wren of his day, in that he left an indelible mark on architecture and town planning. His work is discernible today in 'rationalist' look-alike high-rise tower blocks, churches that resemble dental surgeries and right-angled grids of inner distribution roads. Cubism applied to tectonics, the genesis of Le Corbusier's lasting influence lies in the unadorned and uniform blocks with standardised doors and windows that he designed in 1924 as a housing development for workers at the oil refineries in Pessac, near Bordeaux. Those who didn't have to live there trumpeted these Brobdingnagian cardboard boxes as a major architectural breakthrough. Among the more prestigious commissions that followed were the Swiss Students' Hostel for the University of Paris, the Ville Radieuse – a commune of cellular flats in Marseilles – and the government centre in Chandigarh, the new capital of the Punjab, one of many 'well-ordered masses placed in sunlight'[13] by a man who regarded a house as 'a machine for living in'.[13] 'Picturesque' – in the sense of stone roses, exposed wooden beams or Greek façades – didn't come into it.

With his scientific command of steel and reinforced concrete to create a ruthlessly austere, functional aesthetic, Le Corbusier was a victim of the same passion as Edgard Varèse, denizen of the geometrically organised streets of New York. The Swiss architect was also a tireless self-publicist, full of his latest triumph – which in 1955 was the pilgrimage chapel of Notre Dame du Haut in Ronchamp – and work in progress, namely his *La Poème Électronique* and 'the vessel that will contain it'.

The opportunity to realize this had presented itself when the Dutch subsidiary of Philips – one of Europe's key record companies – sought to make maximum impact on 2 May 1958 at the forthcoming World's Fair in Brussels with an exhibit that it hoped would be different from the usual trade-fair stalls for promenading entrepreneurs. Thus Le Corbusier was contracted to mastermind 'a work capable of profoundly affecting the human sensibility by audio-visual means. I had an obscure sense that something could be brought into being on the creative level using the perhaps prodigious means offered by electronics: speed, number, colour, sound, noise, unlimited power. Immediately, I thought of Varèse. My feeling about this was so strong that I was forced to say that I would not undertake this task except on condition that Varèse should create the music.'[14]

In collusion with a former pupil, Yannis Xenakis, Le Corbusier's insistence on Varèse obliged an exasperated Philips to recognise that, innovation or nuisance, electronically generated music was here to stay. The company, therefore, had to dismiss its own choice of composer, Sir William Walton, and grant the newcomer *carte blanche* to record an eight-minute composition as the essence of the main event. The multi-faceted Xenakis would attend to the intermission music (ie the amplified cracklings of burning charcoal). He, rather than Jeanneret, would also be in charge of the supervisory donkey work with regard to the erection of the impressive parabolic folly of a pavilion, to be demolished soon after Varèse was heard there and Le Corbusier's flickering *mélange* of patterns and images were projected onto its inner walls.

Having taken on *La Poème Électronique*, Varèse's preparations included receiving practical instructions about general principles at the University of Columbia's Electronic Music Laboratory, where Chou Wen-Chung was, by now, employed as chief technical assistant. When sufficiently schooled in the aural possibilities of professional equipment, as opposed to the paraphernalia in his workroom, Varèse spent several months in Eindhoven, commuting between lodgings and Philips' three-track studio, whose technicians had been put at his beck and call within conventional office hours (meaning a 9am start and an hour off for lunch).

Assembled literally second by second, the music of *La Poème Électronique* evolved over hundreds of block-booked hours, punctuated by occasional spats when a murmured head-to-head argument about, say, degree of reverberation on a particular edit would scale such a height of stand-up vexation and cross-purpose that a white-jacketed underling would slope off for an embarrassed coffee break while defiance, hesitation, defiance again and final agreement chased across the face of either the composer or the chief engineer. Yet, during the interminable re-running of each taped mile, the technicians – if showing neither enthusiasm nor distaste – would be astounded constantly by the visitor's learned recommendations about amplitude, track allocation, stereo placement, degeneration *et al*, although correct terminology would defer sometimes to '*zzzzt*', '*woop-woop*' and '*bap-bap-bap-bap*', like snatches from a Dada poem. Now and then, someone or other would want to collapse, screaming with laughter, onto the carpet, but the staff kept themselves in check as the piece began to assume sharper definition. Nevertheless, if Philips' executive body had ever envisaged a Walton-esque hybrid of Elgar and Britten, they were to be dismayed.

The montage of sound did, however, contain a *plink-plonk* element that was characteristic of Walton's lighter pieces, although it bore a closer affinity to Cage's *Fontana Mix*, a classic of its kind then nearing completion in Milan's Studio di Fonologia. Yet the similarity is superficial, because *La Poème Électronique* relied on a determinacy that Cage avoided in *Fontana Mix* and, crucially, in *4'33"*, which requires a pianist to sit before a keyboard without touching it for that length of time. Coughs, the rustling of programmes and the huff of footsteps walking out of the auditorium are part of the performance.

Extraneous noise, however, is an unwanted distraction when listening to *La Poème Électronique* on compact disc. A whistling kettle, a pneumatic drill in the next street, the caw of a crow – all are irritations threatening to capsize the careful Mondrian-like arrangement of cleanly recorded samples modified only to enhance clarity and stereo shift. 'The score is not compounded of recognisable instruments' was the sweeping generalisation of *The New York Times*. 'It is the work of a man who has been seeking for several decades to return music to a purity of sound that he does not believe possible in conventional music making.'[15]

La Poème Électronique was certainly as far from *Un Grand Sommeil Noir* as could be imagined. Bells, sirens, woodblocks, *bel canto* warbling, silence, female sighs and electronic signals – 'a protest against inquisition in every form'[16] – would inform a contradiction of hysterical gravity in keeping with Le Corbusier's visual array of fish, masks, skeletons, cities mushroom clouds, birds, animals, reptiles, idols and women, both naked and clothed. Moreover, the tape was to be fed through 350 revolving speakers. While annoyed that the sound system wasn't quite perfect on the day, Varèse accomplished with a vengeance at the age of 74 the 'sound moving through space' notion of which he'd been speaking for nigh on 20 years. The effects of the *La Poème Électronique* experience varied from person to person, but overall it would probably be described as 'psychedelic' nowadays.

Although Xenakis and Jeanneret's pavilion is no more, the music is still available from record shops, usually on 'complete works' collections used for documentary rather than recreational reasons.

Back in Greenwich Village, news of Varèse's activities in the Netherlands had preceded him and plans were being made by a local journal and record shop to stage a simplified version of the 'happening' in Brussels at the Village Gate club in Bleecker Street.

This would be the first of several attempts to recreate the sensation of the 1958 World's Fair. My own feeling, however, is that you had to have been there. Varèse's *La Poème Électronique* was meant to be heard only in the context of Xenakis' building and Le Corbusier's light show on that particular day in May.

The whole event was a subject for discussion by the Belgian media for weeks afterwards, especially as its triumvirate of creators stayed on to sit on a panel of judges for an experimental film competition. Then Varèse left for Paris to put his head around the door of the RTF and take a nostalgic stroll around his old haunts, some of which were no more. Back in his hotel room, and on the voyage back across the Atlantic, he sketched diagrams and drew graphs as much as he inked dots on manuscript paper. This was the beginning of *Nocturnal*, Edgard Varèse's artistic valediction.

10 The Californian

'I didn't write a rock 'n' roll song until I was in my 20s, but I had been writing chamber music since I was 14. I only had two albums – one was the complete works of Varèse.'
– Frank Zappa, 1991[1]

Among the difficulties of writing a biography is that real life doesn't run as smoothly as fiction, from one chapter to the next. Nevertheless, this seems an appropriate moment to introduce one who was to become Edgard Varèse's most eminent supporter – and also to give some indication of how Varèse's music was regarded by the general public that were made aware of it.

Born on 21 December 1940, the celebrated Frank Zappa all but shared the same birthday. Yet, on the face of it, he was an unlikely mouthpiece through which the word about Varèse could be spread to a wider world – but the same could be said about George Harrison, a member of a Liverpudlian beat group, and the sitar virtuoso Ravi Shankar.

Zappa's background was as lugubriously suburban as Harrison's. He spent most of his adolescence in conurbations no different to transient outsiders from any others on the edge of the desert regions of northern California. Once divulging to a journalist's tape recorder that he used to think that classical music was 'only for old ladies and faggots', the teenager was ignorant of post-tonal composition until 1954, when he chanced to read an article in *Look* magazine about an owner of a record shop whose talents as a salesman were exemplified by his offloading of Edgard Varèse's EMS collection –

'dissonant and terrible, the worst music in the world'[2] – onto a browsing customer. I'd want to hear something described like that, and so did Frank Zappa.

Zappa's opportunity came one day in a local store, where 'I noticed a strange-looking black-and-white album with a guy on it who had frizzy grey hair and looked like a mad scientist. I thought it was great that a mad scientist had finally made a record.'[3] On closer inspection, the disc turned out to be the item mentioned in *Look*. Following impassioned haggling with the counter assistant, Zappa bought for half a week's paper-round wage a shop-soiled *Complete Works Of Edgard Varèse: Volume One* which had been used to demonstrate hi-fi equipment.

'Everything that I liked was based on my gut reaction to what was on the record,' confessed Zappa. 'For some reason, I liked Varèse right away.'[3] Having invested that amount of cash, he intended to spin it until it was dust, sometimes concentrating, say, only on the percussion, then just the horns. Next, he might play it at the wrong speeds – or backwards, if the record player could be rigged up to do so.

'The way I perceived the dissonance was that these chords are really mean,' Frank explained. 'I like these chords, and the drums are playing loud in this music, and you can hear the drums often in this music, which is something that you do not experience in other types of classical music.'[1]

Soon, the teenager became fascinated with the creator of this marvellous music. He began seeking insights into artistic conduct, clarification of obscurer byways and general information about what made Edgard Varèse tick, making myriad private observations that lifted him from his armchair and back to an album that was by now acquiring scratches and surface hiss. Frank was interested not only in the sound within the grooves but also the label, catalogue number (EMS 401) and sleeve notes. He was to find more to study, notice and compare in 1962, when Columbia Masterworks issued *Déserts* (MS-6362), a pressing that Varèse himself would regard as definitive.

At school, Frank had became quite preachy about 'the world's greatest composer'[4] after deciding to share his cultural secret. What he considered to be 'the good bits' on EMS 401 were marked in chalk for easier reference because, 'whenever people came over, I would force them to listen. I thought it was the ultimate test of their intelligence. They thought I was out of my mind.'[4] Zappa's parents did, too, forbidding him to spin the record within their hearing, 'because the sirens made my mother neurotic while she was ironing'.[5]

For his 15th birthday, Frank was permitted to make a long-distance call to Varèse, feeling an odd disappointment on finding that his hero's New York telephone number wasn't ex-directory. As Edgard was in Belgium awaiting the performance of *La Poème Électronique*, the boy chatted to Mrs Varèse instead. He was, however, able to speak to the maestro himself a few weeks later, but discovered that he had nothing to say beyond some duck-billed platitude, probably along the lines of 'Hey, I really like your music!' – an exchange that he made out to be less fleeting in class the next morning.

While staying with an aunt in Baltimore 15 months later, Frank endeavoured to arrange a visit to 188 Sullivan Street, but Mr Varèse was about to leave for Europe again. However, he sent a polite handwritten letter – dated 12 July 1957 and subsequently framed by its recipient – intimating that he hoped to meet his young Californian disciple soon.

Further hard listening to EMS 401 and MS-6362 evolved into Frank leaning heavily on Varèse when he started writing his own music. In 1962, he hired a hall to present a piece for a 20-piece orchestra and taped electronics with a home movie he had made with his father's cine camera. Owing less to Varèse than Russolo was Zappa's *Bicycle Music*, performed on a nationally networked chat show later that year. 'You play by plucking the spokes and blowing through the handlebars,' he informed host Steve Allen. Other methods of producing 'cyclophony' involved twirling the pedals, stroking the spokes with the bow of a double bass and letting the air out of the tyres. A duet by Allen and Zappa was accompanied by atonal honking from a jazz band and a control-room technician 'fooling around' with a tape recorder.

These two incidents were among those annotated by Zappa in 'Edgard Varèse: Idol Of My Youth', an article for *Stereo Review* in 1971.[6] By then, Zappa was a fully integrated mainstay of contemporary rock's ruling class, his circumstances much changed from when he had superseded Paul Buff as proprietor of a run down recording studio in a far-flung suburb of San Bernardino, 100 miles east of Los Angeles. As such, he ministered to hundreds of commissioned demonstration recordings at an hourly rate as well as soundtracks to low-budget movies and one-shot pop records, multitracked and released pseudonymously.

So it was that Frank Zappa, 21 years old and battling financial woes, came to serve a short jail term when, through the medium of a vice squad *agent provocateur*, he was arrested in 1962 for 'conspiracy to commit pornography'.

11 The Indweller

'Varèse has been recognised at last, but he is a lonely figure still. That is partly because he preferred composing to the career of "being a composer". He went his own way and alone.'

– Igor Stravinsky, 1962[1]

While Frank Zappa's musical career was in danger of being extinguished by ridicule and disgrace in the early 1960s, Edgard Varèse's final years were overflowing with honours and citations for music he'd written decades earlier and, to a lesser degree, his final (and incomplete) offering: *Nocturnal*.

During this most public and bittersweet phase of his life, the scores on which his reputation rested appeared in print again and, while EMS 401 had long been consigned to the bargain bin, new recordings were being released more frequently. *Amériques* had nestled among one opus each by Bartók, Schoenberg and Webern at the Karuizama Festival in Japan. In the aftershock of *La Poème Électronique*, meanwhile, would be Scandinavian premières of *Octandre* and *Density 21.5*; *Déserts* in London and Pierre Boulez conducting *Intégrales* at the Donaueschingen Festival in Germany. Closer to home were four nights of *Arcana* – under Boulez's baton again – at Carnegie Hall. The last time it had been performed in North America was at the same venue in 1927.

Now a studio audience hung on the composer's every word on primetime television in French Canada. This tied in neatly with a special Varèse edition of *Liberté* magazine and a broadcast on 8 August 1960, on both English- and French-speaking networks, of a forthcoming première of a revised *Déserts*. The first stage performance of any Varèse opus in Canada created such a stir that *La Poème Électronique* was booked for the next summer's annual music festival in Montreal, where it was then heard in total darkness, apart from the changing colours of two luminous sculptures. The following afternoon, the festival committee immediately underwrote a glowing tribute to Varèse – records and eulogies – at a local university faculty.

How swiftly he'd become a vogue. One day he'd been a ghost of dubious distinction from the recent past, the next – or so it seemed – he was bringing much of the aura of a fresh sensation to those young enough never to have heard much of him before. What was going on in Varèse's head as he acknowledged the superabundant acclamations at Carnegie Hall or in Montreal with a judged equilibrium of gravitas, becoming modesty and a bewildered good humour? Suddenly, although his memory wasn't what it was, he had been transported back in time to the fuss over *Hyperprism*, *Amériques et al* in the 1920s. Was he now coming into his own again? At first, he was at a loss to account for the close but widespread attention that his old works were receiving, but he knew too well how ephemeral such enthusiasm could be.

Yet the fuss these days was a manifestation of respect for an elder statesman of modern music rather than an amused cheer for the oldest teenager in the business, despite so-bad-it's-good-type reviews and some of the musicians sharing the mirth of a claque of detractors among the crowd at the Canadian première of *Déserts*. 'People laugh because they don't know what else to do,' snarled the composer in a whisper to Fernand Ouellette, seated next to him. 'It's a defence reaction.' However, to those of Varèse's entourage dutifully leading the barrage of applause that drowned out the derision, the overall renewal of interest was akin to a schoolyard situation in which a child, teased mercilessly throughout the spring term, is suddenly popular when his playmates return to class after Easter, a sense of 'Eddie has been tormented quite enough. Let's start being nice to him.'

Animated chatter swelled to sustained clapping before 'Eddie' had uttered a syllable of his autumn 1959 lecture at Princeton University's Faculty of Advanced Musical Studies, which began with a disarming 'It must be quite widely known by now – since I have been boring people on the subject for half a century – that my aim has always been the liberation of sound, to throw open the whole world of sound to music.' He then told the students of his own youth, of how 'I began to break the rules, feeling even then that they were barring me from this wonderful world, this ever-expanding universe.'[2]

Was the world any more wonderful at 74? When the adulation and spoken words were over for the day, Edgard would lie in bed, worn out but with eyes open and temples throbbing as depression – now undistracted – lacerated his already overloaded mind with shards of disjointed thought. He would long to be at peace, but fingers of despair would reach in and sleep wouldn't come for all the potions and draughts he was prescribed. During one particularly violent surge of self-loathing, he had risen and stumbled to his study. The same devil that had directed Van Gogh to hack off an ear directed Edgard Varèse to dig out from its drawer the only copy left of *Bourgogne* and tear it to shreds. 'Infanticide,'[3] Louise called it after she was jerked from her dreams by his frothing and fuming downstairs.

Varèse's spiritual wellbeing had depended always upon conscious creative progression and counteracting onsets of his blackest moods by burying himself in work, especially now that the realization of many of his earlier ideas were less fanciful in the light of ever-accelerating technological advances. While *Arcana* had been rewritten for a far bigger orchestra of 120 musicians[4] and he was refining the *Déserts* interpolations at Columbia-Princeton Electronic Music Centre, Varèse was in two minds about whether to invest other of his published compositions with taped sequences or even in-person electronics, as John Cage had with 1960's *Cartridge Music*, whereby contact microphones turned otherwise inconsequential acoustic noises into something otherworldly.

Cage's was among a number of essential names dropped in September 1960 when, to a *whoomph* of flashbulbs, Varèse took tea with Stravinsky amid the murals and mosaics of Peacock Alley, the dining area in New York's deluxe Waldorf-Astoria Hotel. For all of the venomous mutual criticism spouted over the years, the two old codgers, their furies and hungers spent, were quite overcome with rose-tinted sentiment when conversing *en français* about people, places and things that seemed so far away now – Vincent d'Indy at the Schola Cantorum, Widor at the St Sulpice organ, the dress rehearsal for *Pierrot Lunaire*, the première of *Le Sacre Du Printemps*... Like riders on the old frontier, they should have gone their separate ways without formal goodbyes, but they obliged the hovering snap-shotters with a handshake and a quotable aside from Edgard, Terry-Thomas to Igor's David Niven: 'I rather like a certain clumsiness in a work of art.'[4]

The encounter was not a 'time-sensitive' feature for most common-or-garden reporters, what with the Olympic Games hitting their stride in Rome and the ongoing east–west, black–white tension. For the more tidy-minded journals that had already commissioned his obituary, it was more or less case closed on Edgard Varèse, to whom had been put cursory questions about current projects. Surely there weren't any more surprises yet to come at this late stage from someone long cemented in place like a brick in a wall between Pietro Francesco Valentini and Astrid Varnay (who?) in *Grove's Encyclopedia Of Music And Musicians*. 'While giving a man credit for his past, they minimise his present and deny him a future,'[5] Varèse had parried, but, as his distant friend Picasso would have suggested, their retelling of the old, old story was better than not telling any story at all.

Edgard's 75th birthday was howled metaphorically from the rooftops of New York when a spectacular in his honour was held in the capacious auditorium attached to the Metropolitan Museum of Art, the largest such museum in the western hemisphere. As well as choosing pieces by Schütz, Monteverdi and other of his favourites from time immemorial, Varèse was called onto the boards to take a bow and utter a *sotto voce* 'thank you' into the ovation that roared as the last bars of *Offrandes*, *Intégrales* and *Ionisation* still reverberated. If as ecstatic inwardly as the capacity audience that he was so deliriously remembered, Varèse was a little embarrassed, imagining that everyone was amazed that he wasn't either some senile Methuselah or mouldering in his grave like Debussy or Ravel were by now.

It was a triumph because everyone wanted it to be. As midnight thickened, the Greatest Night Anyone Could Ever Remember continued with an *après*-concert party, where the champagne flowed and the cards, presents and congratulatory telegrams – including one from Stravinsky – were displayed. Edgard and Louise reserved a little of their charm – mainly hers – for every guest who entered their circulating orbit, embracing young intimates like Chou Wen-Chung and doling out a few minutes of chat each to witnesses and even participants in some of the stirring musical exploits of the past, present and what remained of the future, whether Salzedo at the first New Symphony Orchestra concert in 1919 or John Cage promising to be in Montreal for *La Poème Électronique*.

Striking while the iron was lukewarm, another Varèse showcase was arranged for the following May at the Town Hall to give 'em all but one of the classics omitted the previous time. *Amériques* would have to wait until the following year, but the customers were more than satisfied with *Octandres*, *Intégrales*, *Déserts* and the second-ever performance of *Ecuatorial* (although there wasn't then an ondes Martenot to be had anywhere in the entire state). For good measure, there was an airing of *La Poème Électronique* and a nascent rendering of *Nocturnal* by an under-rehearsed orchestra *sans* the two ondes Martenots required – although Salzedo had developed legs like whipcord in his energetic labours to bring the choir up to scratch.

For the most part, the critics were non-committal about *Nocturnal*, gauging that a Varèse backlash was untimely, in view of his current standing. No less than the Koussevitzky Music Foundation – established by the expatriate Russian pianist at the Library of Congress in Washington – had sunk hard cash into *Nocturnal* and were to present its composer with the first Koussevitzky International

Recording Award at an optimum moment during a back-slapping, hand-pumping banquet in New York's Plaza Hotel, an establishment as upper-crust as the Waldorf.

In anticipatory thanks, Varèse dedicated *Nocturnal* to its sponsors. More obviously truncated than Schubert's *Unfinished Symphony*, the abrupt ending – like a motorway terminating at a precipice – at the Town Hall recital did not pass without comments – although these were, admittedly, swept away by the riptide of bonhomie saturating the entire evening. Musically, *Nocturnal*'s closest relation in Varèse's canon is *Ecuatorial*.[6] While the trademark horn-section arpeggios are used less copiously, *Nocturnal* also features a solo voice (albeit female this time), a male unison chorus (that intones menacingly rather than sings) and a libretto that about two per cent of its listeners at the première had recognised and to which only the most persistent and loyal consumers would devote hours of enjoyable time-wasting to analysing in depth. The crux of it was seemingly random juxtapositions of phrases from *The House Of Incest*, the prose poem *cum* novel by Anaïs Nin, now resident in New York. To these, Varèse had added apparent babble *à la* Kurt Schwitters – 'wa ya you you wa wa yao ya ha ha ha you', 'o a o a oo a oo hm', 'oomp ts oomp ts oomp', *ad nauseam* – as if *Nocturnal*'s sentiment couldn't be expressed through expected verbal articulation.

'If sometimes I want to use the voice,' Varèse elucidated, 'I need words, not for their signification, but for what they will give when masticating them for the formant in the throat.'[7] As a wordsmith, he favoured disjunctive syntax reminiscent of Pierre Reverdy rather than literal interpretation – which, in any case, didn't take precedence over phonetics or conflict with artistic motive. Vowels and consonants were, however, not viewed as instrumental sound as much as a means through which he could counterpoint a seemingly incongruous aural fly-past of images into an organic and apprehendable whole.

With quiet pride, Varèse couldn't begin to explain what *Nocturnal* meant. Truly, it wasn't 'about' anything, beyond a general intention to draw in the secret parts of an ancient night – or, as Chou Wen-Chung was to note in the preamble to the printed score, 'a world of sounds remembered and imagined, conjuring up sights and moods now personal, now Dante-esque, now enigmatic. A phantasmagorical world? Yes, but one as real as Varèse's own life.'

What life? Was it recollections of the sexual athletics of youth in the flushed swoops from contralto to orgasmic high soprano in the space of a few bars – the groaning and breathy sentience, the post-coital scent of 'perfume and sperm'? Alternatively, perhaps it was an abstraction of *Un Grand Sommeil Noir*, or an explicit matter – say, the night train from Prague back to Paris in 1914 as storm clouds gathered? Personally, I think that, belligerently alive though *Nocturnal* is, its veerings from cheerless morbidity to what I hope is dark humour are connected with the advanced years and imminent decease of its composer, bereft of dreams and gazing pensively from his study window.

Was he so near the edge of eternity now that it wasn't worth getting the piano tuned? Should he still be bothering the doctor about a very arthritic knee, traceable to an adolescent sports injury? The following winter he would be prostrated with bronchitis so severe that, lingering for months, it would necessitate X-rays and fluoroscope readings. He would perk up briefly on learning of the demise of the older cousin he detested, but took umbrage at the news that Alfred Cortot warranted an honorific plaque in Le Villars, a place in which Varèse believed he had never set foot.

Varèse was of an age when the passing of time was marked by the funerals of further members of his own over-the-hill generation. A month before his own death, he delivered a laudation amid the sobbing and blowing of noses at a formal wake for Le Corbusier, albeit with a barbed subtext lamenting the demolition of the pavilion that staged the première of *La Poème Électronique*.

Preoccupation with past regrets and mortality pervaded *Nocturnal II*, an attempt to compose an opus apparently more long-faced than its predecessor, as intimated in Louise Varèse's description of 'nightmarish voices encircling the woman in her dreams'.[8] This was never to materialise, however, and neither was starker *Nuit*, a work based on the same themes of night and death, in that its text was also borrowed from *The House Of Incest*, after Varèse had considered in one empty moment of layering a Morse code translation of a raw stream of consciousness onto its musical bedrock.

Nocturnal, *Nocturnal II*, *Nuit* – in some respects, it didn't matter to Varèse if no one heard them. He was solvent enough, now, and had become so without compromise. Much of his music hadn't been performed accurately, and, even when it was, it wasn't always as he'd first imagined it would sound. Nevertheless, he alone had accepted responsibility for it. While advised by agents, conductors and musicians, he had never been either a corporation marionette or spent most of his working life in a 'proper job', like Charles Ives did, composing in his spare time.

The success of the late Ives' insurance firm in downtown Manhattan had allowed him a cosseted retirement, a luxury denied Edgard Varèse, despite the mortgage on 188 Sullivan Street being paid in full years ago. Besides, the present-day composer refused not only to die but also to retire, even one whose parchment visage stared vacantly back at him from his shaving mirror. Yet, while his health in old age wasn't first rate, 'he had kept his magnificent leonine head', so old acquaintance Andre Billy would remark in 1965, 'a real musician's head, and a musician of genius, a head worthy to hang beside that of Berlioz. All that mop of hair – and those eyes! As I contemplate his photo, I finally recover the Varèse of 1910. Yes, it really is him, but with 50 years [*sic*] added.'[3]

His could have been like the happy ending in a Victorian novel, with all the villains bested, the inheritance claimed and the protagonist settling down to a moderately comfortable dotage. There were, indeed, many occasions when a grouchy *vieillard* would emerge from his workroom and unwind sufficiently to, say, pen a lengthy dedication in one of Louise's friend's cookbooks, mentioning a dish that 'I remember I have often made myself – Syrian, I think. Consists of cucumbers sliced very thin and prepared with sour cream and mint. This, as well as old familiar French dishes such as boeuf bourguignon, potée bourguignonne, coq au vin, veau (or poulet) marengo, I learned from my Burgundian grandfather.'[9]

Compliments for his cooking were as ego-massaging for a composer who'd have been as happy growing grapes as he was when he received the Koussevitzky Award or was elected in 1962 to the National Institute of Arts and Letters. That year also saw him donning tie, white shirt, sober grey suit and professorial air to receive a kind of Nobel Prize without the money from the Royal Swedish Academy.

That these and further rewards for his achievements marked his calendar so often was a source of wry amusement, as was the Bell Telephone Company chucking blank cheques about to foster research into sound. In 1962, one of its directors, a Dr JR Pierce, had been executive producer of *Music From Mathematics*, an album containing IBM-computer-generated digital-to-sound renderings of 'Frère Jacques', 'Bicycle Made For Two' and Orlando Gibbons' *Fantasia* among original pieces with titles like *Noise Study*, *Numerology* and *Variations In Timbre And Attack* by Pierce himself and other Bell employees with trimmed beards and science degrees. Similar institutions in Europe would finance the likes of Tom Dissevelt's *Round The World With Electronic Music*, forever on BBC radio schools' programmes in the mid-1960s.

Perhaps it was just as well that Varèse's pre-war appeals for aid to Bell, Guggenheim and elsewhere had fallen on stony ground. It is interesting to speculate, too, on what direction Frank Zappa's career might have taken had he not been entrapped by the San Bernardino County Vice Squad. More profound clashes with Authority were on the horizon when he formed The Mothers Of Invention in 1964. It was the group's submission to composer, guitarist and occasional singer Zappa's masterplan that guided them eventually to a qualified prosperity. 'He very patiently taught me how to play all those rhythms and time signatures,' averred drummer Jimmy Carl Black. 'I'd never even played 3/4 before, but he knew I could do it. He also made us aware of modern classical stuff.'

Concerts and, later, albums resembled pop-Dada aural junk sculptures made from an eclectic heap that supported Zappa's well-founded premise that 'it is theoretically possible to be "heavy" and still have a sense of humour'. While the 1968 instrumental 'Uncle Meat' was lifted directly from Milhaud's 'Un Homme Et Son Désir', Zappa and the Mothers borrowed less nakedly from the tonalities of Stravinsky, Webern and Varèse, to whom the second movement of raga-like 'Help, I'm A Rock' on 1966's *Freak Out!* was to be dedicated.

If he even recalled the youthful correspondent of the late 1950s, Varèse may have been flattered by how far-reaching his impact had been. Yet Zappa's cultural inroads in around 1964 would have been of less intrinsic value to Edgard Varèse than the four evenings of *Déserts* in January at the Lincoln Center, a new arts complex in Upper Broadway. These were conducted by Leonard Bernstein, who had queued with Aaron Copland, Pierre Boulez and musicians of similar eminence to loudly praise Varèse the previous May, at the Plaza celebration. In his preamble on the first night of *Déserts*, he did the same, comparing the work to Picasso's agonised *Guernica*, which was currently occupying an entire wall at the Museum of Modern Art. Varèse himself considered these to be the finest performances there had ever been of *Déserts*, which amassed the customary mixed reviews, the most typical being the *Herald Tribune*'s 'I can recall no piece at the Philharmonic in recent years that has been received with such contrasting boos and bravos.'[10]

'Tiring, boring, ugly and, above all, useless noise',[11] however, was *Musica-Disques*' verdict on Boulez's reading of *Arcana* with the Orchestre Nationale that spring in France, a land that thought of Edgard Varèse now as less its own than the USA's.

Meanwhile, his adopted country couldn't get enough of him, almost as if it had guessed that there was wasn't much more than a year to go. In August, it gave him pride of place at a composers' conference at Bennington College that was crowned with a performance of *Octandre*. A fortnight later, an all-Varèse concert – at which the man of the moment addressed the audience – sold out at New York's Judson Hall, which admittedly had a far smaller capacity than the mighty Carnegie – although this was full enough on 31 March 1965, when it was 'once more, with feeling' for

Hyperprism, *Ionisation* and so forth in front of the Great Man himself, along with a cortège that, during the intermission, hushed when he spoke, laughed when he laughed and fetched him drinks.

In this way, Varèse had become the focus of the same kind of insufferably smug elitism that he had loathed when he was a nobody, reluctantly obliged to the likes of d'Indy, Fauré and Strauss. In retrospect, some could theorise that that was why, when he was called to the spotlight at the close of another night devoted to him – this time in the Chicago Theater – Edgard Varèse waved into the blackness and vanished into the wings forever.

This, nevertheless, wasn't intended to be his last contact with the general public. Preparations were already underway for extravaganzas in New York and, yes, Paris to commemorate his 80th birthday, on 22 December 1965. To Louise, Edgard seemed happy about both this and an imminent visit from Monte Carlo of Claude and Marilyne, the grandchild he'd not yet seen.

Letters – and, later, transatlantic telephone calls – exchanged by Varèse and his daughter had always been infused with an underlying if brusque affection. Her stay at 188 Sullivan Street in September was, therefore, undramatic and free of trauma – although to Claude, her father appeared unusually contemplative, which might be either evidence of wisdom after the event or because he was pondering suggestions that it was time for an autobiography.

Death, however, ceased the pondering. Late in October, Varèse complained of abdominal discomfort, detailing the symptoms to his doctor, who, convinced that a thrombosis had caused extensive intestinal blockage, ordered an emergency operation that very afternoon across town in the University Medical Center. Edgard had started to drift into a coma as the ambulance nosed up Sullivan Street, but, a week after coming around from the anaesthetic, he was taken off the danger list. He was, however, soon back under the scalpel again after an infection – probably gangrene in a section of bowel – was diagnosed, and the flame flickered lower.

On the morning of 6 November 1965, his breathing slackened and Edgard Victor Achille Charles Varèse passed away quietly on a hospital bed. A self-confessed 'pagan',[3] he had asked that his cadaver be cremated before nightfall and the ashes scattered to the 12 winds.

The anniversary concerts went ahead as planned. On 24 November, *Déserts* was performed at the Domaine in Paris. Here's what *Le Nouvel Observateur* said of it: 'It seems like a poorly conceived improvisation, the work of a none-too-gifted amateur.'[12]

Epilogue: The Earthling

'How could anyone like this stuff?'
– Alan Clayson, 1971[1]

Edgard Varèse wasn't the tidiest of people. When she'd cried her tears, among his widow's more onerous tasks was to sift through nigh on 40 years of accumulated clutter getting tattier by the day in the workroom. By methods peculiar to herself, she acquired a black belt in feng shui. Thus, the irrelevant rubbish was thrust aside and the rest subdivided into some kind of order.

No musician herself, Louise had been no more capable of being objective about the fragments of manuscript paper and diagrams left by her husband than a shopper can be about separate backwashes of supermarket muzak. They were just there. In 1973, she turned her findings over to Chou Wen-Chung, who had been appointed literary executor of the Varèse estate. He so caught the undercurrents that most obviously eased passage through the confusion that he was able to make a game attempt at finishing *Nocturnal* from three reference copies containing extensive indications for changes and additions.

This brought the number of Varèse's extant compositions up to 15 (if you count *Tuning Up* and 'Dance For Burgess'), the smallest output of any modern composer of importance. Yet his offerings impact still via concert performances, retrospectives on disc and over-analysis in a self-aggrandising form of music criticism that intellectualises the simply intelligent.

Such attention was deserved, if only because it was well known that Varèse rippled across the works of Stockhausen, Cage, Ligeti and nearly every other post-war giant of non-minimalist modern classical music, as well as those of, for instance, the 100-odd callow apprentices who participated in Dartmouth Arts Council's first International Electronic Music Competition in Hanover, New Hampshire, on 5 April 1968. Many created fine music, but somehow a lot of them sounded just like Edgard Varèse. Even a radical conservative like Louis 'Moondog' Hardin was to echo at least the ambition of *Espace* in 1989's as-yet-unstaged *Cosmos*, a nine-hour epic for over 1,000 musicians and singers.

Varèse also continued to infiltrate jazz, as exemplified by the *Ionisation*-like effect of the siren tearing into the drum solo on the title track of The Roland Kirk Quartet's *Rip, Rig And Panic* ('inspired by the music of Edgar [*sic*] Varèse').[2] Furthermore, had he been alive still during pop's fleeting 'classical period', in the later 1960s, he might have been approached for permission to direct his works on vinyl towards that market, just as EMI bought a quarter-page in the *New Musical Express* to advertise a new pressing of Holst's 'psychedelic' *Planets Suite* as an object that would look well artlessly strewn in the bedsits of undergraduates that were flirting with bohemia before settling down and becoming teachers.

CBS had already perceived similar potential in Moondog, with his groovy Viking-bard regalia, as well as minimalists Steve Reich and Terry Riley. Likewise, the Island label promoted Pierre Henri and 'Samurai of sound' Stomu Yamash'ta – a percussion virtuoso awarded a classical Grammy – almost as rock stars, while Ringo Starr, of all people, was to 'discover' an English 'answer' in tall, long-haired John Tavener.

As it was, music by Varèse, along with Berio, Stockhausen (included on The Beatles' *Sgt Pepper's Lonely Heart's Club Band* sleeve montage) and Penderecki, was as likely as anything from the Top 40 to blast from the car stereos of self-improving pop musicians, both obscure and famous. Varèse's influence on pop has, however, less to do with theories and artistic content than with the replacement of traditional means of music production with entirely synthetic ones – more *La Poème Électronique* than *Octandre*.

(If anyone's interested, I layered a *La Poème Électronique*-type tape collage over the main instrumental interlude on 'Sol Nova', the third track on side one of *What A Difference A Decade Made* by Clayson And The Argonauts, and an air-raid siren from a sound-effects record gnawed at my 1998 arrangement of Jacques Brel's 'Next [Au Suivant]' where a bank of strings might have done.[3])

A truce between synthesiser technology and human emotion was less crucial for certain other pop artists than the use of sounds for their own sake rather than as substitutes for, or integration with, other instruments. This was particularly rampant in the music of Faust, Neu!, Can, Kraftwerk and other executants of a strain of pop known as 'krautrock', which exuded an icily urban appeal, mostly through state-of-the-art machinery keeping pace with detached singing and outbursts of art terrorism.

In Britain, Varèse was just as much an inspiration to the likes of Brian Eno, Throbbing Gristle, Ultravox and, as a case study, Cabaret Voltaire, the most ground-breaking combo to come from Sheffield since their formation in 1973 – although their efforts were more inclined to have pleasant mid-tempo tunes in among the pre-recorded sound collages, cut-up techniques and tape loops of steam hammers. Clock DVA, Goodnight Forever and The Human League were three of many parochial acts who built upon Cabaret Voltaire's precedent. Exponents of industrial pop, it seemed natural that the task of releasing Clock DVA's cassette-only *White Souls In Black Suits* should fall to brand-leading Throbbing Gristle's Industrial Records.

On about the same level as Throbbing Gristle in the meritocratic hierarchy of pop – sorry, *rock* – history, The United States Of America were a New York outfit that, prior to disbanding in 1969, recorded an eye-stretching LP that, rather than tampering with the workings of orthodox amplified instruments, used electronically generated sound as the dominant sonic thrust. Often only the lead voice put their music in the realms of pop at all as, running a gamut from pseudo-horrific flash to subdued ghostliness, the Varèseian tape collages and electronic twiddling went past mere gimmickry to be integral to the lyrics and melodies.

The same was true of another New Yorker, Laurie Anderson, who struggled as a performance artist until enjoying a surprise hit with 'O Superman' in 1981. Her multimedia projects have since encompassed music, film, mime, visual projections, dance and spoken and written language – and an injection of Varèse, notably in 1972's *Automotive*, featuring a symphony of car horns.

That year, too, Varèse's name was incorporated into the title of a pop record. Nevertheless, 'A Hit For Varèse' wasn't at all, although it was the spin-off single to *Chicago V* by the most renowned rock equivalent of a brass band, which had been formed four years earlier by music students at the Windy City's De Paul University. Composed by singing keyboard player Robert Lamm, 'A Hit For Varèse' – for all the half-baked electronics of its introit, and an element of free improvisation – was a straightforward song based on common chords and verses that were no incisive insight into either Varèse or the human condition.

The best that can be said of Chicago's 'A Hit For Varèse' is that its heart was in the right place, and that its principal ostinato was reminiscent of *King Kong* by Frank Zappa, now sporting facial hair that made him look like Vincent d'Indy, of all people. His Mothers Of Invention had landed a prestigious summer season at Bleecker Street's Garrick Theater in 1967. Zappa and his pregnant wife stayed in 'this miserable apartment on Thompson Street, but it was a block away from Varèse's house. He was dead by that time, but I used to walk by there and see that little red door and just try to imagine what it would be like to be trapped in that apartment, not writing music for 25 years [*sic*].'[4]

Although Zappa wasn't the most reliable authority, as far as the finer details of his hero's life story was concerned, his assimilation of Varèse's artistic portfolio was more accurate and developed than those of any of the composer's biographers – including me – and any conservatoire-trained conductor of specific works. A modified quote – 'The present-day composer refuses to die!' – from the International Composers' Guild manifesto was printed somewhere on the sleeves of many albums by Zappa, who searched in vain for a bust of Varèse for display on the sleeve of 1968's *We're Only In It For The Money* by The Mothers Of Invention.

An understanding of Varèse is vital to any plausible examination of *The Chrome-Plated Megaphone Of Destiny*, *Nine Types Of Industrial Pollution* and other instances in Zappa's own 'electric chamber music'.[4] His discs and stage shows were too clever for the commonweal until the 1970s, when they came to attract – for better or worse – a wider audience in their drift towards lavatorial hum*or*, as opposed to the hum*our* epitomised by Zappa's segue of 1956's 'The Closer You Are' by New York vocal group The Channels with *Hyperprism* ('two of my favourite records that should be heard as a pair') when appearing as a celebrity presenter on a BBC Radio 1 programme in 1980.

Yet, like Mozart, Zappa ceased to spring for the commercial jugular towards the end of his life and negotiated a complete artistic recovery as a 'serious' composer in the same league as Varèse. Most of his last recordings were realized on a costly synclavier, which – like harmonisers, samplers and further modern marvels – can be used by anyone with the most basic keyboard skills, as instanced by the polysynthesiser with sequencer module that provided the backing on The Human League's hit records. 'It was quite clear that the League weren't that good,' pontificated Goodnight Forever's Eric Benn, 'but with machinery like they had, it was pretty hard to make mistakes.'[5]

The concept that The Human League were so reliant on pre-recordings that their engagements could be timed to the second may have delighted Varèse, even if – as Zappa complained in 1992 – certain manufacturers of polysynthesisers, synclaviers and the like sought to phase out their relationships with musicians and package the product purely as post-production tools for videos and motion pictures.

During his Mothers' residency at the Garrick, moments of Zappa's offstage hours were misted with regret at not engineering a face-to-face encounter with Varèse. Years after the sundering of the group, however, he was able to make telephone contact with Nicolas Slonimsky – surely the next best thing to the deceased Edgard – who happened to be in Los Angeles in the spring of 1981. The call was motivated by Zappa's agreement to compère A Tribute To Edgard

Varèse by The Orchestra For Our Time at New York's Whitney Museum to coincide with Louise Varèse's 90th birthday, on 17 April. 'What the organisers were trying to do was to get a younger audience to come and hear the music of Varèse,' ascertained Frank, 'and I thought that, to do a good job, maybe I ought to talk to some people who knew something about Varèse's background and get some anecdotes that I could pass along to the audience. It turned out that this was completely unnecessary because, when the concert occurred, the audience was so unruly. They were behaving like a rock 'n' roll audience. They sat completely still when the music was being played, but as soon as the music stopped, there was pandemonium, so there was no way to tell them anything – but I did make the attempt to get some information from Slonimsky about Varèse, and that's how I met him.'[4]

On the afternoon following that first conversation, a black Mercedes was sent to transport Nicolas Slonimsky to Zappa's home in the Hollywood Hills. The elderly musician's fingers proved as supple as ever they were when he played his own *Minitudes* – which utilised every note of seven and a half octaves – on his host's huge Bosendorfer grand piano. Impressed, Frank asked Nicolas to deliver the same with the band as special guest at a Zappa concert the following evening in Santa Monica's Coliseum. This marriage of rock and classical was an enjoyable experience for all concerned. Indeed, the elegant Slonimsky took such a liking to the dagger-bearded, chain-smoking ex-Mother Of Invention that he penned the latter's entry in Baker's *Biographical Dictionary Of Musicians*, describing Zappa as 'the pioneer of the future millennium of music'.[6]

Slonimsky also attended A Tribute To Edgard Varèse, which was moved, at Zappa's suggestion, to the New York Palladium. Frank would also be the central figure at later memorial concerts to Varèse, actually conducting *Intégrales* and *Ionisation* at the San Francisco War Memorial Opera House on the 100th anniversary of the composer's birth.

Shortly before his own death, in 1993, Frank Zappa's commitment to keeping Varèse's work before the public extended to the recording of the hitherto-unissued *The Rage And The Fury: The Music Of Edgard Varèse* with Germany's Ensemble Modern. 'Frank didn't want to call it a tribute,' explained studio engineer Spencer Chrislu. 'He felt Varèse is completely misunderstood, and he didn't think the music had ever been performed properly. He wanted [The Ensemble Modern] to feel the music and get in touch with the emotions waiting to come out of it.'[7]

Chronology

'I think it is time to pay more attention to music than to promotion of personality – and as for the dates of performances or publication, I think it is almost a pedantic necrophilia.'
– Edgard Varèse

1883 22 December: birth of Edgard Victor Achille Charles Varèse in Paris

1890 Birth of Louise McCutcheon

1900 Varèse begins studies under Giovanni Bolzoni

1903 Varèse leaves family home for Paris

1904 Varèse enrols at the Schola Cantorum

1905 Varèse enrols at the Paris Conservatoire

1907 Wedding of Varèse and Suzanne Bing

Varèse moves to Berlin

1910 9 October: birth of Claude Varèse (daughter)

10 December: première of *Bourgogne* at Berlin's Bluthner Halle

1913 Divorce of Varèse and Suzanne Bing

1915 29 December: Varèse arrives in New York

1918 Wedding of Varèse and Louise Norton (*née* McCutcheon)

1921 Founding of the International Composers Guild

1922 23 April: première of *Offrandes* at New York's Greenwich Village Theater

1923 4 March: première of *Hyperprism* at New York's Klaw Theater

1924 13 January: première of *Octandre* at New York's Vanderbilt Theater

1925 1 March: première of *Intégrales* at New York's Aeolian Hall.

1926 9 April: première of *Amériques* at Philadelphia's Academy of Music.

1927 8 April: première of *Arcana* at Philadelphia's Academy of Music

1928 Founding of the Pan American Association of Composers

1932 15 April: première of *Ecuatorial* at New York Town Hall

1933 6 March: première of *Ionisation* at New York's Carnegie Hall

1936 16 February: première of *Density 21.5* at New York's Carnegie Hall

1940 Birth of Frank Zappa

1947 23 February: première of *Etude Pour Espace* at New York's New School For Social Research

1950 Recordings of four works by Varèse released on long-playing disc

1954 2 December: première of *Déserts* at the Théâtre des Champs-Elysées in Paris

1958 2 May: première of *La Poème Électronique* at the Brussels Exposition

1961 1 May: première of *Nocturnal* at New York Town Hall

1965 6 November: death of Edgard Varèse in New York

Notes

Prologue

1. *Private Eye*, 16 October 1998
2. *Guitar Player* (special Zappa edition, May 1994)
3. Published in its original French by Éditions Seghers (Paris) in 1966, with translations appearing in the USA via Orion, in 1968, and in Britain through Calder & Boyars, in 1973
4. Published by Eulenberg, 1973
5. To TH Greer, 15 August 1965 (Otto Luening Collection, New York Public Library)
6. *The Sunday Times*, 12 August 2001

Chapter 1

1. Anton Webern was born in the same year, in Vienna
2. To which, chronologically, the Vietnam War was to be connected
3. Part of a long dedication in a book of recipes presented to Varèse's New York neighbour, Mrs Kay Boyle, in July 1961
4. *Varèse: A Looking-Glass Diary – Volume 1: 1883–1928* by Louise Varèse (Eulenberg, 1973)

Chapter 2

1. *Courier De Pacifique*, 2 December 1937
2. *Varèse: A Looking-Glass Diary – Volume 1: 1883–1928* by Louise Varèse (Eulenberg, 1973)

Chapter 3

1. *Aeolus*, April 1932
2. The Cubist painter Juan Gris – whose given name, José Gonzales, was similar to that of Julio Gonzalez – settled in Paris in 1906, six years after his near-namesake
3. To Fernand Ouellette
4. *La Liberté*, 14 February 1933
5. *Santa Fe New Mexican*, 25 August 1937
6. *Liberté '59*, autumn 1959

7. From *Chère Sofia* by R Rolland (Albin Michel, Paris, 1960)
8. Quoted in *Anecdotiques* by G Apollinaire (Gallimard, 1955)
9. *20th-Century Dictionary Of The English Language*, edited by Rev T Davidson (Chambers, 1908)
10. *Varèse: A Looking-Glass Diary – Volume 1: 1883–1928* by Louise Varèse (Eulenberg, 1973)
11. *Courier De Bayonne*, 21 September 1905
12. Contained in *The Essence Of Music And Other Papers* by F Busoni, translated by R Lay (Philosophical Library, New York, 1957)
13. *FM Listeners' Guide*, November 1962
14. *Claude Debussy* by H Strobel (Plon, Paris, 1952)
15. *Le Petit Marseillais*, 13 March 1932

Chapter 4

1. *Twice A Year*, winter 1941
2. Fabric touching a rotating barrel
3. Ouellette
4. *Varèse: A Looking-Glass Diary – Volume 1: 1883–1928* by Louise Varèse (Eulenberg, 1973)
5. Maxwell Davies's sleeve notes to *Pierrot Lunaire* by The Fires Of London (Unicorn RHS 319, 1973)
6. Although completed in the same year (1902), this had nothing to do with Debussy's opera of the same title
7. *Berlin Tageblatt*, 3 January 1911
8. Quoted in *391* No.III, March 1917
9. It was a forerunner of the more refined russolofono and, if you like, the digital sampler
10. *The Evening Bulletin*, Philadelphia, 12 April 1926
11. *Prager Tageblatt*, 6 January 1914
12. *L'Intransigeant*, 18 April 1915

Chapter 5

1. 'Marcel Duchamp At Play', unpublished essay by Louise Varèse, December 1972, Sophia Smith Collection, Smith College, Northampton, Massachusetts
2. *Varèse: A Looking-Glass Diary – Volume 1: 1883–1928* (Eulenberg, 1973)
3. *The Memories Of An American Impressionist* by A Warshawsky (Kent State University Press, 1980)
4. *New York Telegraph*, 11 March 1916
5. *Between Sittings: An Informal Biography* by J Davidson (Dial Press, 1951)
6. Stuckist pamphlet, 11 April 2000 (Hangman Bureau of Enquiry)
7. *391*, No.5, June 1917
8. *Les Lettres Française*, Paris, 1965
9. *Shadowland* by A Kreymborg (MP Publishing, 1922)
10. *The Complete Works Of Marcel Duchamp* by A Schwarz (Abrams, 1969)

11. *Music And Its Relation To Futurism, Cubism, Dadaism And Surrealism* by TH Greer (PhD dissertation, *Fine Arts*, North Texas State University, 1969)
12. *Trend*, May-June 1934
13. Quoted in *Jacques Brel* by A Clayson (Sanctuary Publishing, 1996)
14. To Olivia Mattis
15. *Zurich-Dadaco-Dadaglobe: The Correspondence Between Richard Huelsenbeck, Tristan Tzara And Kurt Wolff, 1916–1924*, edited by R Sheppard (Hutton Press, 1982)
16. To Ouellette
17. *Le Cahier* No.8, Paris, 1929
18. *Seven Arts Chronicle*, June 1917
19. *Evening Mail*, 2 April 1917
20. *Cincinnati Commercial Tribune*, 18 April 1918
21. *New York Times*, 20 March 1919
22. 1920 was also the year of the birth of Jeanne Loriod, Messiaen's sister-in-law, destined to be to the ondes Martenot what Yehudi Menuhin would be to the violin
23. *Aeolus*, November 1927
24. *The Villager*, 20 February 1922
25. Varèse quoted in sleeve notes to *Varèse: The Complete Works* (Decca 460 208-2, 1998)
26. 'It is important in the same way that Cubism is important in the history of fine arts. Both came at a moment when the need for a strict discipline was felt in the two arts – but we must not forget that neither Cubism nor Schoenberg's liberating system is supposed to limit art or to replace one academic formula with another' (quoted in sleeve notes to *Varèse: The Complete Works*)
27. To Lucille Lawrence, Carlos Salzedo's first wife, quoted by Ouellette

Chapter 6

1. *Twice A Year*, winter 1941
2. Sleeve notes to *Varèse: The Complete Works* (Decca 460 208-2, 1998)
3. *New York Times*, 22 December 1923
4. *Christian Science Monitor*, 18 July 1922
5. University of California lecture, 5 June 1939
6. *Courier De Pacifique*, 16 February 1938
7. *Music America*, 5 March 1922
8. *Christian Science Monitor*, 29 April 1922
9. *Varèse: A Looking-Glass Diary – Volume 1: 1883–1928* by Louise Varèse (Eulenberg, 1973)
10. Ouellette
11. *New York Times*, March 1923 (precise date obscured)
12. *New York Evening Post*, 14 January 1924
13. *Courier De Pacifique*, 2 December 1937
14. *Christian Science Monitor*, 14 January 1924
15. *New York Times*, 6 December 1936

16. See 9. Villon was very much in the air in 1924. Some of his ballades were being adapted by Berthold Brecht and Kurt Weill for *The Threepenny Opera*
17. *Evening Standard*, 31 July 1924
18. 2 March 1925
19. Varèse quoted in *La Poème Électronique* (Éditions de Minuit, 1959)
20. *Le Figaro Hebdomadaire*, 25 July 1928
21. *La Liberté*, 24 February 1932
22. *Christian Science Monitor*, 15 April 1926. The 'grand orchestra' consisted of two piccolos, three flutes, three oboes, one cor anglais, five clarinets, five bassoons, eight horns, six trumpets, five trombones, two tubas, two harps and a string section. Even so, Varèse had reduced considerably the orchestra's size from the 1920 arrangement, as well as the length of the piece
23. Programme notes for a performance of *Amériques* in Paris, 30 May 1929
24. 10 April 1926 version
25. *Evening Bulletin* (Philadelphia), 12 April 1926
26. Stokowski in *Twice A Year*, No.7, winter 1941
27. *The Sun*, 13 April 1927
28. *Evening World*, 13 April 1927

Chapter 7

1. *Trend*, May 1934
2. *Music And Modern Art*, edited by J Leggio (Routledge, 2002)
3. *Pour Vous*, 30 January 1930
4. *Arts Et Spectacles*, 8 November 1954
5. *Trend*, May 1934
6. *Courier De Pacifique*, 2 December 1937
7. See, for example, 'Of The Adder's Bite' in *Thus Spake Zarathustra* by F Nietzsche, translated by RH Hollingdale (Penguin, 1974)
8. *Varèse: A Looking-Glass Diary – Volume 1: 1883–1928* by Louise Varèse (Eulenberg, 1973)
9. *Comoedia*, 20 April 1929
10. *La Liberté*, 27 April 1929
11. *Le Monde*, 30 April 1929
12. *Le Menestral*, 7 July 1929
13. *Le Monde*, 30 June 1929
14. *Le Merle*, 21 June 1929
15. *Evening News* (London), 14 June 1924
16. *The Roaring Silence: John Cage* by D Revill (Bloomsbury, 1992)
17. *Olivier Messiaen* by M Pierette (Seghers, 1965)
18. *Kineo*, 9 October 1931
19. *Excelsior*, 15 June 1931
20. *Musical Courier*, 18 March 1933
21. *Le Feuilleton Du Temps*, 26 November 1932

22. *Cottbuser Anziger*, 8 March 1932
23. *The Life And Death Of Adolf Hitler* by R Payne (Jonathan Cape, 1973)
24. *Trend*, June 1934
25. Ouellette
26. From Varèse's lecture at Mary Austin House, Santa Fe, 23 August 1936
27. *Le Figaro*, 25 July 1928
28. *New Republic*, 26 June 1933
29. *Musical America*, 25 April 1934
30. *New York Times*, 16 April 1934
31. *Musical Courier*, 16 March 1933
32. 22 July 1933
33. *New York Times*, 4 March 1937

Chapter 8

1. *Trend*, June 1934
2. *Santa Fe New Mexican*, 15 June 1936
3. *Liberté 59*, autumn 1959
4. *New Mexican Sentinel*, 21 September 1937
5. *Courier De Pacifique*, 2 December 1937
6. Lecture at the University of Southern California, 5 June 1939
7. Letter to L Theremin, 5 v 41, quoted in its entirety by Oeullette
8. Sleeve notes to *Varèse: The Complete Works* (Decca 460 208-2, 1998)
9. *Pour Le Victoire*, March 1946
10. However, it was the basic texts that would be used when some of Varèse's talks were edited and published in *The American Composer Speaks*, edited by G Chase (McGraw-Hall, 1966)
11. To Ouellette

Chapter 9

1. Halliwell's *Film Guide* (Grafton, 1991)
2. From Bernstein's diary, quoted in sleeve notes to *West Side Story* (Polydor POL 645, 1985)
3. *New York Herald Tribune*, 24 January 1954
4. *Le Monde*, 4 December 1954
5. *L'Express*, 11 December 1954
6. *La Gazette Litteraire*, 18 July 1954
7. *Carrefour*, 8 December 1954
8. *Combat*, 11 March 1955
9. *L'Age Nouveau*, No.92, May 1955
10. *New York Herald Tribune*, 20 May 1955
11. *Harper's Magazine*, 1 December 1955
12. *The New Yorker*, 10 December 1955
13. *Toward A New Architecture* by Le Corbusier (Dover, 1986)

14. To Ouellette
15. *New York Times*, 8 July 1958
16. Varèse quoted in *Electronic Music* by A Mackay (Control Data, 1981)

Chapter 10

1. To Pete Frame and Kevin Howlett, 14 February 1991
2. *Look*, August 1954
3. *Guitar Player* (special Zappa edition), May 1994
4. *Frank Zappa In His Own Words*, edited by B Miles (Omnibus, 1993)
5. *The Real Frank Zappa Book* by F Zappa with P Occhiogrosso (Picador, 1989)
6. *Stereo Review*, June 1974

Chapter 11

1. *Musical America*, June 1962
2. Varèse's University of Princeton lecture notes, 4 October 1959
3. *Varèse: A Looking-Glass Diary – Volume 1: 1883–1928* (Eulenberg, 1973)
4. A score finished in February 1961 accommodated a 70-piece string section, over 40 percussion instruments, one heckelphone, five clarinets, three bassoons, two contrabassoons, eight horns, five trumpets, four trombones, two tubas, three piccolos, two flutes, three oboes and one cor anglais
5. Quoted by Chou Wen-Chung in sleeve notes to *Varèse: The Complete Works* (Decca 460 208-2, 1998)
6. The piece with which *Nocturnal* was to be conjoined on a 1968 LP (Vanguard VSL 11073)
7. Quoted in *Morton Feldman: Essays*, edited by W Zimmerman (Kerpen, 1985)
8. Quoted in *Varèse*, by O Vivier (Éditions du Seuil, 1973)
9. Quoted by Ouellette from a book of recipes sent by Kay Boyle to Beryl Barr in Paris, May 1961
10. *New York Herald Tribune*, 24 January 1964
11. *Musica-Disques*, May 1964
12. *Le Nouvel Observateur*, 1 December 1965

Epilogue

1. See Prologue
2. *Rip, Rig And Panic* by The Roland Kirk Quartet (Mercury 220 119 LMY, 1966)
3. For information about my musical and literary undertakings, please investigate www.alanclayson.com
4. *Guitar Player*, April 1992
5. Swinging Sheffield by A Clayson (Sheffield City Museums, 1993)
6. Baker's *Biographical Dictionary Of Musicians* (Schimer, 1984)
7. *Los Angeles Times*, July 1995

Index